LOST
BOY
FOUND

LOST BOY FOUND

KIRSTEN ALEXANDER

GRAND CENTRAL
PUBLISHING

NEW YORK   BOSTON

Copyright © 2020 by Kirsten Alexander
Discussion Questions copyright © 2019 by Kristen Alexander.
Author Essay copyright © 2020 by Kristen Alexander and Hachette Book Group, Inc.

Cover design by Elizabeth Connor. Cover art by Debra Lill. Cover copyright © 2020 by Hachette Book Group, Inc.

Grand Central Publishing
Hachette Book Group
1290 Avenue of the Americas, New York, NY 10104
grandcentralpublishing.com
twitter.com/grandcentralpub

Originally published as a Bantam trade paperback entitled *Half-Moon Lake* in 2019. Published by Penguin Random House Australia Pty Ltd. Level 3, 100 Pacific Highway, North Sydney NSW 2060

First Grand Central trade paperback edition: March 2020

Grand Central Publishing is a division of Hachette Book Group, Inc. The Grand Central Publishing name and logo is a trademark of Hachette Book Group, Inc.

The publisher is not responsible for websites (or their content) that are not owned by the publisher.

The Hachette Speakers Bureau provides a wide range of authors for speaking events. To find out more, go to www.hachettespeakersbureau.com or call (866) 376-6591.

Library of Congress Cataloging-in-Publication Data has been applied for.

ISBNs: 978-1-5387-0056-3 (trade paperback), 978-1-5387-0057-0 (ebook)

Printed in the United States of America

LSC-C

10 9 8 7 6 5 4 3 2 1

For Dave, Liam, Milo

"No one can pass through life, any more than he can pass through a bit of country, without leaving tracks behind, and those tracks may often be helpful to those coming after him in finding their way."

Robert Baden-Powell, *Scouting for Boys*

AUTHOR'S NOTE

Lost Boy Found is a work of fiction. Every character, conversation and event as described here is imagined. There is a town called Opelousas and a body of water called Half Moon Lake in Louisiana, but neither of these places bears any resemblance or geographical relationship to my fictional versions of them. And while some of the historical moments mentioned in the novel did happen, I am neither an academic nor a reporter, so I would urge readers not to rely on *Lost Boy Found* as an accurate telling of history.

There is, however, a fascinating true story that inspired *Lost Boy Found*: that of American boy Bobby Dunbar. Like many people, I learned the Bobby Dunbar story from Tal McThenia's *This American Life* radio documentary "The Ghost of Bobby Dunbar." (I admit to not hearing the original 2008 broadcast; I encountered the story years later.) Tal McThenia also wrote a wonderful book, with Margaret Dunbar Cutright, titled *A Case for Solomon: Bobby Dunbar and the Kidnapping that Haunted a Nation* (2012).

In Bobby Dunbar's tale I found such a wealth of interesting ideas about family, power, authenticity and identity that I am forever grateful to have stumbled upon it. But the moment I started writing this novel, I left historical fact behind. Should the reader be interested in truth rather than fiction, I recommend McThenia and Dunbar Cutright's detailed and compassionate book.

LOST
BOY
FOUND

PART ONE

LOST

CHAPTER ONE

The three boys bounded through the grass toward the forest, a spray of panicky hoppers glimmering around them, while John Henry recited the passage from *Scouting for Boys* that approved the adventure. He nodded when he reached the end.

Mary fixed her eyes on the children, one arm raised to block the late-morning sun. "They've never gone so far on their own."

"George wants responsibility." John Henry smiled at his wife. "We should encourage him."

"Seven's no age for responsibility, John." Nor, she thought, old enough to shepherd a six- and a four-year-old, neither of whom could walk unsupervised to their bedroom at night without veering off to investigate some amusing distraction. An insect, a thud. But she bit her tongue for fear the Scouts had something to say about that, too.

Mary watched her boys slow their pace and enter the forest, lifting their hands and knees as though wading into cold sea. In a blink they were gone, indistinguishable from the dark mess of pine trees, discarded branches and spiky under-growth.

The Davenport family stayed at Half Moon Lake in July. Their Louisiana lake house was smaller than their home in Opelousas, but still impressive: two stories, pale blue, with slate-gray shutters, white trim, a wide porch and a balcony off the main bedroom. The house sat five hundred yards from the lake, which was fringed on three sides by for-est, at the top of a clearing, providing the Davenports a dress circle view and unimpeded access to the water. Here, Mary woke to birdsong and the smell of fresh-baked ginger cake, and later played piano while the drawing-room cur-tains swelled on the breeze. John Henry took breakfast with his wife, read the *St. Landry Clarion*, the *Atlantic Monthly*, *Outdoor Life*, the latest *Picayune*, then worked on plans to further expand his business. The Davenport boys—George, Paul and Sonny—watched by Nanny Nelly, spent their days playing cowboys and Indians, chasing dun-colored rabbits, and kicking a ball to one another. In the afternoons, John Henry instructed them in an aspect of Scoutcraft.

This summer day was muggy, but oak trees surrounding the house offered enough shade that John Henry, Mary and their guests, Ira and Gladys Heaton and Gladys's mother, Mrs. Billingham, would sit outside, as John Henry pre-ferred.

"Perhaps *air* will ease my headaches. Now that my daugh-ter has declared my homeopathics quackery, I'm left to suffer without relief." Mrs. Billingham fanned herself.

"You know the pastilles help. There's no reason to resist every modernity." Gladys turned to Mary. "Eucalyptus and cocaine. They work wonders."

"Without any relief at all."

As the group enjoyed their sweet tea, bees harvested nearby crepe myrtle trees, and hummingbirds flew from foxgloves to hollyhocks in search of nectar.

The Davenport boys had joined the adults for a while that morning, squatting near the woodpile with their toy soldiers—unobserved, Nanny Nelly having been permitted a rare afternoon and evening off to visit her mother—until they'd grown restless and begged to go exploring.

"In search of what?" Mrs. Billingham asked.

"Life's compass," John Henry replied.

The men discussed business: John Henry's furniture manu-facturing company had sold a thousand chairs in the past eighteen months, and Ira Heaton's stationery company had secured a significant government contract. Gladys chattered about millinery, bemoaned her rust-red hair, envied Mary's glossy blackness. Mary worried about the boys. She feigned interest when Gladys, holding up an open copy of the *Delineator*, said, "Here's the ribbon I mean," and offered a sympathetic murmur when Mrs. Billingham confided that the pastilles made her pulse race.

When she went indoors, ostensibly to check with Cook that she'd remembered Mrs. Billingham's aversion to pepper, Mary shared her concern with her housekeeper, Esmeralda. "What if the boys meet with fire ants, snakes, alligators!"

Esmeralda folded her hands over her dusting cloth. "Mr.

Davenport's taught them how to behave in the outdoors. They won't come to harm."

"There's no behavior that fends off an alligator aside from firing a rifle," Mary said, though Esmeralda had, as always, calmed her.

At noon—as John Henry led Ira to the library to show him a recently acquired map of Peru, the women strolled in the garden, and John Henry's butler, Mason, pulled on his boots to go fetch the boys—George and Paul Davenport walked up the hill without their brother.

Mary stopped by the rose bushes. Gladys and Mrs. Billingham followed suit.

"George," Mary said. "Where's Sonny?"

"We thought maybe he'd be here."

"Why would you think that?"

Mrs. Billingham tsked.

"We looked every other place. Shouted and whistled."

"He's no good at hiding. Except this time. Dropped Hop though." Paul held Sonny's toy rabbit aloft by its threadbare arm.

"I said we'd name him the winner. Only had to show himself," George said.

"It's true, he said that."

"Where is he, then?" Mary's voice quickened.

Behind her, Gladys placed her fingertips on her mother's arm.

"Don't know." Paul shrugged.

Mary looked across the grassy expanse and glaring lake to the forest. Nothing moved. She grabbed Paul's wrist and pushed

George's shoulder to turn him around. "Inside, now." She called for John Henry as she hurried the boys up the front steps.

Sonny wasn't in the garden. He wasn't in the thickets or on the rope swing or in the shed. And though John Henry and Ira scoured the forest and lake's edge with Mason, they didn't find the boy.

While the adults searched, George and Paul sat on the porch steps, forbidden by Mary from moving one inch.

"He's hiding to get us into trouble," Paul said to Esmeralda.

George waved a fly from his face. "You don't know anything."

"I know I'm hungry."

"Hush, both of you." Esmeralda twisted a tie of her apron until it coiled. "Left your brother out there alone. Should be ashamed of yourselves."

Mary circled the house, frantic, ran inside to hunt in closets, beneath beds and behind doors, a ring of blackened linen flapping about her ankles. When she knelt on the steps and shook George, demanding he tell her again every word Sonny had said, reducing the boy to tears, Mrs. Billingham insisted Mary lie down.

Esmeralda served ham sandwiches and pastries, made a pot of coffee and, at Gladys's instruction, added a generous dash of brandy for Mrs. Davenport.

"No, no, no," Mary said. "No."

"There's no cause for alarm," Mrs. Billingham counseled. "John Henry will find the child."

But when she could, Mrs. Billingham suggested that Ira drive into town to alert the sheriff.

"The boy's only been missing a few hours," Ira said. "He's probably off frightening small creatures or digging a hole."

"Digging a hole? Is that what you think children do?" Mrs. Billingham stared meaningfully at the motor car.

Alone in the dark forest, his heart thundering, John Henry looked for signs of his son's passage: crushed leaves, broken branches, blood.

CHAPTER TWO

At six o'clock, Ira returned from Opelousas with Sheriff Sherman and three of his men. Everyone rushed out to meet the cars. In the overlapping introductions and activity—Cook being told to bring tea, Mason offering his assistance, the men adjusting dusty hats and clammy shirts, Esmeralda glaring at Paul to silence his cheep of "Mister, mister"—the sheriff stood, straight-backed and speckless, as though in the eye of a storm.

John Henry stepped forward to shake the sheriff's hand, noted his healthy solidity, glints of white in chestnut hair, the thoughtful narrowing of his eyes as he scanned the surroundings, the unforced kindness in his voice when he spoke to Mary.

"My deputy's coming with dogs. And we have a few hours' light. We'll find him." He pointed two of his men toward the woods and one to the house. "You've been to the resort?" he asked John Henry.

"Surely that's too far?"

"Not if he cut across the hill. I think it's worth talking to them."

Once his men had scattered and John Henry and Ira had driven off, the sheriff turned to George and Paul, who were still flanking Esmeralda. "Now," he said as he crouched down, "how about you tell me exactly what happened out there."

The Starry Lake Resort was one mile east of the Davenports' Half Moon home by road, but less, as the sheriff said, if Sonny had clambered over the hills. So John Henry and Ira sped down the shaded road, past cotton fields and run-down farmhouses, toward the resort. Where they'd usually comment on dimwitted landowners being stuck on old ways, the increasing number of cattle falling to disease or the frustration of managing Negro workers, they stayed silent.

The resort catered to the area's wealthiest citizens. Membership was by invitation, referral or bequest. During the past year, the outside walls and columns had been painted and the cedar ceilings, marble mantels and Oriental carpets revived. Tennis courts were added. Local newspapers followed the progress of the renovation. Families picnicked outside the grounds, and the children of local lumbermen stared through the curlicued metal gates. The resort had reopened with fanfare in May, promising an elegant atmosphere reminiscent of the glory days of the South, before the war.

When the afternoons were dry and not too hot, wasp-waisted ladies wearing slippery silk and long strands of pearls ambled beneath magnolia trees, while men of influence stroked their whiskers and discussed the issues of the day: workers' strikes in England, the trouble in the Balkans,

Colonel Gracie's new book *The Truth About the Titanic*, a second example—following *The Truth About Chickamauga*—of his talent for rendering thrilling events dreary (Gracie's recent death noted then ignored). They discussed how to assist one another's endeavors, too.

At night, when the wind blew the right way, birch trees shimmied music from the resort through the forest to the Davenport living room. Mary closed her eyes and listened, imagining dancing couples lit by crystal chandeliers, while John Henry stewed about the conversations taking place without him. Important people made important decisions at Starry Lake Resort. For too long, he'd dismissed the resort as inconsequential. But his friend Judge Roy insisted otherwise, and promised he'd nominate John Henry next month. John Henry had ambitious plans, and membership at the resort would be key to their success.

It had never been part of John Henry's plans to stand on the dirt driveway and rattle those formidable gates in frustration, shouting out for entry to the resort to search for his son. Yet there he was. Ira Heaton pressed his car horn again, stopping at the sight of a dumpy man with a scowl plodding across the lawn toward them.

John Henry's first encounter with the resort lacked dignity, but he hoped at least the gates would be opened for him. The man spat tobacco on the ground. "Members only."

Speaking through the bars, John Henry told his story, describing Sonny, and making sure the man understood—if he didn't already from John Henry and Ira's appearance—that he was unaccustomed to being denied entry anywhere.

The man lifted one shoulder in a shrug. "I'll keep an eye

out. And ask in the kitchen and laundry who's come and gone. We get a lot of deliveries. Could be someone offered him a ride."

As John Henry walked back to the car, Ira stepped closer to the gate. "You understand that is the very opposite of reassurance?"

"Wasn't aware coddling strangers was part of my job."

Word traveled that a boy had gone missing at Half Moon Lake, and people from surrounding towns, farms and even a docked showboat volunteered to help. They searched the chapel and school, asked around in local stores. In no time at all, a hundred men, glad of summer's late light, were spread across the landscape, occasionally raising their hats to wipe their brows with kerchiefs, whacking sticks through the undergrowth, sending grass seeds and mosquitoes into the air. Some rode on twitchy horses, cradling shotguns. Snuffling hounds ran diagonals in front of them.

A beady-eyed tanner called Jackson Lane found small footprints beside the railway tracks, and the searchers swooped, like a flock of starlings, up the hill and into the drier woodland above the lake where the trains cut through. The sheriff told one of the younger searchers to run back to the house and fetch Sonny's sandals. "Ask the housekeeper, not the mother. And mind your manners." When the boy returned, breathless and sweaty, the sheriff held the sandals next to the prints. The men craned into a circle and saw the prints were, yes, the right size.

Nobody could agree on why the prints petered out.

"He's been taken," Jackson said. "Lifted onto a train."

"Then why's there no grown man's footprints? You saying somebody strong enough to jes' reach out and swoop him up from a moving train?" one man asked.

"Impossible," John Henry said.

"There's no train today," another chimed in.

"Freight trains go slower," Jackson said.

The sheriff held one hand up to silence the men. "I've told you twice to back off. Y'all hard of hearing?"

John Henry exhaled loudly. Ignoring the sheriff's instructions, the men had stomped around the prints, snapping twigs and squashing Indian grass, making and perhaps destroying leads. His own children knew better.

Sheriff Sherman asked his deputy to drive to the stationmaster's house to get the schedule, but he was clearly skeptical of Jackson's theory. "Even a beanpole like you couldn't reach out that far from a train, no matter the speed."

All through the night, searchers came into the house in waves, trudging up the hill under a starry sky with only a sliver of moon. The men smelled of whiskey, pine smoke and salty sweat, and lay down in the kitchen and dining room on make-do bedding brought in by the Ladies Aid. Esmeralda spread hessian sacks on the ground for the dogs. The symphony of snores—hound and human—croaking frogs, hooting owls, and music from the resort made the house thrum. The sounds carried to the Davenports' bedroom, where John Henry slouched for a brief rest in a chair by the window and Mary wept and slept, shook then sat numb, clutching Sonny's toy rabbit.

Down the hallway, George and Paul sat cross-legged on their beds in the dark.

"He's too chicken to be out at night," George said. "Unless he's really lost, or you said something to make him stay there. Did you say something?"

"Nothing bad," Paul whispered.

"What'd you say?"

CHAPTER THREE

The following afternoon, Tom McCabe and Eddie Dale arrived at the lake.

"Wish he'd let us come out earlier." Eddie dropped his cigarette to the ground and stubbed it out with his heel.

"You've got plenty of time to get your pictures," Tom said.

"Spoken like a writer."

Tom surveyed the scene, taking in the army of men, the exhausted dogs lying in packs, the glossy lake rippled from Negroes dragging heavy nets through it. He smelled the tadpoley muck of roots draped along the lake's edge, felt warmth rising up from the earth. Tom put his hands in his pockets, jiggling his lucky pennies. Then, instead of heading to the lake to get the facts from the sheriff—like he knew he should—he went to the house to find the boy's mother.

It wasn't hard to figure out which woman was Mary Davenport. She sat in a white wicker chair at the front of the house, in the shade of a tree, upright and pale as a lily, ignoring the women who swooshed about her. She'd fixed her eyes on the lake. A breeze blew tendrils of fallen hair from her face, creating a clear line of sight into which Tom intruded.

"Mrs. Davenport? My name's Tom McCabe. I'm a reporter at the *St. Landry Clarion*. I'm here with our photographer, Eddie Dale." He used his hat to point out Eddie, who'd stood his tripod near the lake.

Mary looked at Tom, her attention perfunctory.

"We'd like to tell our readers about your missing boy. One of them might know something." He waited. "I'm sure he'll be back home in no time, Mrs. Davenport, no time at all, but I—"

"You think they'll find him soon?" Mary flicked her eyes up at Tom. Hazel, bloodshot, Tom noted, with a spray of freckles across her nose. "Do you think so?"

And though he had no idea about anything, Tom said, "I'm sure of it, Mrs. Davenport." He took out his notebook and licked his pencil. "So what's Sonny like—is he a good boy?" Tom shook his head. "Of course he is. What does he like to do? When I was a boy I was crazy for animals. Chased chickens around the yard, rode the mule though I wasn't supposed to." Mary turned her attention back to the lake. "I have a dog now, Mrs. Davenport—he's named Walter. He's a terrific dog. Does Sonny like dogs?"

"Sonny *loves* dogs. He begs his father for one." Her voice softened. "When Sonny's found I'll tell him he can have a dog, any one he likes."

"I'll bet you will. And what boy wouldn't love that."

Esmeralda came out of the house and shooed Tom away. "Mrs. Davenport needs quiet."

Tom didn't like being spoken to that way by a Negro,

but neither Mary nor her attendants reprimanded Esmeralda. Tom dipped his head to Mary and walked down the hill to Eddie, who was pulling himself out from under his camera cloth.

"This is Jackson Lane." Eddie nodded at the man in front of his lens. "You'll want to talk to him—he found a clue."

"And I can too reach a boxcar from there," Jackson said. "Lay down and tested it."

"Bully for you," Tom muttered, and rolled his eyes at Eddie. How many times had he told him to steer clear of the crazies?

A dozen yards away, John Henry boomed out instructions to the Negroes standing thigh-deep in the lake. Out of the corner of his eye, Tom saw Mary stride toward her husband. He hoped she didn't say a reporter had planted ideas in her head about a dog. If he wanted to get the story he'd need to win over all the players. Huh, but there was something telling: as Mary moved closer to John Henry he turned, sensing her, and his hand and hers rose up and reached out through the air for its mate.

As the sun dropped behind the hills, the lake changed color from moss green to fleshy pink, purple, resting at black. Slow-moving searchers made fires and lit lanterns. Smoke whorled against the spangled sky and amber firelight cast strange shadows on the men's faces. To John Henry, watching from the porch, the scene resembled a Bible School painting, a Hell of barking dogs, black men and wild flames, in which his boy wandered, lost.

Local women shuttled chicken, yams and corn to the trestle tables set up on the lawn and put a tray out for leftovers to give to the colored men. John Henry was close enough to hear the women talking to one another, blending practical and personal comments, sharing anecdotes.

All of this to an unseemly score of ragtime tunes drifting out from the resort.

It was remarkable to John Henry how quickly an abnormal situation had become normalized, how by the second night there were systems in place for eating and sleeping. He approved of the methodical intelligence of it but struggled to control his rising panic. None of this noisy industry had yielded anything, but it would. It must.

Meanwhile, Mrs. Billingham stood at the living-room window, one hand holding back the heavy curtain so she could watch. "I'm certain they haven't put out enough food," she said to Gladys, then abandoned her post to collapse into the nearest armchair. "But I'll spend what energy I have caring for Mary." She rubbed her worked wrist. "What an awful ordeal."

"So awful. I do hope they find him soon."

Mrs. Billingham glanced at Mary, who had unintentionally consumed enough alcohol to fall asleep on the sofa, her face squashed into a cushion, another skirt ruined. "Ring the bell, Gladys. I'll have Esmeralda help Mary to her room."

Gladys was tapping her boot in time to what she could hear of the distant Joplin tune.

"Gladys."

"Yes, yes." Gladys, pouting, walked across the room and rang the bell. "Another night ruined because of one naughty boy. I'm not sure I ever want children."

* * *

"Tell me," George insisted, again. It was too hot to sleep. They knelt on the wooden floor, side by side, and stuck their heads out the window in the hope of seeing some of the action, but the backyard was empty.

Paul folded his arms on the sill. "What does it matter? They'll look for him anyhow."

"Just *tell* me."

Knowing that George would keep at him like a wood-pecker, Paul gave in. "I told him he wasn't our brother. That we were only letting him stay till his real family came back from a war. And then he'd have to go live with them in the North and we'd never see him again and good riddance because I was sick of him following me like a bad smell."

"What war?"

"I made that up."

"You made all of it up." George punched his brother in the arm. "Idiot."

"I didn't know he'd run off forever." Paul's eyes filled with tears. "Do you think he's okay?"

"No. He can't even buckle his shoes." George stood up. "I'm telling Pa."

"Don't! It won't make any difference."

George figured this was probably true. The adults would search for Sonny until they found him, no matter what Paul had said. And if Paul admitted he'd scared Sonny, he'd be made to sit alone and think about what he'd done, banned from playing games, and George would be left with nothing to do. That wouldn't be fair. He glared at his brother. "You've done a lot of dumb things, but this is the dumbest."

CHAPTER FOUR

Thick clouds covered the sky and heavy midsummer rain fell, making the search harder. Day after day, men trod across gummy mud and slippery grass, and sought to keep memories of comfortable beds at bay.

If there'd been other footprints they were washed away, along with any scent of the boy. Without a doable task, the dogs became fretful and undisciplined, chased squirrels darting for cover, played deaf to their owners' calls. Bill O'Sullivan's setter was snatched by an alligator when the dog padded too close to the water's edge, nose down, not seeing the serpentine eyes in the lake's pocked surface. Bill shot at the gator as it yanked his fine-boned setter into the lake, but in a flash there was nothing to shoot at other than trampolining water.

Men came from Crowley, Alexandria and Baton Rouge. Each train that stopped near Half Moon Lake collected sodden searchers to return them home and delivered a fresh batch of helpers. When the trains stopped for the night, the men slept on floors and in canvas tents, the colored men taking shelter from the rain on the back porch. But the searchers found nothing, not a trace of Sonny Davenport aside from that one set of vanished prints.

The reporters who milled around the muddy patch where the footprints had been discovered, now marked by a flagged stick, agreed it would take a giant of a man to reach that far from a moving train.

"Unless," Tom whispered to Eddie, "he wasn't on a train."

Eddie raised his eyebrows.

"Could be our man was on a horse, walking the tracks, knowing he'd hear a train if one came. Lot of scrub and uneven ground up here, except on the tracks. Sees the boy. Easy enough to help him onto a horse, tempt him with a ride home."

"A horse wouldn't like those rocks between the sleepers. Maybe the boy was walking the tracks by himself. That wouldn't leave prints either."

"Less likely, I'd say." Tom had already fashioned horse-related headlines and didn't want Eddie messing with his percolating theory.

The sheriff had his men interview the guests, staff, musicians and suppliers who'd passed in and out of the resort on that day. He contacted stationmasters along the train line and extended the foot search ten miles in every direction. He sent for Indian trackers, regretting he hadn't done so before the rain. And he reluctantly told John Henry about a possibility closer to home.

"It might be that an alligator's taken him. Wouldn't be the first time around here."

John Henry nodded. "I know."

The sheriff didn't mention Bill O'Sullivan's dog; he only wanted John Henry to be clear about why he'd instructed his men to blast the lake.

The ground shook as men threw sticks of dynamite into the water. The blasts brought scores of stunned and dead catfish, crappie and bass to the surface. A tree was uprooted and drifted across the lake, its branches wafting about like hair. Each time a whole alligator floated to the top, belly up, tangled in hyacinth, the men dragged it onto land and sliced it open with care. They cut through the armored back and dug into the creature's carcass, pushing muddy fingers into organs and around muscle, feeling for any trace of the boy—shredded clothing, human bones—while being mindful of how much the skin would be worth once they determined who had the right to sell it.

In the quiet between booms, people shouted to one another and whistled to wayward dogs. The men's numbers grew to two hundred. The manager of the Starry Lake Resort, more understanding than the groundskeeper, dispatched another dozen members of his ground staff. The Davenports' friends sent their servants to assist. Gladys and Mrs. Billingham stayed on and had their maids travel from Opelousas to tend to their needs. Half Moon Lake had never seen so many people.

They would find him. The reporter had assured Mary of that again yesterday when she'd snuck downstairs for relief from her room and the endless unhelpful visitors. He'd asked if he could join her on the porch, then leapt up the steps two at a time like Paul did. She'd almost smiled.

"Mrs. Davenport." He'd lifted his hat an inch above his head.

"I'm sorry, I—"

"Tom McCabe, and you owe me no apology. This isn't any way to make a person's acquaintance." He'd glanced toward the open front door. "I'd wager it's crowded in there, too. You have a lot of friends, Mrs. Davenport."

"Oh, I don't know these people. I'm grateful for their help, of course—"

"Of course." He'd lowered his voice. "Not everyone is as helpful as they'd like to believe in these situations though."

At that, she had smiled. "Are you helpful, Mr. McCabe?"

"I sure am. A good reporter is part bowerbird, part bloodhound. There's many a time a reporter has solved a case before the detective."

"Is that so?" she'd said, as though they were at a party, making playful conversation. "I wonder if Sheriff Sherman knows that."

Uttering the sheriff's name had sobered Mary, and she'd fallen silent.

"Mrs. Davenport," Tom had said, in a tone determined to reassure, "there are hundreds of men out there now, whole acres of brawn and brain. There's no doubt they'll find him."

Mary lay in bed, as unable to sleep as her boys, replaying her conversation with Tom McCabe. John Henry had brought the doctor from Opelousas that morning, and though he'd come armed with medicines for anxiety and insomnia, Mary refused to take them. She wanted to be alert when Sonny was found.

So many unfamiliar sounds filled her house this evening. She could pick out Esmeralda's steadfast clomp up and down the stairs, the insistent ringing of the living-room bell, the ceaseless opening and closing of doors. But there were voices she didn't recognize: men on the porch, women in the hall. There was a braying horse, metal clanks—and was that Gladys singing?

Rain hammered down so relentlessly that Mary imagined the roof collapsing onto her, a wet crash of wood and slate. She pictured water streaming through her room and down the hill, gouging into the earth, filling the lake. The thought of this watery chaos—of Sonny outside in this monstrous weather—was too awful. She slapped the bedspread with one hand, Hop in the other, and pushed herself up.

Mary walked to the mantel to stare again at the photograph of Sonny in an oval brass frame. He'd enjoyed having his picture taken, the only one of the three who did. George had tolerated it, as always showing serious forbearance. Paul had fidgeted and fussed, complained about the tedium of so much sitting. Sonny had grinned—more than John Henry had wanted for this family record, but she'd winked at her son, encouraged him. Why wasn't there more of him, she thought. A picture, clothes, a toy rabbit: that wasn't enough.

She'd had to part with the photograph for two days. The sheriff wanted the newspapers to use the one picture and written description. "Otherwise they take unhelpful liberties," he'd explained.

Mary and John Henry had drafted Sonny's description together, giving rise to the worst disagreement they'd had since his disappearance. When they'd recalled the origin of

Sonny's unique feature—a curved scar above his elbow, wide in the middle, from being yanked out of the birth canal by forceps—Mary became angry about the scar Paul sported on *his* arm from an irresponsible (Mary's word), unfortunate (John Henry's) lesson in whittling. Later, the sheriff told them he'd omit the detail of Sonny's scar in any case, saying to Mary that he often withheld one piece of information to check for hucksters, and then, to John Henry, that it was a mark easily added to a child's arm by unscrupulous criminals hoping for a reward. They described Sonny instead as having his mother's almond eyes and rosy cheeks, with fair hair and all his teeth; a shorter build than some boys of his age, but still robust. Mary wanted to add "cheerful" but the men pointed out, gently, that under the circumstances that might not be the case.

Sonny was her favorite. Each of the others had held that title for a while, then lost it.

She'd been besotted with George because he was the first, and such a happy baby. But once he could talk, John Henry became his teacher, and the boy grew so clever so quickly it alarmed her. George didn't mean to rattle her with his hungry intelligence, but Mary no longer felt easy in her role. Her warmth seemed childish, her authority shaky. George became his father's son.

Then Paul had arrived, a rascal from the start. He'd adored her without restraint, but lately he'd become defiant and argumentative.

Sonny's birth had been the easiest, since the doctor brought chloroform. She'd passed out instantly, felt no pain. "The miracle of medicine," the doctor had said. After the birth, he'd encouraged Mary to drink French tonics when she fed Sonny.

They'd both been relaxed for months, and that sweet comfort had stayed between them.

Mary stood at the bedroom window, resting her forehead on the glass. The clouds obscured whatever stars there might have been, and the fires were wet ash. There wasn't enough light for her to tell if any men were out in the rain. But the longer Mary stared, the more she saw pulsing dark spots, inexplicable movement. Was Sonny watching from afar, teaching his brothers a lesson for some infraction they were refusing to admit? It wasn't as though she hadn't grilled George and Paul. And unless Sonny was injured or trapped, it wasn't too far from forest to house. Where was he?

When he could, John Henry read aloud to distract his wife. Mary enjoyed reading but now couldn't muster the concentration, and her eyes stung from crying. At first, he read from the *Clarion* about the Gettysburg reunion, which had brought Fifty-Thousand Men to the Site. But Mary curled into a ball on her bed and sobbed that Sonny would have loved that tale. So John Henry abandoned the newspaper in favor of Muir's *The Yosemite*, hoping the steady describing of rocks and streams, irised waterfalls, forests of silver fir would soothe her as it did him. "*And from the eastern boundary of this vast golden flower-bed rose the mighty Sierra, miles in height, and so gloriously colored and so radiant, it seemed not clothed with light, but wholly—*"

"How long until they find him, John? It's been seven days."

John Henry placed his book on the side table. "Soon, my love. There's no chance he'll remain undiscovered for much longer."

As he pushed himself up from the chair, Mary lurched across the bed.

"He's alone." She gripped his arm. "Seven days alone!"

Once John Henry had coaxed his wife to sleep, with the aid of the doctor's alkaloids, he sat, again, in the nearest armchair to watch her. He rested one hand on the books piled next to him. Thoreau, Longfellow, Emerson. If he could choose, he'd summon Emerson for company. Thoreau was an impressive naturalist, and John Henry could almost admire the rigor he showed in abstaining from tobacco, alcohol and meat (and salt!), but Thoreau's rejection of companionship was troubling. The man was a misanthrope, and he had no children. Best he remain on the page. Longfellow was too emotional to give sturdy comfort to another. Emerson would understand. Devastated by the deaths of his first wife and one of his sons, he'd emerged wise and empathetic. Emerson was a man John Henry would like to sit with now. In reality, though, he was as good as alone.

John Henry was aware that his readings and the doctor's medicines could only do so much for his wife. He sent for Father Clement. Mary had never warmed to the priest ("He barely notices I'm standing beside you"), but John Henry knew he'd deliver assurance of a kind no one else could. And since the Davenports had unfailingly attended his ten o'clock Mass for years, married in his original church and contributed generously to the building of its impressive replacement, he assumed his request would not go ignored. He was right. Father Clement arrived at Half Moon Lake the same day he was bidden.

Mary tolerated several hour-long visits before imploring her husband to keep the priest away. "He speaks nothing but platitudes."

"He speaks God's word."

"I pray every day for God's help. My palms are all but welded together. Can I not speak with Him directly? I'm unconvinced Father Clement prays as urgently as I or—"

"Mary, stop."

"You know he wants more money for his German stained glass windows."

"He did mention that."

"I don't need him as emissary of my message, John. If he'll pray for Sonny's return, then good. I beg he asks the entire congregation to do so as well. But let me pray on my own."

Mrs. Billingham and Gladys ministered to Mary, too, under instruction from John Henry not to offer opinion or update. Gladys brushed Mary's hair, and chatted about the interesting items in her magazines. Mrs. Billingham rang the bell for dry pillowslips and sweet tea, scented Mary's handkerchiefs with lavender oil, and ensured the servants didn't become lazy.

The women listened as, during her lucid moments, Mary worried about how hungry Sonny would be, how frightened, then railed against Nanny Nelly's thoughtlessness.

"For her to have spent the night away when you needed her, it's appalling." Mrs. Billingham sniffed. "Why haven't you dismissed her?"

"Oh, I couldn't do without her. No, I need to remind her that her loyalty is to us. That's what I need to do."

Mrs. Billingham examined an itchy spot on her thumb. "If you think that's best."

When Mary did take the doctor's formulations she slept, but woke hot and bilious, and suffered baffling dreams of the bayou near her childhood home. Not Half Moon Lake in the sunshine, not her favorite picnic spot near Spearmint Pond, not the banks of the Mississippi, not any other pleasing or relevant body of water. Not a reunion with Sonny. Asleep, her mind clawed and yowled.

She dreamed she sat on the slippery red leather seat of her family's buggy, next to her black-clad mother and facing her glowering father, as they rolled down the long road away from Arlington Grove Plantation. She felt the cool shadows as the buggy passed beneath thick trees, then the slowed trot of the horses—the horses slowing, though Thomas never asked them to—as they entered the bayou, a place so different from the airy flats around their plantation. Here the greens were darker, the plants gnarled. The cypress trees in the bayou were draped with moss. Algae and reeds fringed the edges of the water. Armies of insects buzzed loudly enough to be heard over the rattling wheels.

Mary wished her father would stop the buggy and let her go to the soupy water's edge, where the alligators lived. She'd seen a quick whip of tail going under water, marble eyes floating on the surface, but never the whole creature. She'd heard their bellow and hiss. The idea of an animal so hideous thrilled her. But neither in life nor in her dreams did she ask her father to stop.

When Mary dreamed of this swampland, so many years

and miles away, she woke gulping for air. Lying in the dark, she tried to take her mind elsewhere, to muster the quiet resolve her husband prized and needed from her. Because who did he have, who did she have, if they were to fail one another?

CHAPTER FIVE

On day eight, John Henry and Sheriff Sherman drove to the nearby cotton mill.

"What we want to check," the sheriff explained, "is that Jack Knowles hasn't scooped him up and put him to work."

"He's four years old."

But as John Henry walked the aisles of Knowles Mill, between rows of deafening steel machinery—all moving at rapid-fire speed, and without guardrails or shields—he understood the ignorance of his remark. There were dozens of children working in the hot, airless factory, and few of them had been alive long enough to hit double digits.

"How is he getting away with this?" John Henry asked, his booming voice rising above the clatter. "These children are far too young for factory jobs."

"Not uncommon, though I share your opinion," the sheriff answered loudly in kind. "Ten-hour days are too long. And this is dangerous work."

"Can't you do something to stop it?" John Henry watched

as a slip of a boy—six at most—climbed on a spinning frame to grab at a flapping broken thread, his blackened fingers darting in and out between the metal rollers.

The sheriff guided them toward a quieter section of the plant. "We've cleared out the youngest ones three times in as many months. Did the same in the mine, the wood mill. But the minute we leave they flood right back in again. It's like sweeping water out of a river." He stopped. "How do you run your factory?"

"I'd never dream of employing children this young."

"Well, poorer folks around here encourage it. It gets harder to judge when you know some of these young'uns are supporting their whole family." He bent down to pick up a shard of green glass. "You didn't work when you were a boy?"

John Henry blushed.

"Huh. Lucky you."

The two men passed spinners, ravellers, loopers, doffers removing bobbins and spindles from whining frames, children working barefoot and bandaged, but none of them was Sonny. And each of the children said the same thing: they'd seen no unfamiliar boy, accompanied or otherwise, in the mill.

"Most likely a tramp took him," a young girl offered, her patched pinafore straining across her chest, her hair in a thin braid that hung between her shoulderblades. "Most likely." A tall boy in too-short pants next to her agreed.

Sheriff Sherman assured John Henry there was no "most likely" about anything. "Problem is, if anyone does see a tramp with your boy it might not register. Hobos make use of strays all the time—having a child in tow makes folks more inclined to open their barn for the night." He pushed on the heavy factory door, letting in a welcome gust of fresh air. "Decent folks, that is."

Their time in the cotton mill rattled John Henry, not only because some of the children were Sonny's age but also because he felt naive. His extensive reading and solid education were not enough to overcome the limitations of his life experience. And he could think of no quick fix or pithy quote to reduce his discomfort.

On day nine, John Henry and the sheriff drove even further, out to the Conroy brothers' sawmill.

"If someone stole your boy or persuaded him to travel with them, fifteen miles is not so far. And like Knowles, the Conroys aren't strangers to trouble." The sheriff steered the car off the main road onto a rutted track that ran parallel with the train line.

Neither of the Conroy brothers was at their mill, but the site manager perched on a stool in the shack said the sheriff and John Henry could talk to the men, so long as they didn't keep them from their work. He whistled out the open window for a boy, then sent him to find out if anybody knew the whereabouts of the Mr. Conroys.

"In town, I'd guess," the manager said to the sheriff and John Henry. "Though I couldn't say for sure."

"Well, I'm going to take a wander around while they're doing their window-shopping and what have you," the sheriff said.

While Sheriff Sherman stood in the entrance to the lot, hands on hips, considering which part of the mill to check first, John Henry walked toward the wide muddy river, having been alerted to a passing steamboat by a sounding call. The Negro leadsman's plangent call to the pilot was functional, singing the depth of the water. But the slow, low voice stirred John Henry, tugged at a buried memory. *Mark Four-or-or.* Deep water, the safest kind. His father had taught him that, if little else.

He gazed across the yard, noticing that here, too, young children in dirty clothes skittered in and out of buildings, carrying heavy buckets, working in pairs to push full wheelbarrows. What different lives they had from his own boys.

John Henry hadn't wanted to tell the sheriff that although he'd never been to the mill, he was familiar with the Conroy name, had purchased from them. He and his business partner, Hank, bought their wood clean and planked at the market. To see it here, though, was something else. Even given the reason for their visit, and trusting the sheriff's judgment about the Conroys, John Henry couldn't help feeling some exhilaration. The sawmill was noisy and bustling, and the smell of fresh-cut wood was enlivening. He stopped at a towering pile of logs: virgin longleaf pine, heavy and durable. These were logs harvested from old-growth forests, stands treasured for their purity. He placed a hand on the coarse bark and felt a push of anger: so often he'd had to compete with Northern buyers for this beautiful wood. They bought down here now, outbidding him, driving up the prices because they'd stripped bare their own forests. John Henry thought that if he owned this wood he'd keep it in the South, yes he would.

Wanting to hear what the men were saying, John Henry joined the sheriff as he walked around the mill, talking with workers at the dipping station and in the drying yard, men on breaks smoking or whittling or sharing chunks of sausage and bread. The sheriff spoke easily with them, making jokes at the Conroys' expense then at his own uncallused hands and starched shirt (the men wearing overalls, britches, unpolished boots without laces), growing serious when he explained John Henry's situation. When the sheriff told him to, John Henry held up the pamphlet that bore Sonny's picture, and when he spoke, he did so slowly for those he suspected were feeble-minded or foreign. The men seemed interested enough, but none of them knew anything about Sonny.

On day ten, John Henry and Sheriff Sherman visited the clutch of cabins where the Negroes lived, near the rank swamplands where no one else would make a home.

While the sheriff hadn't let the reporters follow him to the mills, he did today. "They might learn something," he'd said to John Henry.

The group roamed from one flimsy shack to the next, through patches of fleabane and foxtail grass, around puddles. At each house, the newsmen stood on their toes to see past the sheriff through opened doorways, keen to include details of interiors. They would describe the smell of red beans and rice (onion, pepper), catfish frying in oil, the lack of furniture, so their story would stand out from the others.

At the start of the day, Sheriff Sherman had stood on a stump to tell the newsmen what he knew so far. "Listen up, ladies, because I don't want you stopping me every twenty yards with your questions. And Tom McCabe, quit jangling those coins. I can't think with that everlasting noise."

"Seconded," Max from the *Bugle* had shouted, and they'd all laughed.

"Yeah, yeah," said Tom, as Eddie patted him on the back, a gesture of camaraderie rather than comfort since anyone could see the reporters liked Tom.

John Henry's and Tom's eyes had met, and they'd both smiled. John Henry was grateful for a moment's levity. Tom was glad of connection, but unnerved by the depth of sadness in John Henry's face. Without any desire to do so, since a reporter's purview was fact not emotion, Tom felt a stab of pain knowing how much the loss of his son would wound this man. Tom wondered about John Henry's upbringing, whether he had a cruel or kind father, a warm or distant mother, siblings. John Henry wondered at Tom's combination of slouching looseness and razor-sharp attentiveness.

Sheriff Sherman told the men to keep a respectful distance. Still, they inched forward when they thought they could and then back, forward and back in waves.

"These ramshackle houses disturb me," John Henry whispered to the sheriff. "So many people in one small room, and that tar-black woman suckling a baby—she was barely clothed…"

"I'm sure they'd live in palaces if they could."

"They'd be better off outdoors. Stale air poisons the blood." John Henry looked behind him to check the reporters weren't listening in. "Do you ever question our wisdom in having brought these people to American soil? I have no desire to vilify Negroes, but if they're not going to improve their lives now they're free they may as well live in any country."

Sheriff Sherman stepped onto the next weatherworn porch. "You'd send them back?" He knocked on the door.

"That's not a terrible idea, is it, to be with one's own kind?"

"Certainly not an original idea, though even Lincoln abandoned it. Guess you'd need to do the same with the Irish, the Italians, the French. The Spanish and Germans, too. The Scots. Mexicans." He glanced back at John Henry. "There'd be nobody home but us and the Indians. And you know they don't want us here."

A young Negro woman opened the door, a bug-eyed girl dressed in rags slung around her hip. The woman looked at the photograph and shook her head. But the sheriff asked if she could show it to the others inside. He rested against the doorjamb while she did so.

"Davenport. That's English?"

"Yes, long ago. I had ancestors land at Plymouth Rock."

"You know where I'm going with this."

When the woman returned, the sheriff dug into his pocket and handed her little girl a wrapped candy.

"A pioneer and a slave aren't remotely the same," John Henry said. He knew that God had authored mankind's character, and created the world's hierarchy in which some taught and some learned, some led and some labored. But at a certain point the onus must be on the individual to improve their circumstances.

"No argument there."

"I suppose that Negro child's life isn't much worse than the children at the mill," John Henry said as they walked to the next lean-to. "Any one of them might choose to lead a worthier life than their parents."

The sheriff sighed. "Choice is a rich person's word, John." He turned to the reporters and raised his voice. "We're done here."

After fourteen days of searching, the Davenports headed back to Opelousas, despite Mary's foggy protestations, George's uncontainable tears and Paul's violent tantrums. Gladys and Mrs. Billingham were driven home the same afternoon. The searchers and newsmen left, too.

Life around the lake quieted. There'd been no sightings of the boy, and no further trace of his presence. There'd been no ransom note. And if it wasn't a kidnapping, an alligator, a wandering gone wrong, if he'd not been taken in by Negroes or Italians, the Knowles or the Conroys, then—people said— he must have been taken by a tramp. And if that were the case, he could be almost anywhere.

PART TWO

TRACKING AND ENDURANCE

CHAPTER SIX

Opelousas woke early, not only on rice, cotton and tobacco farms, not only where cattle, roosters and horses demanded it, but also in the town center. On this warm September morning, seven weeks to the day after Sonny Davenport went missing, as John Henry and Mary ate breakfast in silence and Esmeralda remade beds, Main Street bustled. Horses pulled buggies past the stately bank and lawyers' offices, fragrant French bakeries, outdoor markets, the Methodist, Baptist and Catholic churches, sharing the street with bicycles and the increasing number of motor cars. Ben Fleury opened the doors to his haberdashery store and paused to stretch his arthritic fingers. Barber Smith tightened the holdbacks on his shutters. The breeze smelled of hair cream, fresh bread, horse droppings and trash.

Tom and Eddie, along with reporters from the *Bugle*, the *Opelousas Daily* and *Louisiana Times*, milled outside the Davenports' front gate. They rested against tree trunks and sat on the stone steps in front of the iron gate, shuffling sideways to make room for visitors. The police turned a blind eye to the newsmen, except when the pack amounted to more than a dozen, at which time they told them to skedaddle.

When left in peace, the men talked among themselves and played cards. They were amiable but suspicious of one another, and always had an eye on the house. Occasionally a departing visitor or nurse would give the reporters a snippet of gossip: "He's drinking so much coffee his skin is gray," "She's barely awake before the hysteria rises and they rest her again," "There were bruises on young George's arm, and they weren't from roughhousing."

Some days the reporters from the *Bugle* and the *Opelousas Daily* hung about at the back of the house, where deliverymen came with meat, milk, ice and wood, hoping to find news there. But none of them got what they wanted: no useful information and no sign of John Henry or Mary. "I don't know if they have an underground tunnel or they're coming and going at midnight," the *Bugle's* photographer said. "But I'll be skinned alive if I give my editor one more picture of boys piddling about in grass."

Tom and his sunshine-colored dog Walter showed up about nine each morning. On their way to the Davenports', Tom threw whatever stick Walter had laid claim to so the dog could fetch it and swagger back, proud as if he'd found gold. Walking offered Tom valuable thinking time: he thought about how to get his story, how he'd begin his article, how to describe John Henry's voice, Mary's eyes. Sometimes Tom would stop and flick through his notebook to check a sentence he'd copied from his reading: a gem of construction by Conrad, an evocative turn by Sinclair, a wise aside from

London (though he'd become less inspiring after his well-publicized bouts of drunken bragging). Tom had a good idea of what he wanted his story to be, but he had to get the facts first.

"Facts are everything, Tom," his editor, Mr. Collins, said. "Our job is to make sense of the world, tell the truth of things, and you can't do that without accurate, provable facts." This, from the man who'd told Tom to use *crush* instead of *defeat*, *despicable* over *bad*, to make liberal use of adjectives and imagined dialogue. "Keeps the readers' interest."

At a reminder of this, Mr. Collins said, "Not contradictory, no. The facts are your skeleton, Tom. They're vital, but not enough to make the thing live and breathe. You need to add meat: the blinding glare, the deafening roar, the turn of an ankle."

Sitting out front of the Davenport house hadn't got Tom what he needed. And it wasn't as easy as Mr. Collins made out. Everyone had heard the facts of Sonny's disappearance and the sheriff's search, but after that it was speculation. Tom knew not to dress that up as news.

When he arrived this morning, Tom greeted the group, told Dan Hardy from the *News* he'd enjoyed his piece about the musical show at the Athenaeum, was thinking about going along to see it himself. Eddie, who'd been at the house since the crack of dawn, patted Walter as he spoke to Tom. "Nothing, same as yesterday. They have to be getting some kind of cabin fever in there. And the boys, never let past this gate."

"Can you get cabin fever in a mansion?" Dan asked. "I'd bet there are rooms none of them has ever set foot in."

Tom stepped up to the fence and looked beyond the metal spikes at the trimmed flowerbeds, the clipped lawn, the persimmon and peach trees heavy with fruit, the towering Victorian house with its many balconies and chimneys. Dan wasn't wrong to call it a mansion. A tortoiseshell cat sat on the porch, flicking its tail, unblinking, watching a swallow that chirped, oblivious, on a branch not high enough to guarantee its safety. Tom's eyes traveled from cat to bird, but he lost interest in the fate of the swallow when the side door opened and Esmeralda walked out of the house carrying a wooden paddle. She headed to the patch of yard designated for chores, and when she came to a stop, she sighed, a sigh not heard by Tom but visible in the rise and drop of her chest. She lifted her paddle and began thumping the carpet slung on a length of rope between two trees.

Although she was only a housekeeper, Tom hoped Esmeralda might be his way into the story. She worked for the family six days a week, not confined to the kitchen or nursery but roaming around the house, able to see and hear everything. She'd been at the lake, a part of the drama from the beginning. And she'd met Tom more than once. Here was his advantage, his spy inside, if he could recruit her. Problem was, Esmeralda never stood still long enough for Tom to have anything like a conversation with her. She watered pots of mint, threw open windows, whacked rugs, swept, bossed the maid: she was always *doing*. On the most recent occasion Tom had called out to her, Esmeralda replied, "No, sir. Mr. Davenport says we're none of us to talk to you."

The tricks Tom used to win over white girls didn't feel right with Esmeralda. He tried joking, cajoling, even complimenting. One time he stayed at the back of the house for hours, sure she'd come out sooner or later. And she eventually had, opening the door and standing to one side as the maid lumbered out leaning under the weight of a full bucket.

"Let me help you ladies with that," Tom had said. Esmeralda ignored him and watched as the maid poured dirty water onto the grass. "It's me—Tom, from the lake."

"I know who you are, doesn't matter a whit." She hadn't even looked up.

But today, after Esmeralda had beaten the carpet clean, she glanced toward the front gate. Walter stood on his hind legs, his front paws sliding on the iron posts. Tom shouted out, "Walter says good morning." And Esmeralda, wonderfully, came toward them.

"Why'd you give him a man's name?" She pushed her hand into her apron pocket. Walter's nose twitched. "I've never met a man as big-hearted as this dog."

"Invite me into the yard awhile. I'll tell you about it."

"Uh-uh, no sir." Esmeralda fed some biscuit to Walter, then stuck her arm through the palings to scratch his head.

"Well now, that's something. Thank you."

"Thank you for what?"

"In my line of work it's important to get things right, and you've corrected my belief that Negroes don't like dogs. You've been nothing but kind to Walter."

Esmeralda straightened up. The man seemed to think his bluntness was endearing. Or else it didn't occur to him to exercise the good manners he'd show a white woman. She thought, but didn't say, that there were "beliefs" about men like him, too, beliefs that white men had nothing more substantial than a lead pencil dangling between their legs, that even the dumbest of them suffered the delusion they were smart, that they grew old but not up.

"I don't like dogs raised to hunt. But it seems to me your dog isn't the killing kind. Maybe he's not even a dog. Maybe you've got yourself a rabbit, a giant rabbit."

Tom laughed. "You might be right."

"Either way, you'll want to keep him out of Mr. Davenport's sight. He wouldn't need much excuse to call the dog-catcher." She didn't care about Tom, but Esmeralda had no desire to see Walter get hurt. And Mr. Davenport had a strange aversion to dogs.

Minutes after Esmeralda had gone back inside, a motor car stopped at the house. The driver yanked on the brake and leapt out to push open the driveway gates. Tom lifted his hat to Mrs. Billingham and Gladys Heaton, neither of whom acknowledged him. They'd never spoken to Tom, but he'd read plenty about them in his newspaper and others: Mrs. Billingham was celebrated in Opelousas for her charitable donations, and Mrs. Heaton for her appearance at fashionable gatherings, always in the latest dresses.

Tom's girl, Clara, had told him more than once about Gladys Heaton's renowned style. "If you do meet Gladys Heaton in real life, Tom, ask her where she has her gowns made. Paris, of course, but where *exactly*."

Tom had scoffed. "If I get to speak to her, I won't waste my time talking about ladies' clothes. I'll ask what Mary Davenport says, if there've been fresh leads. That's what I'll ask."

He walked toward the idling car, close enough to hear Mrs. Billingham say to Gladys that the day was gallingly sunny, and the weather ought to be on the turn by this time of year. Gladys replied, "Mother, last week you couldn't tolerate the gray afternoons, said the sky was too low. I'm not sure the weather can have any notion of how to please you."

When the ladies were inside the house, Nanny Nelly, carrying a hamper of clothing, came outside with George and Paul. Nelly sat in a garden chair, selected a pair of trousers, and began to darn. Nelly, Tom thought, seemed more amenable than Esmeralda. Maybe she could be his spy—a second-rate one, though, since everybody knew she was the dimmest light in the house.

Tom watched the two boys chase the cat, then howl at the unfairness of it outsmarting them with a sudden leap onto the fence. Walter didn't notice the cat until it was airborne, at which point he barked excitedly, wedged his jaw between the railings as if to push through the narrow opening, then yanked himself back and bolted along the sidewalk toward the neighboring yard. George remained po-faced at Walter's foolishness, Paul fell about laughing: that seemed their usual way.

"He might have more luck than you," Tom called out, smiling at Paul.

"Only if he can fly," Paul answered. But before Tom could take advantage of this chance to talk, George whispered in his brother's ear and the two walked closer to the house.

None of the reporters had been let anywhere near the Davenport boys, and they'd found that distance infuriating.

"They're witnesses," Dan Hardy said.

"Instigators, maybe," Eddie added.

Tom figured that if the boys knew anything of importance it would've got out by now, but they were the last ones to see

Sonny, so he wanted to talk to them. He had a way with kids, and he had Walter. He was about to shout out, see if he could convince Nanny Nelly to let the boys pat the dog, when Eddie nudged him in the ribs.

"Clara's here."

Most days, Clara showed up at the Davenport house with lunch for Tom, made by her family cook under her mother's watch. She'd bring sardines with crackers or pork with an apple, in a tin container. Sometimes she had pralines to share with the other men, too, the ones not so lucky to have a girl.

Walter kept their spirits up when things grew dull, chasing sticks and barking at birds, but Clara was the true ray of light in their days. When the newsmen saw her turn the corner on Westbury Grove then cross Mulberry Street toward the Davenport home, they perked up. Clara—curly-haired, slender, winsome—felt terrible for the family and admired Mary's dignity during such a time. "She's so brave," she'd say to the reporters, who were disarmed.

As the newsmen were watching Clara Tisdale cross the street, John Henry Davenport walked to the gate and cleared his throat. Clara saw him first, made wide eyes at Tom, and tipped her head toward the house. The reporters whipped about as one to face John Henry. Those who'd been seated leapt up, notebooks and cameras at the ready, alert as a pack of prairie dogs.

Tom saw that John Henry did indeed have ashen skin and dark circles beneath his eyes.

"Tom McCabe."

"Sir?"

With the other newsmen watching in silence, John Henry

reached over the fence and shook Tom's hand. "First time
we've formally met, I think. You still have those lucky coins?"

"I sure do." Tom tried to hide his pleasure at being picked
out from the crowd.

"Let's put them to work, then."

Tom could feel the other reporters watching, but didn't
want to lose time to a cocky win. He'd grab the rope John
Henry was throwing him. "I hope you know I'm doing everything I can to keep attention on your story, Mr. Davenport."

He saw from John Henry's frown this was a poor choice of
words. A man's son was not a story, and why would anyone's
attention have wavered? But before Tom could say more, John
Henry held out an envelope. "My wife wanted this to go to
you. To print." Noticing Walter, John Henry jerked his hand
back then turned and walked toward the house.

Were it not for the other reporters, Tom would've torn
open the envelope right away. All the while he'd been figuring
out how to get the inside story through a servant, and here
was John Henry Davenport handing it to him, just like that.
The reporters closed around Tom, jostling and yipping.

"Open it, McCabe."

"Tell us what it says."

Tom pushed his way out of the pack, grabbed Clara's free
arm, whistled for Walter to follow, and made for the *Clarion*
office. The others trailed him, imploring him to be reasonable:
hadn't they waited day after day, too; didn't they deserve to see
what was in that envelope?

When they got to the *Clarion,* Tom ushered Clara inside then
turned to the reporters who'd followed them. "Fellows, you'd

keep a letter like this to yourselves, too. You know it." Walter nuzzled his way through the men's legs into the foyer. Tom told Clara to wait on the settee, then bounded up the stairs and marched through the editorial room into Mr. Collins' office.

Mr. Collins looked up from his reading, over the top of his gold-rimmed glasses. "Mr. McCabe, it's customary to knock—"

"Mr. Davenport gave me a letter, said the *Clarion* was to print it." Tom, panting, handed the sealed letter to his editor who made a firm, fast slice with his letter-opener, skimmed the page, then passed it to Tom.

"Two thousand dollars." Tom whistled.

"No questions asked."

Tom read the sentence again to be certain he'd made no mistake: "A two-thousand-dollar reward for any person who delivers our boy to us unharmed."

"Is he giving this to any newspapers out of state?"

"No idea."

"Find out. And talk to Sheriff Sherman. See if he knows about this. Make him give you some information in return this time. Tell him we're printing the reward in tomorrow's paper, front page."

Throughout that steaming summer it had been hard to escape the story of Sonny Davenport. People in Opelousas discussed their personal theories for weeks after the boy's disappearance. "Missing" posters plastered store windows, and the *St. Landry Clarion* and *Opelousas Daily* published countless articles of increasing implausibility about the fate of young Sonny.

But the story had become less captivating and more unnerving the longer the boy was gone. Even Mrs. Billingham
had grown weary of telling how she'd managed the Half
Moon Lake house during the most urgent days of the crisis.

So when the *Clarion* printed the reward notice, on an otherwise uneventful autumn morning, the people of Opelousas
snapped back to attention. Mr. Collins' accompanying Editor's Letter said the *Clarion* hoped the reward would prompt a
useful lead, but cautioned it might also bring forth scoundrels
wanting the Davenports' money. (Which, in its own way,
could be just as thrilling. "Sharks descend on Opelousas to
feed on cash," Eddie said. "You can have *that* headline for
free.")

Mr. Collins would give his readers the latest news on the
Davenports, but he was determined to also print stories from
far afield to make the *Clarion* essential reading. Aside from the
troubles of one local family, the mood of the year had been
optimistic. It was an exciting time for the world, "a golden age
of advancement, unparalleled."

"Unless Europe insists on warring," Mr. Collins said to
Tom, waving his glasses in one hand. "You'd think the
Balkans would've exhausted them but Britain and Germany
both seem intent on owning the seas. France and Russia
are bulking up their military. Everyone trying to out-muscle
everyone else. I can't see where that'll lead other than stalemate. But I could be wrong." He pointed at a copy of the
Atlanta Georgian on his desk, its top headline reading, "War
Spirit Flares Over All Europe: Clash Near." "I'm dead sure
of two things, though: if there *is* a war it'll be short and
swift, and it won't involve us."

Tom shifted his weight from foot to foot. He wanted to leave Mr. Collins' office, but his editor wasn't done.

"The important thing is that America's holding our own, McCabe. We're the future. Readers need to be assured of that. New York's port is busier than London's. Our railways are expanding their reach, steel mills are springing up, six million telephones connect the country...And President Wilson's push for a central bank is smart. Yes, it's a time of enormous promise. And that includes us right here."

Opelousas didn't feature in international headlines, but Tom agreed there were changes—good changes—afoot in his town. Main Street had been transformed in recent years, with cars zipping alongside buggies, a busy nickelodeon, restaurants serving fine foods. The population had tipped past 4,600. There were still one too many saloons for the comfort of some, but overall the town was advancing along with the rest of the world.

And Mr. Collins was right about it being a time of promise in more ways than one. The Davenport story wasn't going away, not with such a big reward. That development might be picked up by national newspapers, even international ones. The story had the potential to carry Tom from local reporter to something bigger. At the very least, he'd met the most influential family in Opelousas. John Henry had handed him that letter personally. He'd remembered Tom, and so had his wife. The question was how Tom could make the most of that.

CHAPTER SEVEN

Mary stayed indoors, frustrated. She both did and did not understand why others couldn't maintain a keen interest in Sonny's absence, but was aware from people's faces and her dwindling number of visitors that this was the case. When she was alone she searched for diversions, but none stuck. Minutes into playing the piano, her fingers slowed into paralysis. The pointlessness of bringing music into an empty room either wilted or enraged her. She walked the halls leveling picture frames. When she had a surfeit of energy, she directed her maid in rearranging the furniture. Sometimes she followed Esmeralda about the house, or bothered the gardener or cook with questions. The days were long.

Most mornings, John Henry went to his furniture factory. He'd become gaunt, his foghorn voice now a tin whistle. His workers stayed out of his path and put their questions to Hank: John Henry's despondency and tetchy criticism weren't helpful. The men became tentative around him, so his place of escape took on a different mood. Soon, he found himself deferring to Hank, too. He continued the search for his son at every opportunity, urging Sheriff Sherman not to slacken the reins, responding to letters, traveling when a tip seemed promising.

He'd abandoned Scout training for George and Paul. Mary was right: they were too young. On that, she and Baden-Powell agreed. George had retained no memory of anything that might be a clue, cried at the slightest prod to think harder. And Paul was tiresome in his repetition of nonsense reasons Sonny was to blame for his own absence. All of that was John Henry's cross to bear; boys were only as capable as their Scoutmaster. He hadn't prepared them for the freedom he'd encouraged. And now his sons and wife languished indoors. A stronger man, he thought, would've stayed at home, faced the problems head-on, persisted with his sons' improvement and comforted his wife. But John Henry wanted to be away, at work or in another city, and not return until he'd found Sonny.

The reporters speculated about the Davenport marriage, since each time John Henry left Opelousas to search for Sonny, Mary stayed behind in the care of a nurse and friends. Some said her grief had tipped into madness; some asked how long John Henry could shoulder the burden of a missing child and a mad wife. The house had a new nanny, too, a skittish young Negro named Pru. The presence of Nanny Nelly had been more than Mary Davenport could bear.

"I saw her at the window again this morning," Dan Hardy said. "Staring at nothing."

Tutors came and went from the house. The reporters

learned to call out to Madame Caron in French, wagered on whether Mrs. Barry would drop her sheet music on any given visit, and mocked Mr. Long's smirk of superiority.

"Latin," Eddie said, blowing smoke to one side. "Who needs it?"

"What I don't get is why they're not going to Westwood Academy with the other rich kids," Dan said.

"You think she's going to let those two out of her sight?" Tom asked.

"Well, I don't know how long she can keep them cooped up in there. Boys need to spread their wings."

"Those wings have been clipped to the bone."

In late November, Mr. Collins heard from the sheriff that John Henry was traveling to New Orleans. He told Tom and Eddie to be on the same train out of town.

John Henry now stood ten feet away from the pair on the wet steps of the New Orleans City Hall, passing out a reward flyer that featured the same old photograph of Sonny dressed in a white smock.

"Remind me why we're here?" Eddie asked Tom, pulling his coat collar up against the wind.

"You know why." It confounded him that Eddie didn't share his ambition, seemed content to take his pictures and then go home. Day in, day out.

Eddie pointed at John Henry. "Mr. Moneybags, pamphletting like a suffragette. Nobody would've believed me if I said he'd be doing that one day." He glanced down at the sheet Tom held. "Looks like a happy kid."

Sheriff Sherman, meanwhile, had left to interview the

woman who'd penned the letter that brought them here. The woman claimed to have seen a boy on Canal Street who matched Sonny's description, and who replied when she called his name. It had been a Tuesday morning, she wrote, when she'd noticed an elderly Italian woman hunched and dressed in black, a deathly specter in the fog, getting on a streetcar with a white boy, heading north. Her level of detail had swayed the sheriff.

Tom had no interest in witnessing the sheriff talk with yet another old lady. He'd read the letter, written an article about it. Mr. Collins was pushing him hard for a different angle on the story, a take on how people in the Louisiana capital were responding. Tom's boss disliked the *uppity* folk there, and wanted confirmation that people in New Orleans were selfish, cold-blooded, thought themselves too superior to care about goings-on in Opelousas and Half Moon Lake. Tom knew this was the story Mr. Collins wanted, but he saw no sign it was the case. All types of people stopped outside the city hall to talk to John Henry, offering their sympathy and promising to stay vigilant. Reporters from the New Orleans papers took Tom aside to check they had the chronology of the case right, and to ask questions about the lake's environs and how the mother was faring. John Henry appeared buoyed by the responsiveness, and vigorously thanked each interested person.

But regardless of John Henry's hope, Sheriff Sherman's thoroughness, Tom's digging and the local goodwill, the trip to New Orleans did not turn up a useful lead to Sonny. Which was aggravating for each of them in different ways.

On their last night in the Hotel St. Helene, the four

men sat together to eat. So few of them had come from Opelousas that it would've been rude not to. After the meal, Sheriff Sherman went to his room, and John Henry asked Tom and Eddie if they'd join him at a nearby saloon for a nightcap.

"We'd be delighted, Mr. Davenport," Tom said.

John Henry encouraged him to address him more informally. "Seems you're in this with me. You may as well use my name."

Eddie scowled, not at the suggestion of fellowship but the thought of leaving the hotel. He'd sat himself in front of the fireplace and loosened the top two buttons on his trousers. Had Tom not been his friend through thick and thin, Eddie could not have been persuaded to budge from that pleasant room. Mr. or otherwise.

The three walked heads down, their umbrellas useless in the wind, through cold sleet and hail, a wide slash of water rearing up and soaking their legs when a car drove close to the curb. They sought temporary shelter under the awning of a playhouse. (The audience scurried out from a performance then huddled around them, comparing opinions.) They passed brothels on Rue Bassin, dance halls and cabaret bars, theaters advertising minstrel shows inside, saloons thumping to the sounds of trombone, clarinet and coronet. Though the sky boomed and lit up, John Henry urged them on.

Now settled in the Black Cat Saloon, on the fringe of Storyville, they agreed they'd more than earned their whiskey. They sat at the back of the noisy, smoky room. A piano player thumped out ragtime tunes. Scantily clad girls moseyed from table to table, one ruffling a customer's hair, another yanked off balance onto a lap.

"Am I missing something?" Tom asked John Henry. "Could be I am, but this place doesn't seem any different from the others we walked past."

"I've been here before. There's comfort in familiarity when you travel as much as I do. Though you've logged as many miles, haven't you? I imagine you curse your editor for making you trail me across the country."

"Not at all. Nobody's forcing me or Eddie. In fact, we asked to be here."

Eddie shot Tom an inquiring glance: it was the first he'd heard that. He'd have preferred to be back in Opelousas spending time with his new girl, Nora.

"Family is everything to me, John. The minute I heard your boy was lost I knew I was the person to tell the story, to get the facts and look for clues until Sonny was found. I promised your wife that Eddie and I would do everything we could to help find your boy. It's a promise I intend to keep."

John Henry sighed. "My beautiful wife, a rose battered by storms."

That hadn't been the response Tom expected. "Only this one storm, I hope."

But John Henry stared at the piano player and didn't reply.

"Has her family been able to provide any solace?" Tom asked.

"Are you married, Tom?"

"No, sir, not yet. But if my girl Clara's mother has her way, I won't be able to say that for long."

John Henry swirled the whiskey in his glass. "You make it sound like a punishment. You don't know the happiness and peace that comes of being with the right woman. Mary has always been the one for me. Most nerve-racking time of my youth was waiting on her father to approve our courtship. She was the prettiest girl I'd seen, the most graceful and kind. Before this she was happy, and I was happy with her."

A barmaid stood at their table, taking one glass then another off her round silver tray and placing them in front of the men. John Henry handed her enough coins to bring a wide smile to her face. It was the kind of money that usually came with expectations, but John Henry didn't even glance her way. He hunched forward, staring at Tom first and then Eddie. "Mary won't survive his loss. It's undoing her. We must find him."

After a brief silence, Tom spoke. "You must miss your boy, too, John. No man wants to think of his son out in the night, with—"

"Of course I miss him," John Henry barked. "I can't bear the thought of—" He made a fist on the table. "It's *crushing* me. I—Ah, but for Mary." He turned away to hide his eyes.

Gladys Heaton had fashioned a solution of her own. When she called on Mary alone one afternoon, she told her about the clairvoyant Rosa Capaldi.

"Kohl-circled eyes, coins sewn onto her cuffs, thick black hair she lets curl every which way." Gladys edged closer to Mary on the sofa. "I learned about her from my seamstress, and I admit I wasn't convinced until I visited her myself. But the things she told me. You must visit her, let her peer in her mystic ball for Sonny." She pointed at the toy rabbit Mary so often held. "Perhaps take that."

The next morning, Mary traveled with Esmeralda to a back alley littered with piles of rotting food stood over by mangy strays. From the car, with a wool blanket spread on her lap, Mary looked out at emaciated cats, Negroes dressed in tatty clothes, Indians swaying from drink. John Henry would never permit her to set foot in this part of town, so she told Esmeralda and the driver their excursion had to remain a secret.

When they reached the house—marked by a weather-worn blue door with a heavy knocker of a woman's hand and carved Latin script—Mrs. Capaldi herself answered their knock. "*Buongiorno, Signora.*"

Esmeralda eyed the spiritualist with suspicion and curiosity. Her Aunt Celestine—who lived no more than an hour from the Davenport house—was a doctor respected in the community for her protective charms and amulets, and powders that cured ailments, granted desires and destroyed enemies, with skills taught to her by ancestors who'd traveled in chains from Senegal. Celestine possessed time-honed knowledge that white people didn't understand, that was shared in ways they couldn't control. Without doubt, Celestine could help the Davenports. But most white people were frightened of voodoo, so she'd never suggested it. She looked at the toy Mary held and thought Celestine might be able to work with that on its own.

Mary and Esmeralda padded close together into a drawing room thick with aromatic smoke, maroon curtains with large gold-threaded tassels that hung either side like limbs. One disturbing object after another passed before their eyes: a stuffed pigeon under glass, a dressmaker's mannequin wearing a sailor suit, unfamiliar sharp-edged metal implements, a bookmarked copy of *Manon Lescaut*. Had Mary not been so desperate, she would've turned and gone home. Had Esmeralda been given a choice, she would never have come inside.

Mary sat at a round table, as Mrs. Capaldi had instructed, in what she assumed was a very small parlor. Esmeralda stood next to the door. A crystal ball on an ornate silver stand sat in the center of the table. Mary handed Hop to Mrs. Capaldi, and the mystic sat, eyes closed, clutching the toy to her chest. After much wailing and swaying, the clairvoyant could go no further than seeing Sonny in a place she described as shrouded with thick trees, lit by campfire and near still water. She held up one finger and whispered, "birds." She assured Mary that Sonny was unharmed: powerful forces shielded him, and the child knew his parents were searching for him. "Your love is his strength."

Mrs. Capaldi's lyrical descriptions of Sonny and his vague location whet Mary's appetite; perhaps another soothsayer, medium or occultist would be more exact. On the way home, Mary reasoned aloud that it was the greater risk to *not* visit Mrs. Capaldi again, *and* to seek the counsel of other spiritualists. "I really do feel this could lead us to Sonny."

Esmeralda worried for Mary Davenport: more optimistic than she'd been in months, duped by a sideshow Gypsy

Jean. Esmeralda had watched Mrs. Capaldi open one eye to a slit to check Mary's reaction when she muttered "still water." The woman was a fraud. And Mrs. Davenport was perfect prey: distraught, rich, as easily manipulated as a child, as transparent as that glass orb. She'd need all the protection she could get.

CHAPTER EIGHT

On the first day of 1914, a bracing and windy day, John Henry sat at his desk and read a letter from Mrs. Leonard Potter who lived in Mobile, Alabama. At first glance it had seemed no more than another letter from a stranger who claimed to have seen Sonny. John Henry received those by the sackful. Some letters gave the assurance—insistence, even—that the penman had seen Sonny *in the flesh*, had spoken with him, had heard the sounds of Louisiana in the boy's voice, and John Henry would telephone Sheriff Sherman. He'd learned, though, to read letters with the same thoughtfulness the sheriff did, checking the postmark for location, the language for rashness or contradiction. John Henry knew that while the sheriff followed up every credible letter, there were people who simply wanted to be a part of someone else's story or who lived more in the land of fiction than fact. In addition to information about sightings, he received letters of encouragement, tales from other families who'd lost children, advertisements from private detectives. So many letters.

John Henry had kept the photographs people sent him of boys they thought might be Sonny, and the photographs of children whom broken parents prayed he'd find in his travels. He was unsure what to do with this growing pile of portraits but couldn't bring himself to throw them away, so he kept them locked in his desk drawer. He had pictures of children from Florida, Kentucky, Tennessee and beyond: serious-looking lads, cowlicks kept in check with mother's spit, faces showing the discomfort of tight collars and long-held poses. One scalloped-edge photograph depicted a freckled-faced boy with a snaggletooth. Another had the photographer's name and town stamped in italics on the back.

John Henry had traveled as far as the eastern parts of Texas on the promise of these letters, sometimes with the sheriff or one of his deputies, sometimes alone. He'd met dozens of tramps and the pink-eyed, dirty boys who shivered alongside them, begging for food and money. He'd spoken with Negroes in factories and fields. He'd been offered beds and meals by farmers' wives when it was evident he should have offered assistance to them.

A few sentences in, John Henry realized that this letter was different. He sat upright in his chair, barely drawing breath, as he read the backward-sloping scrawl:

> Dearest Sir, I've seen a tramp with a whip-thin boy I think is yours. The two were outside the house of Mrs. Eleanor Crumm. I found excuse to pass by and I saw a scar marked his arm, like a red new moon. The left arm, from where I stood, I know that. A sure sign of mistreatment. He didn't utter a word to me. But I have strong

instincts, Sir, and am certain this was not the child of that man. And when Mrs. Crumm came onto her porch and said she preferred not to have a tramp loiter near her home, the man shouted and the child cried. Sir, I went and found my newspaper of months past with the photograph of your boy and I do think it's him. The tramp is still in town. Do come, Sir. I feel certain your boy is here and in dire need of you.

Reference to a scar made John Henry's heart leap, for it had not been mentioned by anyone else. Here was a genuine lead. He telephoned the sheriff.

While other Opelousans harvested the last parsnips and spinach, and planned ahead to February when the soil would be warm enough to sow beets and cabbage, onions and peas, while they enjoyed seafood gumbo in the evenings, compared their trap hauls of muskrat, raccoon and mink, and took in what news they cared to of their town and country, John Henry and Sheriff Sherman traveled by train to Mobile. They met with the local sheriff, Sheriff Bird, with whom Mrs. Leonard Potter had also shared her concerns. Together they called on Mrs. Potter, who lived with her two grown sons and young daughter in a farmhouse a half-mile from the banks of the Mississippi.

Sheriff Bird assured Mrs. Potter they didn't mind sitting in the kitchen. He preferred, in fact, to be in that room, warm from the pot-belly stove, made homely with wire baskets of eggs, jars of rosemary cuttings, and windows framed by cotton curtains. But Mrs. Potter insisted they sit in the living room; they were guests. Her elder boy carried in extra logs, and her daughter brought coffee. Sheriff Bird chose a comfortable armchair, dropping into it after Mrs. Potter plumped his cushion, and looked around for the cat that had jumped on his lap when he'd last visited.

While Sheriff Bird held his mug up to accept a refill of steaming coffee, Sheriff Sherman and John Henry gave polite, brisk "nos" to Mrs. Potter. They'd been in this position enough times that a new hearth was no novelty, and sweet treats no incentive to stay. They wanted to learn what they could and begin their search.

"Now, it's true I haven't seen your boy since I wrote to you," Mrs. Potter said to John Henry, "but it'd been so sad. He was barefoot, scurrying to keep up with the man, who cuffed him more than once when he moved too slow."

John Henry winced.

"Mrs. Potter, can you tell us where they were headed?" Sheriff Sherman asked.

She adopted a serious expression. "Yes, sir, that I can do. They were going toward the rail yards."

After what seemed to John Henry like an excessively protracted goodbye to Mrs. Potter, Sheriff Bird drove Sheriff Sherman and John Henry to the yards, where a railman vouched he'd seen a pair who matched the description, and had talked to the tramp. "Make no mistake, he hasn't left town, not by rail anyway. He told me he might not get on the Pensacola train after all, wanted to stay here a while instead. And when we were done talking he reached down for the boy's hand." The railman lowered his voice. "The child shrank back in fear. *Re-coiled*."

* * *

Sheriff Bird's men carried out a door-to-door inspection of houses in the Mobile area, and sent extra men out to surrounding farms. They searched in the colored and Italian neighborhoods. They searched laneways and backstreets. They heard from two different men who lived by the river bend that the tramp had been in their home with the boy, doing odd jobs. But no one found the tramp.

John Henry raised the reward to four thousand dollars, a fortune. He would not, he bellowed at Sheriff Sherman, fail again: "This endless hunt must deliver my son." Never in his life had John Henry exerted so much effort without achievement, he said. The sheriff watched John Henry's intensifying exasperation with concern.

That same afternoon, the sheriff suggested he and John Henry search the thick woods near the river bend by themselves. For two days they hiked along the narrow dirt trail, looking for any indication that others had passed through recently, stopping to eat Mrs. Bird's packed cornbread with black beans and to rest. Late at night, they sat on logs on opposite sides of an open campfire, rugged up against the cold. A soft wind blew through the trees, rustling the leaves. Frogs croaked and crickets chirped. The fire popped and wheezed.

Sheriff Sherman poked at the logs with a long stick while John Henry watched the flames.

"It's been nearly six months." The sheriff weighed his words. "You know I want to find your boy, John. But it might be time for us to think about how much longer we can keep doing this."

The embers cast a tangerine glow on John Henry's face "I

wasn't aware you'd decided on the amount of time my son's life is worth."

"Now, hold your horses. That's not what I said."

"I was under the impression this was your job, not an activity wasting valuable—"

"John, you must have considered that after so many false leads... It could be that Mrs. Potter is mistaken, too."

"But the scar."

"Other boys have scars."

"On the left arm, curved, a boy the same age—it's Sonny."

"None of us knows that boy's age."

"I'm certain it's him. And who's to say any of the other leads have been false? The tramp is traveling. We simply haven't been fast enough to catch him."

"I guess my question is, how long are you willing to do this?"

"As long as it takes. What other answer is there?" John Henry fixed his eyes on Sheriff Sherman. "Are you proposing that I stop searching, tell Mary we no longer care where Sonny is, *who* he's with? I can't do that."

The sheriff nodded slowly. "I hear you, John. And I understand. But I want you to think seriously about how much more you're willing to put yourself through. It's taking a toll on you both."

Having no easy reply, John Henry stood up and walked away from the campfire. He headed back toward the town, watched men stumble out of crowded saloons and a cat skitter from its garbage-can perch, glanced up to see a girl standing at a lit window, a thick arm slithering around her waist. Occasionally a Model T rumbled past him.

After a while, houses took the place of saloons, then fields took the place of houses. John Henry stopped on the road, surprised at how far he'd traveled and the lightness of the night. Scores of stars sparkled like diamonds, and a near-full moon shone on him, casting his shadow onto the ground. The night smelled like cold gin; the sky pulsed.

He saw a plume of white-gray smoke rising up from a field. Who else would be out here, where there was no other sign of human life? Maybe it was the tramp. He looked for a track that might lead in the direction of the fire and found it in no time, forcing himself to slow down so he wouldn't be heard.

About twenty feet along the trail—rocks rolling under his boots, sticks crunching, a fieldmouse scampering off in fright—John Henry saw he was wrong. Hidden behind a thick cluster of trees was a scattering of shacks: small, rudimentary structures bathed in moonlight. Field workers. Still, he was so close, it could be worth watching from behind the trees to see if the tramp had sought refuge here for the night.

John Henry heard the voices of Negro men before he saw them. He found a spot behind the largest tree from which he could eavesdrop, then squatted there.

There were eight men sitting on logs around a fire. An elderly man with silver hair, red braces and a collarless white shirt buttoned to the neck tapped one foot as he sang. The men either side of him nodded, spoke in time. A group of younger men sat on the other side of the fire, sharing a bottle of something into tin mugs, laughing and nudging one another as they talked. An opossum cooked on a stake over the fire.

He'd felt momentarily released from his burdens in the

presence of the high stars and wide land, but watching these men, John Henry realized how lonely his life had become, how weighty, with no equivalent gatherings of easy camaraderie. The mood at the fireside with the sheriff had been morose long before they'd argued. Back at home he had a wife who was at any time either hysterical or dumbstruck, and two sons whose presence reminded him of the missing third.

One of the younger men greeted a newcomer. "Boots."

Boots had a mouth harp, and the other men urged him to play. John Henry brushed aside sticks and stones so he could sit in more comfort on the ground. He listened to the harp music, heard snatches of conversation, and felt in no rush to return to his own campsite.

Boots stopped playing. "I've made up my mind. I'm leaving, two days' time."

The wiry man sitting beside him threw a stick in the fire. "Don't ask me to come with you. I won't."

"What exactly are you staying for?" Boots asked. "After what happened to Frankie? You going to sit around and wait your turn? I'm not, no sir."

"I'm not saying there's no danger here. I'm saying the river, the men on the roads, dogs—you'll never make it."

The silver-haired man huffed. "Yes he will, Samuel Stanton. And you should be thanking him, not filling him with fear."

"He's not doing this for me."

"Why're you always undermining him? Boots is trying to make things better for us, while you mooch around getting drunk and pawing at girls."

Samuel chortled, but the old man would not be stopped.

"I mean it. Are you teaching your children to read and write? Do you tell them they have worth? The things you do now make the future."

At this, Samuel took offense. "I'm making a future."

"That farm? Ha!" The old man slapped his thigh. "They're playing you. You'll be working that farm to pay off a debt they'll raise and raise. You try to walk away, you'll get arrested as a vagrant, and the judge'll make you work off your fines on a plantation. Like a slave. Oh, and don't walk home in the dark. Do that and you'll wind up tied to a fence and whipped with wire like Frankie. You're a fool, Samuel. If I was younger I'd go north with Boots. You should, too."

John Henry was astonished by the debate that followed, the vocabulary he'd not known Negroes possessed, the passionate way in which the older man explained why they ought to fight for equality. Equality. John Henry thought back to the Negroes who'd dredged Half Moon Lake, helped search for his son. He tried to remember individual men's faces or a single name, and found he could not.

As the fire burned out, the men drifted to their shacks to sleep, and John Henry stood. He was appalled at his ignorance in first thinking the gathering had been one of jolly fools. These men would understand his pain more deeply than any others on Earth.

As he walked away, John Henry had an idea. In his travels, he'd seen Negroes living in desperate circumstances, always in poverty. It wasn't voting they needed, it was release from deprivation and an alternative to indolence.

Once Sonny was found, John Henry, as mayor, would promote the Scout Promise—physically strong, mentally alert, morally straight—throughout Negro communities. He had no doubt the whole South would benefit from the most downtrodden being improved, starting with the youngest. That, he could do.

CHAPTER NINE

Mary had grown up in Louisiana on a sizable sugar cane plantation with thirty-seven men. In Mary's time, freed men worked Arlington Grove Plantation, though the family had had fifty slaves managing the house and fields before the war. Some of the workers at Arlington Grove during Mary's childhood had once been slaves or were the children of slaves and stayed on, even kept her family's name, which she thought had to be a sign of some affection. Her father was voluble in his disdain whenever a worker would ask to leave the plantation. "There's nothing out there a hardworking Negro can't find under my roof," he'd say.

Mary's father, Theodore Gould, ran the plantation to strict rules. He was a grave and commanding man, like his father before him. The fact that Arlington Grove Plantation House stood undamaged through the war—its *garconnière*, *pigeonnier*, overseer's cottage, barns and slave quarters likewise unharmed—was testament to her grandfather's resolve that it be so. Mary's father took seriously his responsibility of maintaining the plantation and grand home, and guiding it into the future. "They might try to control us," he said. "But they will never erase us."

Mr. Gould often expressed his disappointment Mary hadn't been born a boy. It wouldn't have mattered had Mary's mother borne other children, but God decided she ought not. Mary's father was never cruel to his daughter, simply unimpressed. "It stands to reason that if you can only have one of anything, you want it to be the best." He said this in a matter-of-fact way, offering her what he considered the compliment that she was sensible enough to understand simple logic.

Mary recalled times when her mother—Adeline Gould, née Babineaux—was confined to her room; Mary was told not to disturb her as she was trying to hold in a baby, but they never held. During these periods of confinement, her mother's cries were heard through the closed bedroom door for days afterward. Without any reason Mary could ascertain, these grim times came to an abrupt stop, her mother left her room, and the house girls, maids and cooks were suddenly on the receiving end of a flurry of instructions to fling open windows, dust sills, wash bedding, make, bake and polish. The frenetic weeks were preferable to the dark and dull ones, but not knowing when either time would come and how long it would last made Mary's stomach clench.

Though she'd never have said it aloud, Mary wasn't sure she wanted a brother. And she worried that her reticence was somehow connected to her mother's failure. At night, she knelt beside her bed and prayed for God to deliver their family a baby boy, and to then transform Mary's ambivalence into delight.

From both her mother and father, she knew that life could not go forward without this. Mary alone was not enough.

Mary had happy memories from her childhood, she was sure of it, but none of them was at her disposal right now. The absence of Sonny was agonizing and all-consuming. Even more painful than his absence was the idea of him with another person, someone who mistreated him, starved and frightened him. It had almost been better to imagine him wandering alone—and *that* had been petrifying. But it seemed he was in the clutches of a stranger, kept in penury, made to *beg*. And not one of the many spiritual practices from which Mary sought advice—not the runes, tarot cards, ouija board or séances—brought forth anything useful from the living or the dead.

There were days when Mary couldn't uncurl her spine for the pains in her gut. The digitalis no longer helped, though she carried it with her for lack of anything else. The doctor urged bed rest, again. But Mary was sick of her bed. She'd endured half a year of being told to lie down.

Sometimes, late at night, she padded down the cold hallway to the bedroom George and Paul shared, knelt between their cozy beds and hugged them in turn, stroked their hair, and straightened their blankets, telling them in rapid-fire whispers they must be careful, must stay safe. And when she left the room, as unpredictably as she'd arrived, the boys sat in their beds staring at the door, then at one another, then back at the door until they lay down to sleep again.

Mary knew her mother had suffered terribly from her failure to deliver a son to her husband—physical pain as well as shame and frustration. But Mary had lost a child she'd loved for years, a boy who had his own character, one of her three successes, four if she counted her marriage. She'd had everything one would want in a life and it had been shattered without warning.

Gladys Heaton's visits weren't helping Mary. On a blustery February afternoon, a few days after John Henry's return from Alabama, and only moments after Esmeralda had opened the living-room door for her, Gladys began speaking in a rush: "I suppose you've heard. If Ira knows, then John Henry does. But I wanted to discuss it with you right away, in any case."

Gladys dropped onto her favorite armchair, removed her gloves and looked about for something to drink. Why Mary's staff could not anticipate one's needs was beyond her.

Mary asked Esmeralda to bring them tea. "I have no clue what you're talking about, Gladys."

"The boy in Mississippi. I passed by the library when Ira told—"

"You didn't eavesdrop on your own husband."

"Men are so loud. And he said Sonny's name, which—"

"Why didn't you tell me that right away?"

"Sit down, Mary, please, and I will. I couldn't speak any faster if I tried." She put her fingertips to her throat and gulped to indicate the challenge of speaking when parched.

Mary made a hurrying motion with her hand.

"Ira said there was a boy outside of Jackson, Mississippi. Now that's more than two hundred miles away so it's odd, but still, they were certain the boy fit Sonny's description and—"

"They found Sonny?"

"Oh, do sit. I can't think with you standing over me."

Esmeralda entered the room carrying a tray with tea and beignets.

"A Negro called Clarence Tine found the boy in the fields at dusk," Gladys said. "I remembered his name because it seemed odd. Don't you think it's odd?"

Mary frowned at her.

"Well, the boy wouldn't say what he was doing there or where he belonged. He just cried. The Negro's wife was in labor—her sister had run to the fields with the news—and the baby was coming fast, though any reasonable woman would—"

"*Gladys*."

"Because the baby was coming, Clarence Tine couldn't afford the time to take the boy up the hill to his boss's house. So he decided to carry him on his back to his own home, as a temporary measure, so he'd be present for his child's birth. He intended to get the boy to its rightful parents at some point. That's what he said, anyway. There were witnesses who told police the Negro's version, before the lynching."

Esmeralda clattered a fork against a plate.

"Oh!" Mary gasped and sank down onto a chair.

"You see, Clarence Tine and his sister-in-law were seen running along the road with a crying white child clinging to Clarence's back. You know how that would be perceived. Some neighbors gathered to rescue the child. Ira said these men knew where Clarence lived because he's one of those Negroes who stir up trouble about voting." She glanced at the plates left out of reach by Esmeralda, who now stood next to the door, eyes cast down. She'd talk to Mary about her housekeeper on another occasion. "It's sad. Clarence was strung from a tree. His sister-in-law met the same fate, the blessing being they died together."

"That's awful, so awful for them."

Gladys leaned forward. "Shall I tell you the most dreadful part? I feel I must. The sister-in-law was pregnant, too, and when she was hanging up, quite dead mind you, one of the men sliced open her belly and the baby slipped out like an eel, dropped onto the dirt. Ira said it was still alive but they left it there. Because, what would one do with it?"

Mary covered her eyes with her hands. "The boy, Gladys, is he Sonny?"

"That's the thing. I'm sure it's him, or I'd never have told you such a story. And why would Ira have been discussing it if the boy wasn't someone?"

Mary turned to speak to Esmeralda, not noticing that she had slumped partway down the wall. "Fetch Mr. Davenport."

Gladys was so shocked by the way in which John Henry spoke to her that she held her empty glass to her chest as though it might protect her.

"Why in Heaven's name would you speak of this to Mary?"

"I had no idea she'd respond so madly." Rather than thanking Gladys for sharing valuable information, Mary had fretted about the fate of the Negroes and the horrors the child must have witnessed, and asked repeatedly if Gladys *knew* it to be Sonny. John Henry, Gladys felt, was being rude. Her fingers tightened around the glass.

"Everyone says—"

"No one says, Mrs. Heaton, *no one*. What happened was

a horrendous error. That our name passed the lips of those men is—"

"Ira—"

John Henry moved his body to block Gladys from Mary's view. "My love, I've spoken with the sheriff, and he's been in touch with the authorities in Jackson. That boy is not our son."

Gladys kissed Mary on her tear-wet cheek, and walked to the door with John Henry behind her.

Left alone, Mary sat with the whirr of her mind and watched a petal drop from the vase of flowers on the nearest table. A small bird landed on the windowsill, its chest feathers stained red from a meal of fresh strawberries. When it pecked on the glass, Mary startled as if she'd heard gunshot.

CHAPTER TEN

Barber Smith draped hot toweling around John Henry's cheeks and jowls, then whisked his badger-hair shaving brush across the block of gray soap wedged into his mug. He looked up to admire not the artful arrangement of his towel nor his immaculate establishment, but the reflection of his own Grecian nose and slicked black hair. He whistled as he unveiled John Henry's warmed face. Meanwhile, Smith's son—neat, witty, inexplicably unmarried—touched the tip of his tongue to his upper lip in concentration as he bent forward to trim the hair around Tom McCabe's ear.

It had been a surprise to John Henry and Tom that they'd arrived at the barbershop at the same time, and uncomfortable for them both. It was one thing to share a table in a bar or sit together in a train carriage, but neither of them had anticipated close proximity during their grooming. To ease into the situation they chatted, and found they shared a boyhood love of fishing and a fondness for baseball. When soap lather and sharp blades permitted, John Henry and Tom spoke about the upcoming season (the White Sox sure to beat Cleveland in May) and current affairs: the curious death of a Texan rancher in Mexico; the launch in Belfast of a sister ship to the *Titanic*; the destruction by a suffragette of a valuable painting in London—with a meat cleaver.

Finally, Tom asked after the health of Mrs. Davenport. "If that's not too bold? I heard the doctor had been visiting again."

For a moment the only sounds came from the barbers snipping and sliding their feet on the black-and-white-tiled floor. Tom couldn't move his head with Barber Smith Junior's fingers rested atop it like a spider so he couldn't see if he'd offended John Henry. He forced a cough, and as he was about to excuse his comment, John Henry spoke.

"The trouble is the hours. She has the same hours she had before, but without any interest in filling them. She hasn't the patience to be with the boys for long, won't embroider, draw or play the piano, won't write letters. She doesn't call on others, and it seems they no longer wish to visit her. I worry about how much time she has to ruminate."

Tom thought for a minute. "I have a trove of books she might find distracting."

"As do I," said John Henry. "But she can't focus her mind enough to read even simple books. She enjoys being read to, but I can't be there to do that every day." He lifted his chin up for Barber Smith Senior, who, relieved at the broken silence, whistled a short tune.

"Perhaps you'd permit me to read to Mrs. Davenport? I often have unfilled hours at the end of my working day. I'd be glad to be of help to you."

It was an unusual proposal, bordering on improper, but John Henry thought it could benefit him and cheer his wife. "She'd enjoy that. I warn you, though: she's incapable of concentrating on anything you might consider worth reading."

"Then I'll spare her *Moby-Dick*."

"She may be exactly the audience that book deserves."

Barber Smith Junior brushed cut hairs off Tom's neck and shirt, then swiveled on his polished boot to fetch Tom's overcoat from the rack.

"You understand your visit would be to distract Mrs. Davenport, not to discuss Sonny. That topic would be off-limits."

Tom slipped an arm into his coat.

"Because she'll raise it with you. And given your professional interest—"

"I've no wish to add to her troubles or yours. I'll read something simple to take her mind elsewhere. As Tom McCabe, citizen, not Tom McCabe, reporter, I promise."

Esmeralda put down a vase of pink azaleas on the largest table in the living room.

"How is Mrs. Davenport today?" Tom asked.

"As well as can be expected."

The question was, of course, a politeness to fill the silence. Tom had, through John Henry, heard the discreet version of Mary Davenport's continuing angst. And he knew Esmeralda wouldn't offer up any salacious details on his first visit to the house, if ever. But Mr. Collins wanted to know what was going on behind closed doors. Is the marriage suffering? he asked Tom. Do they still believe they'll find their boy—find him alive? He had grown impatient with the lack of new angles in Tom's articles. Tom assured Mr. Collins that giving him time in the Davenport house would pay off.

"I'm glad not to have a fence between us anymore," Tom said, smiling at Esmeralda. "Perhaps we can begin afresh. Might I ask your name?"

"You know my name. You've used it plenty." Esmeralda walked toward the door to leave, across sunlit squares cast onto Persian carpet by large French windows.

"I mean your family name."

She stopped and looked back at Tom McCabe. His face, bathed in light, was as unlined and without guile as a child's. And yet he was in this house, and was talking with the help, for a reason. "The name given to my family, you mean, before the war?"

"What I meant is, might I call you Mrs.—What would the next name be?"

"You can call me Esmeralda."

"And what name comes after that? In Europe, housekeepers are Mrs."

Europe. He was in no hurry, she could see that, and Mrs. Davenport hadn't even made it out of her bedroom. But Esmeralda had work to do. "Somerset. Esmeralda Somerset. That's my name."

"And does Mr. Somerset work for the Davenports, too?"

"No, sir. Mr. Somerset passed away seven years back."

"I'm sorry to hear that. Are there young Somersets?"

Nosy, too. "A boy and two girls. Lord save them."

"They're in some trouble?"

She wouldn't risk being any bolder but truly, how did white

people know so little? And this one was paid to know things. "They're good children, but life's hard without a father. They work long hours. Jane takes in laundry and Sally, though she's so young—" She saw his eyes flick toward the grandfather clock. "I'll remind Mrs. Davenport you're here."

Whatever John Henry said about his wife's keenness for diversion, she seemed relaxed with time. She kept Tom waiting. He stood at the window, admired the view of the garden, and looked beyond the front gate to where he'd waited with the other reporters. He made note of the Chinoise vases, the watercolor landscapes: the kind of details Mr. Collins appreciated. His mother would love a home like this.

Just when Tom was thinking he might have come in vain, Esmeralda opened the door again, balancing a silver tray on one hand. As she placed the tray on the largest of the side tables, Mary Davenport walked through the still-open door. He saw that although she was disturbingly thin, she'd retained her patrician beauty and dressed like the lady of the manor she was: an apricot day dress with a high neck, a string of pearls, the faintest touch of color on her lips. John Henry was a lucky man.

Tom stepped forward to greet Mary but had not, despite the ample time to do so, committed to his opening line: thank you for choosing the *St. Landry Clarion* to print the reward letter, I apologize for lurking at your front gate, I remember those days at the lake…

"Mrs. Davenport, how delightful to see you again."

"A pleasure to see you also. Please, Mr. McCabe, sit. Have a slice of orange cake. It's one of Cook's best."

Tom sat in the chair opposite Mary and accepted the plate Esmeralda handed him. But the instant he took a mouthful of cake he regretted it, the food turning like clay in his mouth.

Mary waited patiently, noticing Tom's wrinkled jacket, the ink stain on his cuff. He put his plate to one side.

"Perhaps I should begin?"

"The book my husband is reading to me is there." She gestured at the leather-bound copy of Ruskin's *Ethics* on a side table. "You'll find the page marked."

Tom examined the gold writing on the spine, then twisted to one side and unbuckled his satchel. "Ruskin is admirable, but I've brought something that might be more amusing, if I may."

Mary craned forward as Tom held up a copy of the *All-Story Magazine*. The cover featured a colorful drawing of a half-naked man wrestling a fanged lion, the wild man ready to plunge a dagger into the animal's head. Mary's eyes grew wide.

"Have you read 'Tarzan of the Apes'?" Tom asked. "This is last year's October issue with the first installment, and I can guarantee you it's an exciting story. There are savages and jungle animals and even a romance. I have alternatives of course, should you—"

Her face flushed. "Oh, I think I'd like to hear that story, Mr. McCabe."

Tom was pleased. He'd hoped to share with her a tale so exotic that she couldn't help but be taken away from her troubles. He hadn't anticipated such an eager response; the poor woman seemed to be so starved of life, so deep in her own sadness, that even the hint of other worlds animated her.

"In fact," Tom ventured, "it's a tale that'd appeal to your boys, too. Plenty of—"

"I'm afraid not." Mary cut him off, her voice stern.

Tom worried he'd overreached, so he began reading right away to Mary—and inadvertently to Esmeralda, who remained in the room, seated by the window, sewing. That bond: he needed to make the most of it. Mary seemed unusually attached to her housekeeper, maid, now chaperone. Tom read to them both, theatrically narrating the mutiny and shipwreck. He read how Tarzan's ape mother cared for him and fought for him when she had to. Mary and Esmeralda made an attentive audience, clucking, drawing sharp breath or muttering as the story directed. Tom was glad he'd brought more than one edition of the *All-Story*, since Mary urged him to continue each time he paused.

"*His life among these fierce apes had been happy; for his recollection held no other life, nor did he know that there existed within the universe aught else than his little forest and the wild jungle animals with which he was familiar.*

"*He was nearly ten before he commenced to realize that a great difference existed between himself and his fellows.*"

Tom enjoyed reading to Mary and, importantly, he was in the Davenport house with the woman to whom he'd been trying to speak for so long. It might take some time to completely win her trust, but Tom was sure he could do so. The story of the missing boy was his to tell.

Over the course of several visits, Tom read all except the last installment to Mary. He gave the finale its own afternoon. He, Mary and Esmeralda settled themselves in the living room, the windows thrown open to invite in the fragrant air, and discussed in detail what might happen, how glad they were to be sharing this tale. These visits had become, Tom thought, almost like a gathering of friends, joyous and temporarily without social barriers. There had been times Tom even forgot why he was there.

"Right then, let's dive in."

Tom felt self-assured enough now to wink at Mary, and she felt a shiver of pleasure. How had she not noticed before how handsome he was? As he read the end to Tarzan's story, Mary admired Tom's thick nut-brown hair smoothed back, a dapper suit she'd never seen before, the almost visible frizz of energy around his body.

But when he closed the magazine, Mary was aghast. "That can't be the ending. Knowing he'd come from wealth, that he was a Greystoke, surely that changes things?" She was unhappy at Tarzan's choice to lie to Jane about his lineage. "Why would he withhold from her?"

Esmeralda mumbled, "No secrets between man and wife."

Mary pointed in Esmeralda's direction and nodded vigorously in agreement, though she wasn't convinced such a blanket statement was always true.

"It does seem a strange choice," Tom agreed, not inclined to tell Mary the ending she wanted was trite. "Maybe he believes that shielding Jane from the truth offers her the chance of a brighter future. His actions could be read as chivalrous."

Mary balled her kerchief into a knot, stood, then whipped around to face Tom, her skirt flicking about like the tail of an angry cat. "You must write to Mr. Burroughs. Write and encourage him to change the ending, to—no, that can't be done—to write an epilogue in which Tarzan tells Jane the truth about who he is, and they marry. They *must* end up together. The truth *must* win out. None of them could be happy with this lie casting such a pall over their lives."

"I can't tell a man how to write his story. I know how I'd respond to a letter like that."

"But it's different for you. You deal with reality. That can't be changed. Mr. Burroughs works with make-believe—he can do whatever he wants. And he must want to please his readers, mustn't he? And to give his characters a happy ending?"

She'd been so agitated that Tom agreed, against his better judgment, to send a letter for Mr. Burroughs to the *All-Story*.

"And then we need to put this tale behind us and begin another. If you want me to?"

"Oh yes. Your stories are one of the few things that stop me worrying about Sonny. Please do keep coming, if you can." Mary paused. "But we must correct this wrong ending first."

"I'll try."

When he next arrived at the house, Tom waved a copy of the *All-Story* at Esmeralda as she opened the door to him. "I should've checked more carefully. Last December even. Hah. Come, Mrs. Somerset, I think you'll be pleased, too." And Tom read the December 1913 installment of "The Return of Tarzan" to Mary and Esmeralda's enormous delight, for Tarzan and Jane were reunited, Jane learned of Tarzan's true identity as Lord Greystoke, and they wed.

"There, that is as it should be," Mary said. "I'm so glad."

Tom could see something still bothered her.

"Tarzan never lost his essential humanity, did he?" she

asked. "He was raised by apes, but his core was that of a gentleman."

"That's true."

"He needed to be shown the manners and habits of a civilized man, but his soul was uncorrupted by his experience in the jungle. He was always a Greystoke. One's essence is inviolable, isn't it?"

"Are you thinking about Sonny?"

Mary blushed. "I am. After the fact, Tom. I enjoyed the story for what it was. But it has made me think about Sonny, and given me hope, because even if he is in the clutches of savage and uncouth people, he's still Sonny in nature, isn't he? Some things are in your blood and nothing can change that."

CHAPTER ELEVEN

Clara longed to travel to the Continent, most of all to Paris. She told Tom repeatedly how she *longed* to see Paris. She read to him, from her well-thumbed copy of *Vanity Fair* magazine, about English gentry taking steamships to Algeria to hunt gazelle (*"in the Oued the men dress in white, the women in orange and violet and rose"*), and spending their summers attending masked balls in Italy and their winters in the Swiss Alps.

There was, Tom thought, an entire catalog of luxuries for which Clara longed. Paris was only the first on her list of future experiences and acquisitions. But Tom wasn't convinced Paris was a place for any self-respecting woman. He'd heard it wasn't just flower-sellers and fancy boutiques. Unsavory men sold indecent postcards at newsstands along the Seine, ladies danced naked at the Moulin Rouge, and long-haired bohemians walked the tree-lined boulevards Clara so swooned over, taunting ordinary people. And for all the reputed gaiety of the city, Tom had read France was growing anxious at the possibility of war.

None of his reservations were of interest to Clara. Her many hints to Tom that, one day, she would like to marry in Louisiana then honeymoon in France were becoming increasingly unsubtle. Tom told Clara that Opelousas was a fine place to be, especially on a reporter's salary, and he had "no desire, no longing, to be anywhere else."

Clara had approved of Tom's charitable visits to Mary Davenport, and even when Tom explained he wasn't without agenda—he hoped his access to the Davenport house would deliver him a scoop—Clara remained encouraging. Secondhand contact with the family gave her a certain cachet among her friends. But as time passed and people further lost interest in the story—which, nine months after the boy's disappearance, no longer garnered much attention from the press, even the *St. Landry Clarion*—Clara asked Tom why he continued to visit Mrs. Davenport and to follow Mr. Davenport on his wild-goose chases. "I hardly see you anymore."

She wouldn't have minded so much if they were engaged, but to still be courting and have him spending more hours with a married woman than he was with Clara was worrying. Her mother never tired of reminding Clara that, at twenty, she was losing her luster. There weren't that many unmarried men with prospects in Opelousas, and if she were to let Tom slip from her grasp she'd have a hard time finding another beau. And while Tom wasn't as wealthy as Ira Heaton or as powerful as John Henry Davenport, he had ambition and came from a stable family. With his strength of mind and Clara's inheritance, her mother assured Clara she'd be able to establish a respectable life. She needed only to be appealing enough to reignite Tom's passion, and demure enough for him to imagine her as his wife, while strategically realigning his peculiar relationship with the Davenports. But the clock was ticking.

Tom was aware of Clara's growing frustration with him. To appease her, Tom took Clara to whatever appropriate amusements Opelousas offered, preferably the kind he enjoyed, too. Tonight, they'd come to the nickelodeon to see Chaplin's latest—not the one Tom wanted to see, *A Thief Catcher*, but a double of *Mabel at the Wheel* and *Cruel, Cruel Love*. The names alone curled Tom's toes. At least it was Chaplin.

"Did you read to Mrs. Davenport today?" Clara asked, shifting about in the uncomfortable seat. "I applaud your kindness, and I do feel awful for her, but don't you think she should be past the invalid stage by now?"

"That's a terrible thing to say. Anyhow, I thought you liked me knowing the rich and powerful of Opelousas."

"Oh I do. You know I'm glad you're still following the story." She lowered her voice as the lights dimmed. "They'll show their gratitude at some point, I'm sure. You've earned it."

The following night, Mason opened the door to Tom and a gust of warm air rushed inside.

"Is Mr. Davenport home?" Tom asked.

"He's dining with Judge Roy, sir. I suspect he won't be back until late." Mason's response had become so predictable that Tom could have answered his own question.

"Boys awake?"

Before Mason could reply, George and Paul raced toward Tom as one, shouting their hellos.

"Look what I found, look." Paul held up a weathered copper coin.

"What *I* found," George corrected.

"Boys," Mason said. "You know not to run and yell inside."

"Yes, sir," said George.

Paul ignored Mason, and continued to hold his coin up.

Tom bent down. "Now that's something." He took the coin and turned it around in his fingers. "A Confederate nickel. You'll want to hold on to that, put it somewhere special. Don't spend it, will you?"

He passed the coin back to Paul, who examined his treasure with fresh reverence. Tom winked at George, who understood: the nickel was no more special than any other, and this was a secret only an older boy and a man could share.

Where a short time ago he'd been a stranger, Tom now felt the boys considered him a benevolent uncle, the single one they had, as far as he could tell. And the more he observed them, the more he could see their demeanors suggested nothing suspicious. Paul lacked the control that keeping a secret required, and George was too honest. Tom would've liked to know what they thought had happened to Sonny. But were he to print anything the boys said to him, it would be the end of his time with the Davenports.

Tom trod upstairs behind Mason, with George and Paul scampering ahead of them, Paul shouting out to his mother that it was her story time.

"Fleas on a hotplate," Mason said.

On his way out of the house, having read "Three from Dunsterville" to Mary and Esmeralda, Tom encountered

John Henry in the entrance handing his hat and coat to Mason.

"Hello, Tom. Mary tells me you've started on a new collection of stories, something English."

Tom reddened at the thought that Mary would discuss tonight's story with her husband. It had been more about the woman's knotty involvement with two male acquaintances than he'd realized beforehand. "Wodehouse. A friend in London sent it over for my mother. Pranks, butlers and high society. You may have read—"

John Henry snorted. "I've no time for make-believe. But thank you for providing Mary with an escape from reality."

Tom bristled. His recent conversations with John Henry had never been anything other than cordial, and he'd thought they'd developed if not a true friendship then something close to mutual respect. While he hadn't expected effusive thanks from a man of John Henry's stature, Tom had thought his kindness to the man's wife might have elevated him in his eyes. Mr. Davenport might have shared one too many whiskeys with the judge.

"Is the furniture business going well?" He would take the conversation back to matters of men.

John Henry smiled. "Yes, the furniture business is going well. It seems the whole state is perpetually in need of chairs." He softened his voice. "Though I'm unconvinced our customers are doing much of use with their hours of sitting. Not everyone is a reader, Tom."

Before Tom could reply, John Henry walked up the stairs without a glance back.

Tom had felt cheery when he'd walked out of Mary's room.

She'd been coquettish with him, had laughed when he'd attempted an English accent during his reading. And Tom had shared a joke with Esmeralda, who, when pushed by Mary to come up with a nickname for Tom, had nominated "Pencil." She'd found her choice so riotously funny that Tom had laughed along.

But as Tom walked out the front door of the Davenport house he was flustered by his encounter with John Henry. He felt certain John Henry didn't disapprove of him. Or did he? This family was getting under his skin.

Frustrated by his fruitless efforts and exhausting travel, John Henry had turned again to his work. The neat spreadsheets, numbers that added as they should, the logic and predictability of business were better medicine than a doctor could prescribe him. John Henry regularly stayed in his office longer than his workload required, then dined with Judge Roy. He wasn't unsympathetic to his wife's illnesses and angst, but he was spent, physically and psychically. He had no more left to give, not even to Mary.

As he stood at the foot of the bed, arms spread so Mason could remove his shirt, John Henry wondered if he ought to worry about the amount of time his wife spent with Tom McCabe. He was relieving John Henry from many tedious hours of reading the books Mary enjoyed, seemed trustworthy, and was attached to that kittenish Tisdale girl. But it was strange that Mary was willing to allow Tom to visit long after politeness demanded. They'd proceeded to a second, third volume of stories. She seemed to consider Tom McCabe something close to a friend. John Henry hadn't anticipated that. He would check with Esmeralda that she stayed in the room when Tom read.

"Will there be anything else, sir?" Mason asked.

John Henry shook his head. After Mason left, he teetered between going to his bed and walking to the living room, where Mary still sat. It seemed the right thing to exchange a few words with her before going to sleep, but the thought of the places the conversation might go made him slump. If he was awake when she came to bed he'd reach for her, without the burden of words.

CHAPTER TWELVE

On July 28, 1914, on a hot Louisiana summer's day, when bumblebees hovered over dahlia bushes, when the last plums and strawberries were picked and okra was in plentiful supply, a year after Sonny Davenport had gone missing, Austria–Hungary declared war against Serbia. Most Opelousans were hard-pressed to locate these places on a map. But one by one, with stunning speed, the nations of Europe formed a web of alliances which, while complicated, brought out more familiar names. On August 1, Germany and Russia declared war against one another. On August 3, France announced its support for Russia and urged Britain to do the same. That night, Germany invaded Belgium. Very soon it was clear that Europe was involved in a bigger battle, one with greater dangers, than America had first thought. The front-page headline of the *Washington Post* declared, "Outlook Is Hopeless."

In the *Clarion* office, where sash windows were pushed up to allow in the light breeze, Tom stood next to Eddie as Mr. Collins used his globe to explain the significance of each alliance, emphasizing the regional madness that saw Germans on the British throne warring with Germany.

"It's interesting, sure," said Eddie, a cigarette dangling from his mouth. "But what does any of it have to do with the price of eggs?"

Mr. Collins studied Eddie over the top of his glasses. "The Continent isn't as far away as you think, Dale. And given how interconnected modern commerce is, it has everything to do with the price of eggs. Telephones, ocean liners, movies— we're knitted together now. Don't you read the stories that fill in the space around your photographs?"

"Are we going to be in this war, though?" asked Tom. "That's the thing. President Wilson—"

"He'll keep us out of it. It'll affect us, no question. But this is a European war, a battle between old powers. President Wilson knows to focus on American issues." Mr. Collins patted the globe. "We'll follow his example and keep our attention on what's happening here. We report this as a foreign war, give it due gravitas, explain the effects on trade, industry and the like, eggs included. And we watch America grow. When Europe is done fighting, they'll look across the Atlantic to see we've continued to advance into the future."

While Tom, Eddie and Mr. Collins discussed the state of the world, Esmeralda, Mason and Cook sat at the beeswax-polished kitchen table downstairs in the Davenport house considering local goings-on. The room was lit by afternoon sunshine. Mason polished his boots atop old newspapers, Esmeralda mended Mrs. Davenport's slip, and Cook shelled peas into a white china bowl.

Cook stood to make a pot of coffee. "Another train arriving tomorrow. Poor dears."

Mason rubbed black polish in vigorous circles onto a boot he wore on his left hand. "They're the lucky ones. They don't want your pity."

"It's not right to have them stand in the square to be inspected, bought like—" Cook glanced at Esmeralda, who kept her eyes on the sewing case as she replaced the needles, thread, thimble.

"You have no understanding of where they've come from," Mason said. "These children live on the streets—rough New York streets. They've had to beg and steal to survive. To have a home is a step up in the world, no matter how they get there." He placed the two shined boots together, admired his handiwork. "Grateful of a meal and a bed, I'd imagine."

"You make it sound like Christian charity," Cook said. "But you know full well the people inclined to take in an orphan are wanting unpaid labor."

"Or can't have one of their own," Esmeralda added.

"If you mean the Fleurys, I think they're the exception to the rule. That long-suffering woman."

Esmeralda murmured agreement.

"The Davenports should take one in, put an end to their grief," Mason said.

"Replace their boy with a foundling?" Esmeralda scowled.

"They're not going to find Sonny now. And they're set on having three boys. Why not take in an orphan and raise him as their own? After a few years no one will remember."

Cook tsked. "A fine father you'd make. It's not the same if it's somebody else's child. And for a family as important as the

Davenports to take in any... Those precious children, it's not their fault, but if they're going to be sent off anywhere it's to a farm, not a fine home like this. The idea."

"Then the Davenports should pray for another immaculate conception, because as far as I can tell that's the only other way they'll find themselves with three sons again."

Though Esmeralda and Cook made noises of shock at Mason's coarseness and blasphemy, they knew what he meant.

CHAPTER THIRTEEN

Because Sheriff Sherman and John Henry had returned to Half Moon Lake on countless occasions and because Mary asked to be driven to the house again and again, with none of these expeditions yielding anything other than disappointment, John Henry put their property up for sale in August 1914.

Mary insisted on visiting the house one last time, after the furniture, crockery and pots, vases, linens and paintings had been packed and moved to one of John Henry's storehouses, and the rugs rolled up and laid like logs in a truck and driven away. She wanted to check, she said, before any strangers were allowed to cross the threshold, that nothing had been left behind. Nothing and *nobody*, Esmeralda thought.

The air around the house was steamy and still, the last dog days of summer. Dragonflies hovered above baked grass. Birds rested in oak trees, waiting for the midday heat to pass. Once John Henry turned off the car engine, the only sounds were the drone of countless insects and the footsteps of the three as they walked without speaking from the driveway to the porch.

On John Henry's instruction, Esmeralda opened the windows in the living room, then went upstairs to air out the bedrooms. The house smelled of hot dust, loamy dirt carried in on the removalists' shoes and droppings from woodland creatures that had scampered through.

She could hear John Henry's sure stride on the boards downstairs as he walked a cursory circuit, ready to be gone from the moment they'd arrived, and Mary's anxious quickstep as she ran about, scouring the house like a cat whose kittens had been given away while she slept. Even when they landed in the same room, Mary didn't seem to care that John Henry and Esmeralda could see what she was doing. Or to be aware of the insanity in thinking Sonny might have been overlooked all this time, waiting or hiding in the hollowed house, returned home after a year-long walk in the woods. She searched for him with the same energy she had the first day of his disappearance. Esmeralda couldn't bear to watch. She told Mr. Davenport she was going to check the outside of the house for buckets and tools. Without taking his eyes off his wife, he said, "How quickly things change."

Esmeralda walked across the uncut lawn, around weedy flowerbeds to the wooden building used as a storage shed. She pushed open the weathered door, which hung crooked on two hinges. A single window let in light. A sparrow on a rafter chirped to tell her it was there, but didn't fly away. She stepped inside—such a plain room, with no curtains, paint on the walls or flooring—and shivered. Now that the room was emptied of the wheelbarrow, shovels and gardener's supplies, she saw it for what it had been: a home.

The Half Moon Lake house had been passed to John Henry from his father, and had been built by his father before him. This shed had been the slave quarters. As Esmeralda stood in the room, she thought about the people who'd been stored here. There was no other word for it. She heard her heartbeat, her breath, then the deep hum of the world: that layer of sound that lives beneath the creak of trees and the distant lowing. Esmeralda heard the hum of what had come before her, the remnant energy of living beings. There weren't ghosts in this room so much as fragments of souls. Keening. When Esmeralda moved her feet, the sound of her leather soles on the dirt floor seemed loud, abrasive as sandpaper. She apologized for the intrusion, crossed herself.

Esmeralda pictured what might have been here before: basic bedding, a rag rug, maybe a woven-seat chair. But these images were too homely. More likely the man was shackled at night to stop him running away, the woman dragged out of her bed to meet a master's late-night needs. And the children would have slept on the floor. Esmeralda wondered how they'd kept going, how they'd not forced their loved ones straight to Heaven, torching the house and field they had to tend. She hoped at least one of them had run away.

"What are you doing?" Mary stood in the open doorway. She glanced around the room, wrinkled her nose at the musty air. "Come loosen my corset. The girl tied it so tight this morning I can hardly breathe. Do you think I should get another?"

"No need for that. It'll be fine once I loosen it."

"A maid," Mary said. "I meant another maid."

PART THREE

FOUND

CHAPTER FOURTEEN

South of the town of Magnolia, Mississippi, 145 miles northeast of Opelousas, in a run-down house at the top of a hill, Grace Mill worked as house girl for Harry Cavett and his wife, Loretta. On this August 1915 morning, as a hot wind stirred the dogwood trees and cicadas rose up in a single-note shout, Grace began her day's labors and the Cavetts grumbled out of bed.

Mr. and Mrs. Cavett were not kind people. They worked Grace hard for six days a week, with Sundays off to walk to church. Mrs. Cavett told Grace they'd done her a favor by offering food and lodging, but the truth was no one else wanted to be yoked to the Cavetts.

When Grace had showed up on their doorstep Mrs. Cavett was thrilled: here was a young, open-faced, unwed mother, likely to be grateful and stay put. She was pretty as a peach—blonde hair, button nose, long lashes—but Mrs. Cavett had no fear about that: Mr. Cavett hadn't shown a spark of interest in any living thing for years. Importantly, the woman had two functional hands while Mrs. Cavett had one, the fingers of her own left hand crushed by washing-machine wringers. Mr. Cavett complained endlessly about having to help with the heavy wet sheets and churning the butter.

The Cavetts had considered throwing her out when Grace told them she had another baby on the way. "What use will you be?" Mrs. Cavett said. But Grace had pleaded with them, and promised she'd be able to continue her duties through her pregnancy. Harry Cavett said he didn't mind the boy too much because it never spoke a word, but expressed concerns about the squawk of a baby interfering with the peace of the household. Grace had no idea what peace he meant since both the Cavetts were enthusiastic yellers, and Mr. Cavett enjoyed playing his whistle late at night, unaware he had no talent for the instrument. Mrs. Cavett had held her silence for a moment before exhaling a begrudging, "Don't make me regret this."

Grace would've liked to live elsewhere, work elsewhere, but as Mrs. Cavett so often said, who would put up with an unmarried woman and a child, especially when her swollen belly told all that was needed about her morals? Anyhow, work was scarce in the area. And she hadn't yet earned their reference.

The Cavetts made no allowance for Grace's pregnancy. No matter that it was the result of their bullish son, Matthew, who'd forced himself upon her. The Cavetts were doggedly blind to any wrongdoing of their only child, who stopped by their house on a whim to share tales of his success as a traveling purveyor of medical treatments, then ask for money to develop his next formulation. Grace had watched through keyholes and cracked-open doors as the Cavetts handed their son money as though they were in a trance, Mr. Cavett wearing the hurt expression of a child at their son's underestimation of them, Mrs. Cavett wanting to return to the storyline of a son made good. Watching Matthew fleece his parents was the one time Grace felt pity for the Cavetts, pity that made way for dread, as they would inevitably vent their pain and humiliation on her once their son left.

Of course, Grace had never expected Matthew Cavett to push himself against her in the barn on his Christmas pass through the area, full of swagger from the dollar bills in his pocket and the moonshine in his belly. His fat tongue tasted of rancid fish, unaccountably so given the grease that stained his pants was from the evening's ham hock. He'd been brutish, so heavy she was scared she'd suffocate, worried he'd snap her bones.

The memory made Grace shake and heave. At first she'd thought the vomiting was a way of purging him from her mind. But when her breasts ballooned and ached, and her monthly blood dried up, she knew. How could a child be conceived from an act she'd so resisted, with a man she found so repulsive? For an instant, she'd considered her knitting needles, then asked God for forgiveness.

Gideon Wolf might have guessed who the father was, since not many men visited the farm and Grace was always at the house, but he never said. He watched her struggle to move about when he came to the Cavetts' house to tune their piano, sharpen tools and mend roofing. And then again to tune the piano, because Mrs. Cavett—who loved to pound away at the thing, often in a hellish duet with Mr. Cavett's whistle—managed to knock the keys about as though she

played with iron gloves. Gideon wondered if there was anything the Cavetts treated kindly aside from their wastrel son.

Grace had been happy to let her boy, Ned, squat beside
Gideon Wolf while he worked. The boy had been mute from
birth, but made it clear from his face and constant presence
how curious he was about the man. He pointed at Gideon's
missing finger and Gideon invented a wild story by way of answer, which amused them both.

"It's bound to be more exciting if I lost my finger to a can-
nibal than a plain old ax," he said to Grace. And he showed
Ned how the stumpy digit was no impediment: he played his
fiddle for the boy, taught him noughts and crosses by drawing
in the dirt with sticks, and lit up his eyes with card tricks.

"Never speaks?" Gideon asked.

"Not a word," Grace said.

After Gideon tuned the piano on his August visit, Harry
Cavett told him he could spend the night in the barn. At sun-
set, Grace and Ned took supper and an extra blanket out to
Gideon. Ned ran to the back of the barn to play with the newborn piglets.

Gideon thanked Grace for the food and edged over on the
hay bale so she could sit while Ned played. "When's the next
one due?" he asked.

Grace felt the baby roll inside her. "Soon, too soon."

"Could be I'm having one, too." He stretched out his rake-
thin legs and patted his medicine-ball stomach.

Ned ran over to them, a squirming piglet in his arms. He
showed the animal to Gideon then his mother.

"Put him back, darling. He wants to be with his family. Be
careful."

Ned carried the piglet back to the pen, cuddling and nuzzling it.

"What happened there?" Gideon had noticed the crescent-shaped scar on Ned's arm.

"A disagreement with a calf's hoof. Some animals don't want to be carried."

"You have to admire the spunk in trying to lift something your own size."

"He's never lacked spunk. Scared of dogs, though, for no reason I know of."

"Huh." The two sat amicably amid the comforting smells of hay and animals.

"You'll have your hands full with him, a baby and them." Gideon took another spoonful of thick bean soup. "You look worn slap out as it is, if you don't mind me saying."

"I'll make it work."

Gideon brushed crumbs off his pants. "He could come with me for a time, if that'd help you."

"Ned? Oh, I don't think so. He'd run you ragged. You've seen how he is."

"I'd survive. I'd enjoy showing him the place, and it'd be good for him to be out in the air."

"He's outside plenty, don't worry about that."

"I'd do a loop and be back here in a month. I travel slow and stop a lot, sleep warm at night. I'd take care of him, give you time to recover after—" He gestured at her belly.

Grace heaved herself up to standing. "Thank you, Mr. Wolf, but I've done fine with Ned on my own so far." Gideon seemed a kind man, indulgent with Ned, capable enough. But that didn't mean he could take care of a child.

"Maybe so, but I reckon he'd have a better few weeks with me than staying at your bedside." He stared out the barn door again. "I wouldn't trust them to look after him while you're birthing and recovering, or to feed him."

Grace placed her palms on her aching lower back and rocked on the spot. "Perhaps you could stay awhile?"

"After tomorrow my work here is done." He placed his empty bowl, bread plate and spoon on the tray and stood up to hand it to Grace.

As she reached forward, Grace felt a twinge in her hip, the pain radiating down her right leg. For a moment she thought the baby might be coming, but she rocked back and forth a while and the pain passed. "Let me think about it."

Ned was never far from Grace's side. He followed her as she worked through her chores, joining in when he could: gathering eggs from the chicken coop, feeding the new chicks breadcrumbs soaked in milk and dusting them with insect powder, fetching Grace the food or drink Mrs. Cavett requested from the cellar, and watching as Grace dug weeds from the vegetable patch and milked the cow. Sometimes, without prompting, Ned would hug Grace's leg through a scrunch of skirting until she tickled him off. They played hide-and-seek behind freshly hung sheets.

In the evenings, Grace sang Ned the alphabet and showed him how to hold a pencil, enveloping his hand in hers and making swirling motions on the butcher's paper she'd taken from the kitchen. If Ned didn't learn to speak he'd have to write, and he'd have to learn younger than most. She taught him the few words she knew and decided they'd both learn to write by copying words from her Bible.

But as the baby continued to grow, Grace found it hard to walk. She worried the birth was going to be difficult; the baby sat at an odd angle inside her. If the worst happened, Ned would be left alone with the Cavetts; it might be the safer option to ask Gideon Wolf to keep Ned away from the farm until Grace had come to the other side of this birth.

Lying in bed the night before Gideon was due to leave, with Ned curled on his side next to her, Grace listened as the first drops of rain hit dusty dirt. Soon, cool air pushed under her door, water pattered on her window and Ned's breathing grew slow and deep. But the top note to these gentle sounds was Mr. and Mrs. Cavett bellowing at one another, then a crash as something heavy hit the floor. Grace let the tears drip off her face.

On the evening of August 15, seated together in the barn, Grace and Gideon made a verbal agreement: Wolf would take Ned traveling for no more than five weeks, would feed him, keep him warm, and make sure he had a place to sleep at night. He'd keep him away from dogs. And if Grace didn't survive the birth, he would find Ned a new home.

Grace wept when she said goodbye to her boy, hugged him to her bulbous stomach and smoothed his hair down with her wetted palm. She handed Wolf a calico bag containing Ned's few clothes and watched the pair walk down the dirt road until Mrs. Cavett hollered for her from the porch.

As the five-week mark came and went, there was no sign of Gideon Wolf or her son. Grace, cradling her newborn daughter, Lily, stood outside looking for them as often as the Cavetts' distractedness permitted. When Mrs. Cavett did catch Grace slacking off, she told her to quit moping.

Grace missed Ned fiercely. Some days she couldn't stop crying, even in front of the Cavetts. At any time, terror that Gideon Wolf would not return came upon her, like a fist gripping her heart. But she couldn't go out on the road and search for them; she had no idea where they were, had little money, no companion to keep her safe, and she had a baby and reduced strength.

So Grace stayed at the Cavetts' farm, worked, slept with her daughter on their straw-stuffed bed, and prayed for Ned to come back.

CHAPTER FIFTEEN

On September 23, 1915, Mrs. Leonard Potter entered the Mobile sheriff's office to say a tramp and child had been on her porch asking for work, and this time she was certain the boy was Sonny Davenport.

"This time?" Sheriff Bird said. Still, he hollered over his shoulder for his deputy on duty, Al, and the two stepped outside, not expecting anything other than a walk to Mrs. Potter's house. (Minus Mrs. Potter, who continued on to the market.)

Along the way Sheriff Bird checked for signs that people were preparing themselves for the coming storm. Another hurricane was headed toward the Gulf Coast, but so far the clouds were wispy, the wind mild. As the sheriff and Al turned into Franklin Street, he noted the birds were still chirping and his arthritis hadn't flared up. Air pressure couldn't be too low, then. He was about to make these very observations aloud when Al pointed at a man and boy sitting on the steps of the Catholic church, right at the top in the shade of the portico.

Sheriff Bird moved closer, staring at the boy. He had the

same build and hair as the child in the photograph, looked about six, but the sheriff wouldn't know until he could see the face. The boy sat side-on to the man, listening—skeptically, it seemed—as the man waved his arms about, likely telling some shaggy-dog story. The man wore a crumpled jacket fastened by a single button over a faded waistcoat. His pants were patched at one knee, his boots scuffed. A tramp, without doubt.

"Morning," the sheriff called out. The tramp stopped talking, hands fixed mid-air, until he saw the star-shaped badge and rearranged himself into a more dignified posture.

"Nice spot to take in the day," the sheriff said.

"Giving the boy a rest."

"Rest from what?" Al asked.

Sheriff Bird hoicked up his pants. "You live around here? You and—?"

"We're passing through." The tramp stood up and beckoned for the boy to do the same. "Forgive me if I've caused offense by using your church steps. We'll be on our way. No harm intended."

"None done. Though I do have a couple of questions. How about you walk with Al and me to the stationhouse. Won't take more than a minute." He walked up a few steps, wanting to get near enough to see if the child had a scar on his arm.

Gideon had been questioned by the law plenty of times, though how it was a crime to be homeless and poor he didn't know. He weighed his options: run, and hope he and the boy could outpace the men; go with them; or try to talk his way out of their interest and scoot to the next town. The first option was out given the sheriff and deputy now stood on the church's steps, blocking access to the street, and the doors behind him were locked. Gideon watched the younger officer fingering the handcuffs that dangled from his belt. It wouldn't take much provocation for him to use them, and Gideon didn't want the boy to see that. And he wasn't sure he could call on his quick wit today: they were outdoors, aimless, because he'd failed to talk anybody into giving him a day's work.

"We'd be delighted to walk with you gentlemen. Come along, boy. Let's show you a sheriff's office."

Although Gideon had cooperated, Al pushed him, without warning, into the sheriff's single cell. Gideon shouted his rage, madder than a wet hen, and the boy cried.

As Sheriff Bird waited for the operator to place his call to Sheriff Sherman, the boy sat in front of his desk on a wooden chair, dangling his skinny legs and sniffling. "Won't say a word," Sheriff Bird said, once he was put through. "But I've stared at him long and hard, and I'm about as certain as I've been of anything—this is the same child as in the photograph."

"If that's the case, it's the best news I've heard in years," Sheriff Sherman said. "But I don't want to drag the Davenports interstate again if there's any doubt."

Sheriff Sherman relayed questions to John Henry throughout that day and the next, asking him for such detailed information about Sonny that John Henry thought he should consult with Mary. He didn't, though, for fear of raising her hopes. At one point, the sheriff asked, "Is there anything unique in the shape of his feet, nose, ears? The scar you described has lightened but that happens—two years..."

Two years indeed, John Henry thought. Sonny would be taller, possibly with new marks and injuries.

"What does the child say?" John Henry asked.

"He hasn't spoken. Give him time. We don't know what he's lived through or how much he remembers."

Sheriff Bird, having rubbed a washcloth across the boy's face, arranged for a photograph to be taken and sent by train.

When it arrived in Opelousas, John Henry studied the picture. The boy was older than his memory of Sonny, of course, and his hair seemed lighter, his eyes tired, but there was something familiar about him. John Henry agreed with the sheriffs that the only way to know for certain would be for him and Mary to see the boy in person.

The meeting presented a risk to his wife's stability. In the past year, she'd regained her physical and mental health, even had new friends through her Ladies Aid charitable work. To pull the scab off such a gaping wound, to encourage her to meet a boy who might be another disappointment, would be cruel. But if it was Sonny, life could go back to the way it had been before…

Because it couldn't continue as it was. Mary still careened from simmering anger at John Henry's failure to protect Sonny to numb inanities, sometimes speaking to him as though he was one of the servants, not her husband. And while apology would be the smart response, John Henry became annoyed and defensive, then cold. He missed the time when they'd been tender with one another, effortless and light, when they'd each known their role. Their encounters had grown increasingly fraught, a jumble of attempts at normalcy: arguments out of the blue; drawn-out, teary meals—

and, sometimes, reconciliation. But no matter how their interaction fell apart, and sooner or later each encounter did, neither of them seemed able to conceive of an end to the sadness. To have lost their son was devastating, and impossible to absorb.

This opportunity in Mobile, though, was possible salvation.

When John Henry arrived at the bedroom door he realized it was a week out from Mary's birthday. What a gift it would be to have her son back. The morning was warm and bright, blue jays peeped, and George and Paul played outside. He'd heard Cook humming that morning on his way to speak with Esmeralda. The signs were in John Henry's favor. Still, when his fingers hovered an inch from the doorknob he pulled back, paused to consider whether he needed to burden Mary with a journey, then decided that yes, it was imperative.

Mary stood at the open window staring down at the garden. John Henry walked to her side. He wanted to stroke the pale nape of her neck, but touching his wife had become an unfamiliar act.

"It's beautiful, isn't it?" she said. "The autumn leaves sprinkled on the lawn. I know they'll be swept away, but I find the shedding before winter so—" She turned away from the view and saw the expression on John Henry's face. "What's the matter?"

"I have news. Sheriff Bird in Alabama might have found our boy. We need to go to him."

Mary reached out to hold on to the windowsill, then crumpled to the floor.

* * *

Once Gideon Wolf was behind bars in Mobile, other people came forward with claims they'd seen him whipping the boy; that he'd told them the child belonged to his cousin, his neighbor, an acquaintance; that he'd told them to mind their own Ps and Qs; that they'd had suspicions.

Wolf told Sheriff Bird he'd never laid a finger on the boy, and might have said any of those things to get people to leave him be. "Hauled off to the hoosegow for no reason. What was I supposed to say?" God's truth was the boy belonged to Grace Mill, who'd been more than happy for him to travel with Wolf for a few months, had asked for that, to give her time to birth her next baby.

"She works on a farm," Wolf said, but in his troubled state he couldn't remember the name of the farmer. "You go find it. Closer to Magnolia than Osyka on the same road as gets you to Newberry place. Near the Picaninny farm."

The sheriff had no idea which of the Picaninny farms he meant or who Newberry was, and with each added detail that met with a blank stare, Wolf grew more frustrated.

"Settle down," Sheriff Bird said. "None of this sounds likely to me, but if there's a farm and a Grace we'll find them."

Wolf scratched at the rough stubble on his chin as he paced the length of his drafty cell, only a few steps to either wall for his lanky lope, muttering, spitting onto the bare boards. "They knowed I was taking the boy and no question she needed the help. Fit to burst and still they're screaming at her to fetch water and feed the mare." The deputy on duty told Wolf to quiet down. But the tramp kept talking. "Pretending they didn't know, while that rope of a man and his mean-lipped wife kept her—Grace. You find Grace Mill, she'll tell you."

When interrogated by Sheriff Bird in a quieter moment, Wolf seemed confused by questions about the boy from Opelousas. "Louisiana? What're we talking about Louisiana for?" And he was even more confused at questions about his travels with the boy during the past two years. "Grace gave her boy over to me the day I left the farm—middle of August, as sure as anything. No more than six weeks ago. Or seven. Tell me the date again."

The sheriff groaned.

"Listen, when you stopped me I was going back her way. I'd gone further east than I'd planned to, hadn't told her I'd leave the state. She'll be worried...But two years? That makes no sense."

"Leaving the state? Where'd you start out?"

"Magnolia, I told you that. Liberty."

"Liberty, Mississippi?" The sheriff sat forward on his chair. "You're telling me now you met this boy on a farm in Mississippi, not Alabama or Louisiana?"

"Louisiana! Why y'all keep thinking I've been in Louisiana?"

Gideon seemed so bamboozled that Sheriff Bird did worry he'd arrested the wrong man. But the Davenports were coming to Mobile, so there was nothing to do now but let them lay eyes on the boy.

CHAPTER SIXTEEN

Gideon Wolf had been locked up for six days when the hurricane made landfall, hitting Grand Isle, Louisiana, early on the morning of September 29. John Henry had hoped news of the oncoming storm had been exaggerated, and that they'd be able to travel to Mobile to see the boy as planned. But there were sixty-mile winds in New Orleans at sun-up, and when the hurricane passed through Opelousas, at seven o'clock that night, he was relieved they'd stayed put.

John Henry, Mary, Esmeralda and Cook had prepared the house as well as they could, closing windows and sealing gaps around doorframes, wrapping furniture in sheets, storing paintings, clothing and rugs in the cellar. Mason carried in outside chairs and took down the porch swing. George and Paul had the job of preparing an emergency kit.

Now, having eaten a cold supper of meats and bread by candlelight, the family huddled in the back of the living room, with camp beds set up for the boys, so they could be together if they needed to evacuate in a hurry. The servants were together, too, in the kitchen.

The strong winds shook the house, hurled rubble at the walls, smashed chimneys and tore at the upper porches until they were hanging by a thread. The Davenports heard the damage from downstairs but could do nothing other than imagine what wreckage was being wrought as the storm entered the house: the saturated carpets, rain-lashed couches. The storm lasted through the night, and while Mary feared for her Opelousas home and family she also worried about Sonny.

"Sheriff Bird will keep him safe. He's a good man, responsible," John Henry reassured her. "Try to sleep. I'll sit up."

They stayed in Opelousas for three more days to direct the cleaning and repair of their home and John Henry's factory. The damage their town had suffered—roofs ripped off and flung about, destroying buggies and cars, buildings; livestock crushed under fallen trees; church towers collapsed onto rooming houses and schools—was a fraction of what Mobile had endured. The *Press-Register* building was ruined but the heroic staff managed to print an edition nonetheless. When their train arrived in Mobile on the night of October 2, 1915, John Henry bought a copy of the paper and, standing on the platform under lamplight, read the front-page headlines to Mary: "The City Emerges from Worst Hurricane Experience," "Barometer Lowest on Record," "Wind Velocity Greatest Ever Reported." "More than two hundred and seventy lives have been lost," he said.

"And yet the sheriff's house stood," Mary said.

"Yes. Sheriff Sherman promises me they're all fine. A miracle, truly." John Henry was as eager as Mary to see the boy, but found her disinterest in the wider devastation troubling. The past two years had hardened his wife.

Mary, meanwhile, felt gladdened by her husband's use of the term "miracle." That augured well, somehow.

"Thousands made homeless throughout Mississippi and Alabama and as far as Tennessee," John Henry read, "hungry and destitute, with nothing but wet clothes on their backs."

"Do you think the car will be here soon?"

The Davenports hadn't traveled alone to Mobile; Sheriff Sherman, Tom and Eddie had been on the same train in the cheaper seats, and Esmeralda had sat in the colored carriage at the rear. They would all travel by car to the Birds' house, where the boy had been cared for by Mrs. Bird following his rescue.

While John Henry read the *Press-Register* to Mary and waited for Sheriff Bird to arrive, the rest of the group watched porters unload their luggage onto the platform. Esmeralda, who had one small bag, stood as close to the Davenports as decency permitted, waiting on instruction. She'd never been to Alabama but knew it to be a dangerous place.

Once everyone's belongings had been accounted for, two cars—one driven by Sheriff Bird, the other by one of his men—crisscrossed the debris-strewn streets through the town center and up the hill. The third car, carrying Esmeralda and the Davenports' luggage, followed.

"What a shame that my first ever sight of Mobile is like this. I'd heard it's such an attractive city." Mary looked for beauty in the ravaged streets, illuminated by a full moon and what lights remained.

"It will be again," Sheriff Bird said.

As reported, the Birds' compact home, though wounded, had held up better than many of the houses around it. It still had its roof. Several of the windows were unboarded and had glass in them. And its position on high ground had spared it from flooding, though the garden had been demolished. John Henry and Mary had been so focused on the terrors the storm might have brought that they hadn't anticipated the Birds' lawn would be filled with local reporters, concerned citizens and nosy neighbors.

"A goddamn circus," Sheriff Bird said. Sheriff Sherman agreed.

Mrs. Bird was as level-headed as her husband, and she'd been a sheriff's wife for long enough to know how to stand her ground. She hadn't been shy about addressing the seething, edgy crowd that showed up on her muddy front lawn. "Only ones coming into my house are the momma and poppa, the sheriff that brought them and the sheriff that lives under this roof. So y'all might as well go home. What's wrong with you, showing up to gawp and gossip?" Of course, no one had gone anywhere.

Mrs. Bird was on her porch scolding the crowd again when the cars pulled up, but her tone changed when she saw Mary Davenport. Her pointing arm softened and took the curved shape she used to hold her children and to dance at weddings with her husband. She stepped forward and ushered Mary into the house where the boy slept. "Come here. Oh, what a time for you." Mary let herself be comforted by an unfamiliar woman as though she wasn't the wife of one of the most important men in Opelousas. They were, at that moment, mothers above all else.

If Tom and Eddie were annoyed by their unforeseen lack of access at a crucial time, Esmeralda was even more so. Esmeralda had thought she'd be standing behind Mary, ready to help Mr. Davenport if his wife became overwrought. What in the heavens was she here for if not to be at Mrs. Davenport's side during the most stressful part of the journey? That Sheriff and Mrs. Bird weren't the ones for that job. They might well be fine people, but they hadn't seen the pain of the past two years, didn't understand how Mrs. Davenport shut down when overwhelmed. And who was laying out Mrs. Davenport's clothes, unpacking her luggage?

Left to stand outside after arriving last, then told by Mrs. Bird's skinny white house girl that she hadn't been instructed to let any Negro lady inside, no way, Esmeralda walked back to the front yard. As if being in Mobile wasn't unnerving enough, she wasn't sure what was supposed to happen next. "I don't know what to do, I don't," she said to Tom and Eddie.

"Seems you're out in the cold with us." Tom looked around. The yard bore signs of the recent hurricane but Tom could see the efforts of the Birds to assert their will over the wind in the raked lawn, the neat stacks of chopped branches. Two tricycles, a broom and a rocking chair framed the front door. "What should our next move be, Mrs. Somerset?"

Eddie walked away from them toward the house, searching the crowd for anyone who might be worth a photograph.

Esmeralda was glad of a familiar face in this strange situation but she did not consider Tom McCabe a friend. "There's no 'our.' I should be inside with Mrs. Davenport."

"Well, we've traveled here together, we've spent more than a few hours in one another's company sharing stories, and I know you like Walter—"

"Everyone likes that big-hearted rabbit-dog. And those stories weren't for my benefit."

Tom sucked in his breath. Esmeralda flipped from civil to hostile, light to heavy without warning. She confounded him, but she was still—usually—useful, so he tolerated their unpredictable interactions. "Mrs. Somerset, you know by now that my motives are pure: I want to tell this story as it should be told. I've never lied or judged or in any way betrayed John Henry or Mary. What will it take to earn your respect?"

"Hmph."

"You must admit it'd be wise to help one another find a way to see inside. Don't you want to know what's going on?"

"Of course I do. I should be in there."

Tom studied the house. "Which room do you think they're in? I figure—"

"Little boy's been sleeping with the other children. Bedrooms are upstairs. But they wanted the boy on his own tonight so they put him down in the living room. He'll be asleep on the sofa, poor child."

"How do you know that?" Tom asked.

"I listen."

"You'd make a fine reporter. Now, why wouldn't they keep him awake?"

"It's eleven o'clock. Child can't stay up that late. The Davenports got here as quick as they could, but that's as early as it was ever going to be."

"The living room. All right, what are we standing here for, then?" Tom signaled for Eddie to rejoin them and, making sure no one noticed, the trio slipped down the side of the house, dropping into the shadows. Tom walked in front toward two windows through which dim light shone. The three crouched in a line outside the lamplit room, peeking over the window ledge. Eddie set up his tripod so his camera was only visible in the bottom corner of the window, where the lace curtain was twisted and had created a patch of clear glass. It'd be hard, but he could get some version of a photograph.

Tom didn't like being outside, snooping on the Davenports. They weren't only news; they were John Henry and Mary. And watching them through a window felt undignified, entirely wrong. But Eddie was going to take a picture and Tom would write a story no matter what Tom's personal misgivings. Mr. Collins expected them to come back with something. This was a front-page moment. The problem was, once Eddie took his picture the flash would alert the Davenports to their presence, which would be unpleasant, shameful even.

They watched Mary through the window as she knelt beside the sofa where the boy was cradled in Mrs. Bird's arms.

"She's not sure," Tom said. "She's not sure that's her boy."

The three held their breath as Mary buried her face in one hand.

Esmeralda exhaled a circle of steam onto the glass.

Mrs. Bird had walked into the room first, carrying an oil lamp. She turned and whispered to Mary, "Storm took out the electricity." The two sheriffs entered behind Mary and John Henry, and stood near the sofa, near enough to observe while not getting in the way. Everyone shuffled into place, murmuring what few words needed to be said, making sure that Mary was able to stand close to the child, who was sleeping under a knitted blanket. Mrs. Bird raised her lamp so Mary could see the boy's face more clearly. "You tell me if you need anything—water, a chair." She watched Mary for her reaction.

Mary clutched Sonny's toy rabbit, Hop, by its thin wrist. She felt the warm air close in around her. She stared at the boy, then knelt down on the rug. "The shadows."

Mrs. Bird took a step toward the sofa. The lamp swayed and shadows formed on the boy's face, rendering his nose bulbous then beaky, his lips cupid bows then a sneer.

Mary scowled in agitation. It was so hard to tell. It wasn't supposed to be like this. The crowd of people outside, though only chattering among themselves and separated from her by a wall, were shouting in her mind, jostling one another in the mud, braying for an answer. She could sense the impatience of the sheriffs, hear her husband's short, sharp breath, could smell the warm doughiness of Mrs. Bird, the smoke from the fireplace. And that useless lamp! She couldn't think straight. And where was Esmeralda? How selfish of her not to be here, to dillydally at the station when Mary needed her.

"I'll wake him," Sheriff Bird said, watching Mary twist and bend to examine the boy.

"Don't." Whether it was a mother's instinct not to wake a sleeping child or fear that he might be startled by her looming over him in the dead of night, Mary didn't know. "Please."

"I think it might be the best way to see him," Sheriff Bird insisted. He lifted the boy to sitting position, sleepy rag doll that he was, then patted him on the cheek. "Child, open your eyes."

"Oh, let me." Mrs. Bird passed her lamp to Sheriff Sherman and sat on the sofa holding the boy close to her, gently patting his back.

The boy rubbed his eyes. Mary held Hop up to show him, then felt foolish when the boy looked from her to the toy and back again, uncomprehendingly. He snuggled closer into Mrs. Bird.

Without warning, Mary sank to the floor and buried her face in one hand. As he watched her cry, the boy began to cry, too, his mouth open without issuing a sound.

"It's all right, all right," Mrs. Bird crooned.

In response to John Henry's gentle touch on her shoulder, Mary whimpered, "Why don't I know?"

"You're spent from the journey and the unfamiliar—" John Henry said. "And it's been two years. It's natural—"

Mrs. Bird cocked her head, mystified. Mrs. Davenport appeared to be in as much need of comforting as the child. Sheriff Bird remained silent. Sheriff Sherman placed the lamp on the mantel. He had high regard for Mrs. Davenport and could see she was overcome, but it was strange for a mother to be unable to tell if a boy was hers, and for mother and child to both be reduced to tears by their reunion. The conclusion was clear, and he now considered how to get the Davenports from the house to the inn with as little fuss as possible.

Mrs. Bird cradled the boy in a way her own willful six-year-old would never have tolerated and rocked him back and forth, his sobs becoming jerky and shallow. He turned his head sideways, still buried in Mrs. Bird's clothing, to look at the other adults. Mary, likewise quieted, was at his eye level.

"Why is he silent?" Mary asked. "I don't understand."

"Hasn't spoken yet. Little darling." The boy grabbed a fistful of Mrs. Bird's sleeve and turned his face back into her chest.

"The scar," Sheriff Bird said, and Mrs. Bird pulled up the boy's sleeve.

Mary leaned in close. "Why, it's much bigger than it was. Lighter, too. And I don't recall this red outline."

"Scars can change over time," John Henry said.

"I gave him quite a scrubbing this evening. The redness could be my doing. It's all right, all right," Mrs. Bird whispered to the boy.

"Mary?" John Henry asked.

Sheriff Bird moved his weight from one foot to the other.

"His hair is coarser."

"No one has cared for him the way you did, my love."

"He doesn't seem to recognize me."

John Henry knelt on the carpet beside his wife. "What do your instincts say?"

"My instincts are talking in tongues."

Mrs. Bird noted the chill that had entered the woman's voice.

John Henry forced himself to speak evenly, to control his rising panic. This boy seemed no more familiar to him than any other, but if Mary sent a signal it was Sonny he'd trust in that. He'd seen too many photographs, met too many children, and this boy was two years older than his mind's picture. But Mary would know.

Sheriff Bird pulled Sheriff Sherman toward the door. "There's an army of reporters outside," he said. "I'll need to tell them something. What are you thinking?"

"Is there a back lane? The driver could meet us there," Sheriff Sherman replied. "I'd like to get the Davenports to their hotel with as little drama and upset as possible, talk to the press tomorrow."

While the sheriffs discussed the logistics of their exit in muted whispers, Mary moved closer to the boy. The curl of hair around his ear, the line of his neck, his bitten fingernails—she'd seen all this before. Did that mean he was Sonny or did the child resemble Paul when he was six? Not George, but possibly Paul. Or was she calling up a longing for a past time? She didn't know, couldn't trust her own mind. But if she were to leave now, let this child slip through her grasp, and later, when she was more composed, realize a mistake—No, it had to be the wiser choice to hold him close and slowly assess. What harm could there be in ending two years of suffering while caring for a homeless boy, a boy who may well be Sonny? Two years of aching loss, sleeplessness, a fractured marriage. Two years of judgmental sneers from her father. Oh, and two years of tumult for George and Paul: the gnawing absence of their brother, their parents' failure. Not another day of any of it.

"Yes." The word came out louder than she'd meant.

"Yes?" John Henry asked.

"It's him."

"Now, Mrs. Davenport," Sheriff Sherman said, "don't feel pressured by—"

She spoke firmly. "This is our son."

A hush of air escaped from a hot log in the fireplace. The boy was still in Mrs. Bird's lap, his face buried in her skirt. The sheriffs stood behind the kneeling Davenports, as if witnessing a nativity scene gone awry.

"It's dark, you see, and when he cried his face seemed different, but now I can tell—"

"Yes," John Henry said.

Mary let out a sob of joy and John Henry embraced her, ignoring Mrs. Bird's troubled expression, her husband's groan.

The lamplight shone onto Mary's and John Henry's faces. Depending on the angle, they looked either beatific or devilish. Mary had spoken, and John Henry had agreed. They said the boy was Sonny. And so he was.

CHAPTER SEVENTEEN

It seemed the whole population of Mobile played hooky that morning to be at the train station when John Henry, Mary and the boy left for Opelousas. People crowded the narrow platform from one end to the other: men in serge suits with their coat collars turned up; men wearing overalls; children hanging off lampposts; and enough women, Eddie said, that it looked "like a suffrage parade."

Tom and Eddie had boarded the train as early as they were permitted, in order to see the action on the platform from an elevated position. Eddie leaned out the window to get a shot of the crowd and saw photographers on the platform below turning their cameras back at him. He gave a thumbs-up in collegial recognition. Tom watched as Sheriff Sherman forced the crowd to part for the Davenports and Birds. The boy, in the center of the group, resisted when his fingers were pulled off Mrs. Bird's coat, clearly distressed at being taken from her and pushed toward Mary. Tom watched Mary, too, to see if she could comfort the boy, but she seemed shaken by the attention of so many strangers, tentative in her actions. John Henry held the boy's shoulder and steered him and Mary through the crowd and onto the train.

Inside their private carriage, John Henry closed the door to the corridor and pulled down the blind. The room became dark and oppressive, the small light above them doing little.

Mary had seated the boy next to her and now, to John Henry's unexpected annoyance, wouldn't leave him be, tucking his hair behind his ears, pulling up his socks and patting his knee. John Henry wanted her to stop fussing, but he bit his tongue. She was trying to find ease with the situation, renewing her familiarity with the boy. He would have been more irritated had she been cold or aloof with him, but her actions felt bothersome in a way he couldn't articulate.

The boy gave nothing back. He didn't respond to Mary's affection or murmurings, nor answer when John Henry asked, "Are you happy to be going home?" He looked scared and confused. What John Henry wanted to ask, but did not, was, "Do you know who we are? Do you know who you are? What happened to you?"

The whistle blew, the engine chugged, and the train rocked from side to side. Once they were clear of prying eyes, John Henry pulled up the blind then sat down with an emphatic thump. But the day's glare showed the worry lines and dark circles on his wife's face, the red eyes and quivering lips of the boy, and the October breeze was so strong that mother and child both slid across the seat away from the window.

* * *

The child was in a state of shock, Mary reasoned, and had suffered. But it was unnerving that he was so unresponsive. None of her efforts at comforting him worked.

Still, she had him by her side. They'd found him. They were going home. And now that she had all her pieces again, she could put them back together. If Mary had learned only one life lesson, it was to persist, to block out doubt and forge ahead. She took a slow breath and glanced out the train window at the blur of trees and fields. And then, as if she'd planned to do so, Mary lifted her chin and sang the opening words to Sonny's favorite nursery rhyme, "Three Blind Mice," ignoring the child's quizzical expression and John Henry's scowl, her tempo speeding up in time with the train.

The same commotion waited at the other end of the line, though it was dusk when they arrived. The lamplit Opelousas platform and the road that led to the station swarmed with people who'd come to be part of a moment the town had yearned for: the happy ending. John Henry carried the child tight to his chest. The boy seemed overwhelmed by the number of people, the flash of newspaper cameras, the headlights of the fire truck, the noisy chatter. He hid his face in John Henry's coat. Mary followed close behind her husband, not responding to the multitude of flowers, cards and toys thrust at her.

Tom and Eddie stayed on the train as long as they could, enjoying, again, the high and unimpeded vantage point.

"What are the chances these so-called wellwishers are going to leave them in peace?" Eddie asked.

Tom shook his head. "Zero to none."

Esmeralda had made her mind up in Mobile: the boy was not Sonny Davenport. But Mary had declared he was and the train had, quite literally, left the station. Now they all had to pretend.

"Isn't it wonderful he's back?" Mary asked. They were alone in the bedroom, as John Henry was reading downstairs. Esmeralda helped Mary out of her dress, petticoat, corset, stockings and into her nightgown, then put the jewelry back in its case, draped ribbons over their hook, placed Mary's shoes on the floor of the closet, even though all this was a job for the new maid. Esmeralda was tired beyond words after the uncomfortable journey, but Mary insisted on her company, wanting to share her happiness at her son's return.

Esmeralda could hear the edge of pleading in Mary's voice turn to annoyance and knew she had to do more than nod and grin. "He sure will sleep soundly tonight." She folded back the bedspread and smoothed the sheet with her hand. Esmeralda had never met her great-great-grandfather but it was family lore that he'd been taken from the arms of his ailing grandmother in Senegal, shackled and shipped to the Mississippi Delta, where his life beared no thinking on. He'd have been more confused than this boy, treated more roughly, sickened by the unfamiliar food. The world had a long history of people convincing themselves that children forget.

Mary put her hand on top of Esmeralda's. "That's enough. Do let me lie down. I'm exhausted."

Esmeralda said goodnight.

After she left Mary's room, Esmeralda looked in on the boys and saw the young one was asleep. George and Paul were not.

Paul whispered loudly for Esmeralda to come into the room. She sat on the end of his bed as he wriggled out from under the sheets to sit close beside her.

"Why're the grown-ups saying that's Sonny?" Paul asked.

"Hush, don't wake him." She tapped Paul on the nose. "You know that whisper of yours is no whisper, don't you?"

George, lying on his side in his own bed, joined in. "I don't know who that kid is, but he's not our brother."

"Your mom and pa say he is."

"What, have they got rocks in their head? He's nothing like Sonny," George said.

"Not a thing like him," Paul agreed.

"Have you said this to your ma?"

"She shouted at him," Paul said, then put his hand to his mouth.

"Stop chewing on your fingers," Esmeralda said. "You'll make them bleed."

"Already bleeding." Paul held up one hand as proof.

She spit on her handkerchief and dabbed at his fingers. "You come to me tomorrow, I'll put some salve on them."

Esmeralda saw that George was staring at the sleeping boy. "How about you be kind to that child, no matter who he is. He's been through a lot."

"But he's not Sonny," George said.

"I know, I know. And you can keep saying that to me. But I'd button my lips with everyone else if I were you. Until Sonny shows up, the boy's here. Let's make that as agreeable as we can."

Paul perked up. "When Sonny comes home we'll have two brothers. Four's better than three for games."

"You're so stupid." George flopped onto his back. "That's not how things work. He'll have to go wherever his own house is."

Esmeralda patted Paul's arm then stood up. "It's not so stupid to make this a game for now, both of you. Play along. Wait and see what happens."

"They'll find Sonny though, won't they, Esmeralda?" Paul asked.

"Sure they will."

Paul felt relieved. He had only now to think of what he'd say to his real brother when he came home.

Word spread of the first encounter between mother and child. Perhaps Mrs. Bird spoke out of turn. Perhaps Eddie was too loose with his telling. It wasn't clear who let slip the story, but the rumors became a public symphony: church and saloon chatter at first, then the newspapers rang in, tentatively—the *Daily* trilled "Not Confident Lad Is Her Missing Boy"—and then with a swell of sure sound, the *Alabama Times* trumpeting "Boy Does Not Recognize His Mother" and the *Times-Picayune* booming "This Boy Is Another Child."

A divide formed among the citizens of Opelousas, fanned and fueled by the newspapers.

Camp A believed Sonny had been reunited with his true

family, having been yanked onto a train as it passed near Half Moon Lake by the tramp Gideon Wolf, who'd used the poor boy for begging purposes. These people said that *naturally* the child was shocked and muddled; he'd been taken from his loving family, stolen away by a man he'd never previously laid eyes on, and then lived a terrible two years. You only had to hear about the boy's ulcerated feet, lousy hair and torn clothing to know he'd endured horrors. He was covered in sores, and had burn marks on both arms. It would take time for the boy to remember the life of a normal home and tell his story. And the relief of the parents was palpable. To anyone who suggested they'd laid claim to another boy, people in Camp A asked, why would any person do that, take in a stray who could carry any illness, any blood? The accusation was churlish and made no sense. It was clear the tramp had invented the other mother, since there was neither hide nor hair of her. The *St. Landry Clarion* and the *Bugle* held to this line of reasoning. They celebrated the reunion of a respected family after years of anguish. Tom, of course, continued to write that story.

Camp B claimed *they* were being responsible citizens, *more* responsible than those grabbing at a quick end to the sorry saga. Dan Hardy from the *News* talked to the doctor who'd examined the boy, and he said on record that the boy's injuries had been grossly exaggerated: "Case of head lice. Dumbstruck. Aside from that, fit as a fiddle." Camp B argued, further, that any child, no matter how long they'd been separated for, would recognize his mother and father, that this boy's silence was eerie. And any natural mother would have no uncertainty when faced with her offspring. Mary's initial

indecision, followed by her bullish conviction, seemed un-
hinged, and people knew she'd suffered mental strain. Also,
the tramp who'd been found with the boy claimed he'd known
him only a few weeks. They were confident that once Grace
Mill was found, the Davenports would have to give the child
over. The *Daily*, *Times-Picayune* and *Alabama Times* were
committed to this thread of inquiry.

The *Louisiana Times* alone hedged its bets.

Dan Hardy claimed he'd also spoken to young Paul
through the bars of the family's front gate and the boy had
said, "He won't play soldiers. Doesn't remember any games.
He's no fun." That was strange, the naysayers agreed, was it
not? Children, while of limited capacity, had no agenda. In
response, Camp A noted how often children lied, for amusement, out of jealousy or when coerced by reporters.

Many people questioned why Gideon Wolf would have
come up with a tale so easily checked. He'd told authorities
where to find the woman, more or less. And Sheriff Sherman was on his way back out of Opelousas to fetch her. If
there was a "her."

For John Henry and Mary, this bout of scrutiny was more awful than the last. Previously their family had been the subject
of unhelpful and prying sympathy. Now they were in the center of a savage storm of accusations and conjecture at a time
they'd hoped would bring joyous relief.

John Henry felt the lashes more sharply than his wife.
Mary had the boys—her three boys together again!—and shut
herself away from society. She managed the boys' days, instructing their tutors on how to include Sonny in lessons,

working with Cook on the week's menus, alerting Esmeralda to the things the new maid, Sula, should know but seemed not to, scheduling with Nanny Pru the boys' time with their mother and father. Mary was busy from dawn to dusk. But John Henry had to consider the impact of the rumors and newspaper articles on his business, his reputation, his plan to run for local office. He was in the public sphere more often than his wife so he noticed the drop in temperature when he entered a room.

The unexpected turns in life exasperated John Henry, mocked his attempts at planning. He'd lost more than two years to searching for Sonny, and now a tramp and a farm girl were sending his family into another spiral. Which had consequences beyond his immediate aspirations or his wife's contentment. He'd long hoped his three sons would attend Westwood Academy once Sonny turned five, but that marker had come and gone; Sonny would be seven in a matter of months. Paul would be nine, George ten. John Henry had hired the finest tutors, but having the boys educated at home agitated him. And Mary was stubbornly resisting letting them out into what she perceived as a hostile world.

"They can memorize the McGuffey Readers here just the same as in some faraway place. Why would you send them there?"

John Henry had explained this countless times. His sons needed to be with other boys. And it wasn't far away. "Even if they stop for every snail on the sidewalk, it's impossible to take more than ten minutes to get to the Academy. And they study more than the Readers."

John Henry had nearly launched into an explanation of

the Academy's adoption of the progressive Agassiz method, adding natural history and laboratory science to standard teachings of classics, geometry, logic, music and the rest. He knew his sons would benefit from the Academy's approach of studying in both classroom and field, adopted to cultivate the mind and body. "The Best Moral and Spiritual Environment. And Splendid Intellectual Atmosphere," their brochure promised. The school would build on his sons' Scout training. But mentioning the outdoors component to Mary would have been the kiss of death, so he didn't. Instead, he said, "They need to meet other children from good families."

Mary paused. "That is true." She felt a stabbing memory of the loneliness she'd felt as a child. She wouldn't wish that on her sons. John Henry stood as still as if he was drawing out a deer. But she pulled back. Her boys were so recently reunited; she wanted them at home. "The year is almost done. It doesn't seem the time to start something new. For now, they have one another for company."

Housekeepers, maids and cooks from other houses grilled Esmeralda whenever she left the Davenports'. She waved away their questions, partly out of loyalty, partly from fear of word getting back, and partly because she intended to follow the advice she'd given George and Paul.

When it was safe to do so, she talked to Cook.

"The truth will win out. It always does," Cook said. "When his mama comes to town the Davenports will realize their blunder, give the boy over and keep searching for Sonny. That day"—Cook pointed her whisk for emphasis—"is when she'll need you most. She's bound to fall back into her dark pit. And he'll take off around the country again."

Cook came from farming stock, had led a sheltered life, but Esmeralda was constantly surprised by the woman's naïveté. "When have you seen either of the Davenports admit they're wrong about anything? No, here's what I think: the woman will see her child, they'll both get so worked up that Mr. Davenport will say the woman is hysterical and the boy overwhelmed. They'll keep him until they find their own son and then…"

"And then?" Cook swapped her whisk for a wooden spoon, added flour to her bowl.

Esmeralda pointed at Cook's metal tins. "You making two cakes?"

"Don't we deserve a treat, too?"

Esmeralda felt sorry for Mr. and Mrs. Davenport sometimes. The reunion hadn't brought them the peace they'd yearned for. She heard their arguments, barely muted by closed doors. And Mrs. Davenport's mood changed at the whim of the child; she was happy when he ate without complaint or played contentedly with his wooden blocks, distraught when he threw himself onto his stomach and pounded the floor with his fists.

"Whatever that child has been through changed him," Esmeralda told Cook, "and all of them have to live with it now."

When she could, Esmeralda studied the boy. If she was right, and she was sure she was right, he had family somewhere. Maybe the woman she'd heard about, maybe not. Maybe his mama was dead. Still, she thought, he has mem-

ories of another place and little understanding of why he's
in this house. She'd have another word to George and Paul,
make sure they were being kind. It was a difficult time for
everyone. But the Lord always had his reasons. The boy, whoever he was, had been sent as a lesson or a test.

CHAPTER EIGHTEEN

Clara was thrilled Sonny Davenport was home. "I'm so glad for them." She spoke over the music coming from the band: renditions of "Ballin' the Jack," "Aba Daba Honeymoon" and, her current favorite, "On the Beach at Waikiki."

Tom could tell Clara *was* glad about the Davenport news, and everything else that'd passed her mind that night. They'd come to their favorite club, a buzzing, crowded room where slick-haired waiters zigzagged between ecstatic patrons dressed in their finest feathers, furs, suits and sparkles. Clara wore her new outfit, a red Oriental satin gown copied by a local seamstress from a photograph in *Les Modes*. "A copy of a Jeanne Paquin," Clara had said in the car on the way to the club. "She dresses the Astors and Vanderbilts, you know. Even has a store on Fifth Avenue." She'd showed Tom an article cut from the *Times-Picayune*. Tom took it and read aloud, "Paquin, Inspired by Old Pictures of Costumes Designed for Famous Personages of Other Days." He'd laughed. "So you're wearing a copy of a copy of a copy?" She'd put a finger to her painted lips. "But don't tell a soul. I'm pretty sure I can pass it off as the real deal."

Tom was happy to be out, drinking cocktails and listening to music. And he was relieved for anything that offered a break in the tension between him and Clara. It hadn't been rosy lately. Clara was confounded by Tom. "You asked me to marry you, after all. Why won't you agree to a date?"

Tom had a hundred reasons but not one of them rang true, even to him. He'd proposed to Clara after traveling to New Orleans with John Henry. He was right, Tom thought: to love and care for a woman was an honorable thing. Marriage and children—these were what came next in life. Sporting houses, gambling, gadding about were fun, but you couldn't do that forever. And Clara was affectionate, cheerful and well bred. Tom saw the way other men ogled her; she'd be snatched up in a minute if he walked away. So why did he so often have the urge to walk away? The idea of committing to a wedding date made him scratchy. He watched Clara, her shoulders jigging up and down to the sounds of clarinet and trombone, mouthing the lyrics. She glanced Tom's way and blew him a kiss.

A night of dancing and talking about the Davenports' good news should've been just the ticket. But hovering below his relief was a nagging unease. He'd seen Mary's face when she first saw the boy: she hadn't been sure, had talked herself into surety. And he'd seen the desperation in John Henry's eyes: he wanted an end to his troubles. Their choice had not seemed premeditated, and they'd come at it from different angles, but in the Birds' house the Davenports had arrived at the same place, the end of the hunt for their child. And in a way that troubled Tom; he could see that this decision had brought them together as unconscious co-conspirators but pushed them apart as a couple. Last night, Tom had dreamed of Mary Davenport in a louche and abandoned way he would never have done before. No longer a victim, she was DeMille's Carmen, Mabel at the Wheel, a beckoning Lillian Gish. Tom had woken up edgy and abashed.

Added to his complicated feelings was the fact he hadn't seen the Davenports since they'd returned to Opelousas with the boy. Tom understood that Mary needed to focus on her children. She received no visitors. And John Henry must have thought it wise, for now, to distance himself from reporters as he'd done back in the early days after Sonny had gone missing. Tom tried to view all this analytically. But he'd consoled Mary at her lowest time, and had searched the South with John Henry. He was invested, he'd been pulled out of the pack to be a part of their story, he was their *friend*. Tom assured himself that John Henry had a plan, and would, at the right time, beckon him. Tom needed to be patient. And to push his doubts and wandering thoughts out of his mind.

Clara touched his arm. "Ask me to dance, will you?"

The next day at the *Clarion* office, Eddie took Tom aside.

"I've got something for you." He gave Tom a photograph. "Know who that is?"

Tom held the picture by its edges. "It's me. Where'd you take it?"

"It's you all right, you on the Mobile train staring down at Mary Davenport. You want to know why I took it? So you could see what I see—you're starry-eyed for her." Eddie slapped the photo with the back of one hand. "Didn't even notice when I took a picture of you."

"You're crazy." Tom held the photo out for Eddie to take back.

"I don't want it. I want you to take a good look at it before you leave the house in the morning, to remind yourself you're supposed to be a newsman—an engaged one at that—not some love-struck kid."

"I'm no such thing."

Eddie held his arms up as if to surrender. "Camera doesn't lie."

As Tom turned his back he heard Eddie sing, "I love, I love, I love my wife—but oh! You kid!"

Who was he fooling? Tom thought. If even Eddie could spell out what Tom wasn't willing to admit to himself, it was time to quit playing the chump. Mary Davenport was a married woman, a mother—and a news story.

CHAPTER NINETEEN

Mr. Gould opened the front door of his city house himself and greeted Mary with a huff. This had been one of the constant sounds of her childhood, accompanied then, as now, with a wry smile and slow shake of the head. Mr. Gould's smile wasn't one of amusement but a sneer of superiority, smugness and melancholy. People failed him in predictable ways; Mary hadn't meant to be late, but she was.

Mary had nudged the three boys out of the car in front of her, telling them to walk sensibly up the stairs to greet their grandfather. She hoped the children, as peppy and eager as released animals after the long drive, would encourage her father into a better mood. But he was still stern-faced by the time Mary had gathered her skirt about her, spoken to the driver, pointed to this and that bag to explain something to Nanny Pru or Sula, and made her way up to the door.

"Cook isn't happy," he said.

Mary followed her father into the cool, spare entryway. "Mrs. Croft, how nice to see you again. Oh yes, we're very pleased to have him back home, thank you." Mary removed her coat. "Follow Mrs. Croft and Nanny upstairs, you three." Her father huffed once more at what she knew he would consider excessive prattling. She could see this wasn't the time to reacquaint the boys with their grandfather. "Sula, lay out my tea and evening dresses, please. I'll be in for the night."

"And on time for dinner." Her father was not ready to let her lateness go. "Lunch is cold now, but you'll have to make do."

"I'm sure that will be fine for us. I'm truly sorry, Father, to have kept you from your lunch."

"You didn't. Lunch is at one o'clock, and that is when I ate. Now come into the living room so I can sit down. Mrs. Croft will let us know when this second lunch can be served."

Mary followed her father into his living room, noting the freshly oiled potted palms in brass pots, the dark wood, Persian rugs, the scent of tobacco, the absence of female frippery. This stiff beginning, even with the added issue of her tardiness, was altogether normal. Mary and her father had never been effusive or warm with one another. She'd long felt as though she was a pet or purchase her father was forever deciding whether to keep. It was an impossible goal to gain his approval. The parts of her that pleased him were the parts that mirrored him; he liked to hear his opinions, his choices, his tastes recited back, with feminine delicacy and humility. She'd tried, of course, for years, and had occasional success, but to be all things to all people (because it wasn't only her father she had to strive to please)—no, to reflect each individual person's favorite aspects of themselves, in a demure and natural way, and with authenticity...impossible. She failed, over and over.

But whenever Mary felt her anxiety rise in her father's presence she reminded herself that she had given him grandsons, and about that, at least, he must be pleased.

At the dining table that evening, Mary knew three nights at her father's house would be too many. Servants ferried soup, duck, roast lamb and peas, and removed plates and filled glasses, but their activities granted only brief respite from the stilted conversation between father and daughter. She wished he'd made an exception and let the children eat with them.

Throughout the meal, Mary racked her brains for something to say. It was difficult to force down food into a seized stomach and keep the conversation flowing. She glanced at the black hairs on her father's fingers, his hand firm on his knife, and wished she'd listened properly to John Henry's updates about the European War.

"You must be as glad as we are that Sonny is returned?" Mary asked. She sipped the syrupy German wine her father liked. "It's a great relief to have him home."

"Yes, and I hope you'll take care not to lose him again. George is, of course, the chief beneficiary to everything I have, but three grandsons is a firmer guarantee of continuing our line than two."

Mary felt blood heat her cheeks. "I don't consider Paul and Sonny as *spares* in the event that—"

"There's no need to take that tone. I'm fond of all my grandsons. Which is why I have no wish to lose any one of them because of a daydreaming daughter."

"You know exactly what happened at Half Moon Lake, Father. And with every fact at your disposal, you still hold me responsible?"

"Who, then?" Mr. Gould asked, with a fiery glare. "If not the child's mother?"

"John gave the boys his permission to explore the—"

"You're not going to blame your husband."

"Of course not. I was saying that when John told them—"

Mr. Gould held up his hand to silence his daughter.

"The children had never gone so far alone and—"

"Enough, Mary."

"It's true I gave the nanny the day off. But the rest—"

"Enough." Mr. Gould pushed his chair back from the dining table and stood up. "There's nothing to be gained from going over this again. You've had a great deal of time to reassess your choices. I'm confident my grandsons will be more carefully watched from now on."

Mary stared at the silver candlestick in front of her. Oh, to be home.

After dinner, Mary complained of a headache and went up to her room. She wished they were at Arlington Grove. There, the boys would have space to run, more servants to tend to them, horses and a swing. She sat on the edge of the bed with her eyes closed and recalled her childhood home.

The plantation hadn't only revolved around her mother's confinements and frenzies. Mary's days had been full of her own concerns: French, grammar, script, elocution, Bible studies, needlepoint, etiquette and drawing—and mathematics, at her father's insistence. Her piano teacher came three days a week, and on the days he wasn't standing behind her making various sounds of disapproval she'd practiced for one hour while her governess sat in a chair in the corner listening. In spite of the adults' attempts at making music a chore, she'd loved to play, loved the pleasing sounds she could invite from the instrument, the smooth sinking of a key under her finger-pad, the feeling of the music traveling up through her body.

She'd filled her discretionary time by exploring the house, swinging on the porch seat to make music of the squeaking chain and her leather boots tapping and dragging on the wooden boards, or watching the gardeners in the vegetable patch. She didn't go into the cane fields, the long lines of swishing green that filled a large swathe of her family's land. Her father forbade her, so she contented herself with sitting on the clipped grass at the top of the slope, watching the Negroes work. She liked it when they sang, as much as she recognized it as singing. It was more a conversation in harmonics, with words repeated and overlapping. The Negroes sang about water and running and sundown and being free.

Mary had sketched the fields, the apple tree that scratched her upstairs bedroom window, and arrangements of fruit that Cook let her make when she sat at the kitchen table early in the mornings. Once, Cook let her touch a plucked chicken. Mary made it sit up, nude and pimply, then Cook moved its scrawny arms so it danced to the tune she sang in French. Afterward, Cook kneaded dough for the week's bread, rolled out pastry for sweet-potato pie, and Mary drew, the two of them falling into giggles whenever their eyes met.

Cook had died years ago and been replaced by another. Mary had no idea who was downstairs in the kitchen now.

When her father had written that he was staying at his city

house, Mary had wanted to retract her proposal, to suggest they'd visit him another time. But he'd written that he wanted to see the boys, and as soon as possible, so here they were. What a mistake. He'd gone a whole afternoon and evening without asking to see them.

Her bedroom was pleasant enough, though minimal. Solid, expensive furniture. A bed with thick turned legs, two red velvet armchairs, a rosewood dressing table on which Sula had laid out Mary's hairbrush, clips, ribbons and toiletries. A painting of a bloody fox hunt. No flowers. It had been a masculine house even when her mother had been alive.

She had few memories of her mother being here; Arlington Grove suited her better. Mary had come alone with her father to this house. How odd that she'd forgotten that.

"Nothing lives forever," her father had said on the night Mary's mother died. Not that she'd expected him to comfort her. Lately, Mary had thought that her mother might have played a part in her own death. Not physically, but by deciding life was simply too much, that Heaven had to be easier.

In her own home, Mary had had Esmeralda put out vases of yellow chrysanthemums, a nod to the coming Halloween. The boys had, under Cook's supervision, cut jack-o'-lanterns for the front porch. John Henry had banned them, however, from walking the streets like poor children; Paul, of course, still lobbied daily to change this. Mary had decided she didn't have the energy to attend the Starry Lake costume party— a Black Cat theme this year—though this had made John Henry cross. She imagined what he might be doing right now. Reading, probably. Or dining with the judge.

Large wide-paned windows provided a view to the street.

Mary parted the drapes so she could see outside. The glass was fogged so she knelt on the floor, on the thick carpet, and pushed the window up so she could be in the night without obstruction.

With her left hand resting on the sill, Mary used her right forefinger to draw a line along the tops of the buildings across the street, up and down, across. She imagined peeling back the traced skyline and pulling it inside, like a flattened train attached to a gossamer thread, where it could sit upright on the floor in front of her, a diorama. She'd watch the people pass by their windows, close drapes, lift their cats indoors, the lights pulsing, blood beating. With the streetscape safely sized, she'd be able to make sense of it all. And offer the sky uninterrupted space to breathe and glow.

The halos of the street lamps below blurred in mist, yellow light shone out from other homes, and the occasional car whooshed by, swinging its headlights around the bend. Even with this much earthly illumination, when Mary looked upward, she saw stars, so many more than she'd expected to see. Millions of stars in a boundless slate-gray sky. Millions. She sat up straighter. Rather than twinkling, they seemed to be moving. What if they were coming closer, were malevolent pinpricks that would become angry fireballs? She felt overwhelmed by the vast sky. She imagined the stars speeding down to Earth, like splinters of glass, plummeting, skewering.

Mary yanked her head in, shut the window and let the drapes swing back into place. She turned to face the room, the enormous bed with its tucked-tight bedspread, the empty

Grecian vase on the marble mantle. Then rushed out into the hall, to her boys.

Early the next morning, Nanny Pru came to Mary's bedroom to say that Mr. Gould had asked for the boys to come to his library, so she'd dressed them and taken them there. He'd dismissed her, and Pru was uncertain if the boys should be alone with the master. Sonny's silence might annoy him, and Paul could be so mouthy. Would Mrs. Davenport like to join them? Pru asked.

Mary considered. "It might do my father good to spend time alone with his grandsons. Yes." He had no idea how much she'd suffered. What was one awkward moment for him?

She rang the bell for Sula. She would dress and go downstairs, take a stroll along the street, to the park. If Paul forgot to say "sir" and Sonny ignored instruction, so be it.

That had been her plan. But as Mary neared the front door, her father called her back. "I don't know what you think you're doing, but that boy doesn't hold one drop of Gould blood. He'll never see a penny of mine."

CHAPTER TWENTY

The war in Europe grew more terrible by the day. In September, on the Western Front, Britain used poisonous chlorine gas for the first time, in a scrappy and ill-considered offensive against the Germans. In October, Bulgaria declared war on Serbia, and France, Britain, Russia and Italy declared war on Bulgaria. In November, 67,000 Allied soldiers died in a third Austro–Hungarian attack against Italy in the Isonzo.

America, while refusing to send troops to any of these far-flung places, helped entrepreneurially. American bankers, brought together by J. P. Morgan, loaned $500 million to the Allied governments. "Pacifist, my foot," Mr. Collins said to Tom. "Wall Street will make a mint out of this dogfight."

Tom was interested, of course. The war's latest bloody battle was front-page news in every paper, every day, with the main question being how long President Wilson could hold to neutrality. Almost every country except America was involved now, and the public was increasingly swayed by politicians who urged military support.

But after leaving the *Clarion* office, Tom's thoughts turned to more local alliances. He'd decided to stop wasting time thinking about the Davenports, blocking unsavory thoughts about Mary and fighting against the idea that John Henry would contact him. Instead, Tom made plans for his own life.

At dusk, he walked down Main Street with Clara to the Opelousas Picture Theater, where, as they did most Fridays, the pair sat in the third row from the front, to watch the latest releases. Tonight, though, they were in for a rerun of a Pearl White picture.

"Pauline's Unending Perils," Tom mumbled. "How many times do we have to sit through these?"

"Shush. It's starting."

"You've got to admit, she's survived years of perils. She should consider staying at home."

"She's an adventurer. Adventurers don't stay home." Clara turned to Tom in the dim light. "Some of them even travel."

Tom slumped in his seat. "Yeah, yeah." The one good thing the war had done was to temporarily put Paris on the shelf. But Clara had found other places to long for: Cairo by steamboat; New York by train.

Tom didn't mind watching movies with Clara. But the ones she loved so much told the same story every time and starred the same people. And occasionally, he read something in the papers to make him think movie stars were as bad a fascination for Clara to have as Paris; her favorite actors were prone to die of alcohol poisoning, too much cocaine or heroin—not the medicinal kind—or syphilis. They weren't good role models. The movies made her happy, though. Tom watched Clara as the images cast a flicker then a glow over her face.

On screen, Pauline smacked her hands to her cheeks as she realized her hot air balloon had come loose from its anchor and she was floating high above the ground, alone. Who'd seen that coming, Tom thought. He knew he could give Clara a real surprise, right then and there. He leaned over and whispered in her ear, "How about April? I hear spring weddings are the rage."

Less than a week later, John Henry invited Tom to visit him at home, "in the evening, when Mary and the boys will be asleep." Tom hadn't been sure what to make of the invitation. He wasn't being offered inclusion at a family gathering, a meal, or the chance to speak with the woman with whom he'd spent so many hours alone. John Henry wasn't granting access to the boy or an opportunity to talk to George and Paul. He was initiating a very belated man-to-man conversation, without Tom knowing what had prompted it.

As he strode the wet sidewalk in the dark, rugged up against the wind, he considered the relatively few possibilities: John Henry wanted to discuss what had happened at the Birds' house; he was interested in Tom's take on Gideon Wolf; or he wished to discuss one of Tom's recent articles about the case.

He was surprised when Esmeralda, not Mason, answered the door.

"Mrs. Somerset, I've missed you."

She peered behind him.

"Walter's at home, I'm afraid." Tom cupped his hands together and blew warm air into them to remind her he was out in the cold.

"You know I missed *him* more than you. Y'all know that."

How she tested him. "Next time, I promise. Is Mason—?"

"New Orleans. Ties, socks, men's what-have-yous."

"Ah. May I?" Tom stepped inside. "Before we tell Mr. Davenport I'm here, how is Mary? What about the boy?"

Esmeralda shook her head. "Mr. Davenport's in his library."

After exchanging pleasantries, John Henry poured Tom whiskey and refilled his own glass, then the men sat angled in front of the fire.

"I'm reading Emerson on self-reliance." John Henry used his glass to point to the book on the lamplit table beside him. "It's lent perspective to our situation." He opened the book. "*At times the whole world seems to be in conspiracy to importune you with emphatic trifles.*"

Tom furrowed his brow. "This is no trifle, John."

"I'm aware of that." Tom sensed coolness in John Henry's tone. "But the way your colleagues have been writing about our situation has, indeed, sought to reduce this to a trifle, a cartoon. Not you. But, let me use Emerson again." Tom watched John Henry as he searched the text. Had John Henry invited him here to complain about the behavior of the press? Was he hoping Tom, a reporter, would sympathize with his situation and . . . fix it somehow, bring his "colleagues" to heel?

John Henry read, "*Do not spill thy soul; do not all descend; keep thy state; stay at home in thine own heaven.* Does that not seem like wise advice? That's what I intend to do to cope with this scurrilous chatter: I'll work, meet with lawyers when I must, enjoy the company of select friends, be at home with my wife and children."

"That's one approach." Tom paused. "May I take it from this invitation into your home that I'm a select friend?"

"However, staying in one's heaven doesn't stop the ceaseless gossip and printed lies." John Henry closed his book.

"John." They'd been on a first-name basis for a long time, but it suddenly felt awkward to address John Henry this way. Tom had shared a drink with this man but he'd also crouched on the ground and spied on him through a window. And the conversation tonight was more scolding and aggrieved than Tom had anticipated. He struggled to find the right tone. He'd wanted to meet with John Henry as a confidant, a near-equal, not as the representative of the world's reporters. "John, they—and I'm glad you'd not consider me among those reporters who are troubling you—*they* aren't going to leave you in peace until Gideon Wolf's trial is done. Not while he shouts his innocence of childnapping and this mysterious other mother is at large. If you want my advice—" Yes, that was it. "I'd say you should come out of hiding, all of you. Show yourselves as happy, carefree, untouched by rumors since they are so patently untrue."

John Henry nodded. "I understand what you're saying. I want every man on the jury to know that ours is the only truth. In fact, I want to know if we can count on you to continue to write articles that help our cause, to be the voice of reason, so the truth isn't drowned in the swill the other newspapers are serving up."

So, Tom thought, he wants to check I'll stay his advocate.

Had anyone else asked this of him, he'd cite independence, objectivity, integrity. He might even remind them he'd been witness to Mary's uncertainty, so he appreciated that reporters had some basis for doubt. But he'd come too far with this family to pretend to be neutral. "I'll always speak in your favor, John. Mr. Collins is scornful of ill-informed gossip, but I should tell you he's worried we're going to lose readers if we won't explore—"

"Exploring is what an amateur does in the wilderness, Tom. Your job is to put reality into words. Otherwise you're no more than a mudslinger. And I know you're not that. You're a man of fact. And our friend."

John Henry seemed to be challenging Tom: a near-insult followed by a declaration of friendship, both uttered with self-interest in mind. Tom wasn't stupid, but nor was he without his own goals. He stretched his legs out toward the fire, took a slow mouthful of whiskey and thought about how he might benefit from John Henry's request.

CHAPTER TWENTY-ONE

Grace was cleaning the Cavetts' dinner plates in the room adjacent to the kitchen when she overheard that Gideon Wolf had been arrested.

"Y'all better find some other tramp to tune your old pile of wood. Wolf's locked up in Opelousas," Matthew said to his mother.

Grace stopped moving, her hands hovering, dripping lukewarm gray water into the tub. A thin wall divided her from the table where the Cavetts sat, but the door was half-open and she could hear them as clear as a bell.

"Opelousas?" Mr. Cavett said. "Opelousas, Louisiana?"

"What's he gone and done?" Mrs. Cavett asked.

"Stole a boy, that's what," Matthew replied.

"What did he want with another boy? What'd he do with Grace's boy?" Mr. Cavett asked.

Grace inched closer to the doorway.

"He took Grace's boy? Then it's the boy they're talking about," Matthew said. "It's in all the newspapers."

"Could be he ran away," Mr. Cavett said.

"Nobody ran anywhere," Matthew said.

"Though where—"

"Never mind about that," Mrs. Cavett interrupted. She could see Matthew was growing exasperated. "Tell us more about this unguent of yours. Will it help with this?" She pointed at a burn mark on her arm.

"Probably, yes."

"How much will I need to buy?"

Matthew sat up straight, suddenly energized. "Do you know, just last week I met a man who hadn't been able to stretch out his arm in a year. Used this Simms' unguent for a month—every day, mind, that's the key, and don't be scared to slather it on thick—and now he's chopping his own wood."

Mrs. Cavett made an *ooh* sound and Mr. Cavett nodded appreciatively.

Grace stayed awake through the night, breathing warm puffs of air into her cold room. She needed to go to Opelousas. But what if Matthew was wrong? What if Gideon wasn't locked up or even in Louisiana? Maybe if she pleaded with the Cavetts they'd help her get to Ned and speak out for a wrongly imprisoned man whom they seemed to like well enough, or simply ask Matthew for more information. But the instant these thoughts occurred to her, Grace knew the Cavetts would be no help. She couldn't continue to simply wait here for Gideon, not now she knew he might be locked away with her son. And if not in Opelousas, at least that would be a starting point.

After a few hours' sleep, having nursed Lily so she'd be dulled and agreeable, Grace pulled her bedding into order, placed her few belongings—clothes, underclothes, Lily's baby blanket, her Bible—on a piece of cut cotton sheet, and brought the four corners of cloth together into a knot. She nestled Lily in a sling across her chest, hung her rudimentary sack on her forearm, and left the Cavetts' house before sunrise.

She walked down the same dirt road Gideon and Ned had, heading, like them, for Magnolia. There'd surely be someone there who'd be willing to read her the story in the newspaper. Then she'd use what money she had to catch a train. Grace tried not to think about how long the journey might be, to where, or how she would manage to feed or shelter herself and Lily. Each step she took brought her closer to Ned.

In the Davenport house, the three boys sat at their desks in the room Madame Caron called their *salle de classe*. It was a cold November morning and though crunchy frost had covered their lawn, John Henry insisted one of the "classroom" windows remain open to assist the boys' health and mental sharpness. Mary, separately, insisted fires be lit throughout the house. Currents of warm and cold air circled the boys as they read, bringing with them scents of coffee, burning spruce, winter honeysuckle and baking bread.

"Shall cut class," Paul had muttered. "Stinky, wet grass. No thanks, I'll pass." He'd tried to raise a laugh from George, but the only person who seemed to hear him was Madame.

Paul slouched in his chair and stared out the window at a car puttering up the street. He'd felt annoyed even before Madame caught him out. George was ignoring him again. His brother and the interloper were still heads down over the same picture book, while Madame had Paul conjugating verbs on his slate. George had repeatedly told Paul that helping the boy learn to read and write was good for them.

"How else are we going to know where he came from? He can draw, but that's not so useful sometimes."

"One of us doesn't care where he's from," Paul sulked. "And that one is me. I don't care."

Now, seeing his brother was again in a funk, George waited until Madame wasn't watching and slipped him a note: *You said it'd be good to have three for games. What are you whining about?*

Paul scrunched the note and threw it at George. "I said four."

Madame Caron looked up at Paul. "Four what, *mon petit* unhappy Davenport?"

"For as in *forget* it."

Rather than making Paul write lines or sit in the corner, Madame Caron moved her finger like a hook, beckoning him to her. Even an occasional visitor to the house could see the unhealthy dynamic between the boys, she thought. Three was such an awkward number, and to her eye George wasn't trying to disguise who was his favored brother. Although Paul was misbehaving, George's was the greater crime: the failure to be discreet. But that was beyond her scope. With Paul standing in front of her, Madame Caron reached into her beaded bag, a Votes for Women badge pinned to the lining, a copy of *Gombo Zhebes: Little Dictionary of Creole Proverbs* given to her by her mother inside, and presented Paul with a mandarin. "For humor in the face of adversity. *Pauvre ti bête.*"

None of the boys was sure what she meant, but she'd sin-

gled Paul out for a treat and in so doing reproved George and
baffled the boy. Without any discussion, each of them shifted
on their axis enough that peace was restored.

Later that afternoon, between lessons, George sat next to
the boy on the rug in front of the fireplace. He told Paul to
quit moping and join them.

"I need your help." George tapped the boy's left hand. "You
like using this one better than the one the teachers make us
use, don't you?"

The boy nodded.

"I'm good at spelling, but Paul knows how—"

"I can use both." Paul plopped down on the carpet, the
three of them forming a circle.

George put his arm around Paul's shoulder. "That's why we
need you. I've been trying to get him to hold the crayon like
this, but—"

"Give it to me. Here." Paul took the boy's hand and, together, they wrote.

CHAPTER TWENTY-TWO

Sheriff Sherman found the farmhouse where Grace Mill had lived, though Gideon Wolf's directions had sent him off-course several times along the way.

By the time the sheriff arrived on the Cavetts' unswept porch, his car covered in dust, his back aching from so many hours driving, Grace had gone. Mrs. Cavett said in no uncertain terms she knew neither where nor why nor exactly when Grace had gone. She wasn't too upset, though: the girl wasn't worth a hill of beans. Mrs. Cavett stayed close-lipped about Grace's boy, saying only she *had* a boy. She'd squinted at the photograph the sheriff showed her, a fresh one taken in Opelousas, saying she'd had as little as possible to do with the child, might not recognize him in a crowd of three. "Could be him. Wouldn't like to say."

The sheriff frowned at her. "You wouldn't like to say?" He'd traveled all this way to hear the same thing the Conroys' manager had said. What was it with people not wanting to "say"?

"I'm an honest woman that deserves no trouble with the

law. That girl showed up here with a boy and claimed he was hers. How am I to know if that's the truth? Maybe he's the child you're chasing after, maybe not." And yes, she'd had her piano tuned by a tramp, and he'd stayed around to do other jobs. Yes, more than once. "But why should I be expected to remember every stranger's name? Seems you're asking an awful lot of a woman whose help has run away and left her with more work than any one person can do."

Mrs. Cavett let the sheriff search Grace's room for clues as to where the girl had gone, watching from the doorway in case he found something she might claim. The sheriff wondered if Grace had heard about Wolf's use of her as an alibi and headed for Opelousas. It seemed she had no life outside this dingy farmhouse, and no kin known to Mrs. Cavett, so it was possible. Having seen the woman's spartan living quarters and met both the Cavetts, the sheriff was amazed Grace Mill had stayed as long as she had. In answer to his question about whether Grace could read, Mrs. Cavett had snorted. But news traveled all sorts of ways. With a newborn babe, though, little money and no car, it was a heck of a journey.

As Sheriff Sherman walked down the dirt path to his motor car, Mr. Cavett scampered down from the barn. "I'll tell you something else, I never thought he looked that much like her."

The sheriff drove away, troubled by the seeds of doubt the Cavetts had scattered in his mind. He felt certain now there was some truth in Wolf's account, that he'd taken off from this God-awful farm with a boy who had a scar, around Sonny's age but most likely not Sonny. Or maybe Sonny had ended up with Grace Mill somehow, after being taken? He needed to talk to her.

Once he was out of the Cavetts' sight, the sheriff pulled off the road, spread his map out on the passenger seat and used a pencil to draw the ways a woman without a car could get from here to Opelousas. It was a challenging journey: if she'd gone by train—the best way, if she had the funds—Grace would've had to walk nine miles to Magnolia station, catch the train south, maybe as far as New Orleans, to change to the track that ran through Jefferson on the other side of the Mississippi, head south-west to Berwick and change lines again, travel northwest through Patterson, Franklin, New Iberia, on foot a fair ways after that... He'd travel roughly the same route back in his car and hope he could find her. Whatever the truth of the story, Grace Mill had pluck.

The morning after the Davenports had taken the young boy home, Gideon Wolf was scuttled unceremoniously from the Opelousas train station to Sheriff Sherman's stationhouse, where he was to be held until put on trial for the childnapping of Sonny Davenport. The locals told their children to stay away from the barred window that let air into the sheriff's single cell. The lay of the land, however, offered a direct view of Wolf through the window. The youngest Opelousans could see in with the help of an upturned apple crate.

Within days, Gideon Wolf became a local attraction for young and old. He neither shouted at nor scared his observers, was in fact friendly. When people came to ogle, Wolf didn't shy away or cower in the corner of his cell, but instead made conversation. He'd ask what they thought the coming day's weather might be, would comment favorably on ladies' hats or the flattering hue of their eyes. With his male visitors,

Wolf shared his card tricks, stories about his years working in Merrimack Mill, and tales of the strange things he'd seen during his travels: a cemetery with caged graves to keep vampires from escaping at night, the ghost of Crazy Horse, a coyote that spoke.

Those not taken with his stories were charmed by his fiddle. He'd played it since he was a lad, so long that he'd worn a groove in his jaw. Wolf coaxed sounds from the instrument that made people stop and listen. Children could hear Wolf's fiddle from the schoolyard, and more than once the teacher raised a finger to silence the class so they could listen to the music. Tom and Clara could hear it from her mother's porch.

Gideon Wolf didn't strike the people of Opelousas as a villain. He was polite, clean enough and articulate.

Even Mrs. Billingham and Gladys went to the sheriff's office to stare through the bars.

"He seems harmless enough." Mrs. Billingham adjusted her sable fur as the pair walked back to their car.

"Rather dull, though," Gladys replied. "I thought he'd play his fiddle for us."

Wolf went to great lengths to explain the details of his trouble to his visitors: he told them how long he'd been traveling with the boy, how he was a caretaker not a childnapper, and how it was wrong to keep an innocent man in a damp cell, one far too poky for a man of his height. He asked after the boy and wanted to know about these people who'd wrongly laid claim to him. He asked his visitors to help find Grace.

Aside from repeatedly proclaiming his innocence, Wolf made himself an agreeable prisoner to the guards. He never complained about the bland and meatless meals. Once he realized there was no other, larger cell, he simply asked for more blankets, a request easily granted.

"Humoring the tramp is ludicrous," Mrs. Billingham said as she stroked the unsullied leather seat of her new Ford. "The boy is at home with a good family. Who could deny that's better than sending him to live with a hobo or an unwed mother? A mother, if the story is to be believed, who gave her child to a stranger."

"That's to say there is an unwed mother," Gladys said. "The boy might be an orphan, no one. Or *his* son, the tramp's."

"I do worry that the child was in unsavory hands for so long, though. Young minds can be tainted. Mary has a job ahead of her to recivilize him." On that, Gladys and Mrs. Billingham agreed. Given the right circumstances, any sweet person could become a beast.

CHAPTER
TWENTY-THREE

The arrival of Gideon Wolf's lawyer in Opelousas caused a lot of talk. The scruffy tramp who people—for or against—dismissed as poor and luckless had secured impressive legal counsel from out of state. His lawyer, a tall olive-skinned Italian man from California, was part of the powerful Gabino family, whose Bank of Italy had bought Fresno National *and* the People's Savings Bank, a background which made him impressive and suspect. Both the lawyer and his assistant were expensively suited and impeccably coiffed.

"It's the brother," Judge Roy explained to John Henry, making a whirlpool of his port as he swirled his glass. "He can't have it. No good for his standing."

The two men had met once again for dinner at the Starry Lake Resort's city club. John Henry looked around the room at the long straight line where polished floorboards met thick carpet, at the gilt frames around large landscape paintings, the fenestration, the Steinway. He crossed his legs, felt the rug sink under his heel. After years of wanting, he was where he ought to be. He belonged. And he did not. He caught glimpses of the gentlemen's faces when he entered the room, and saw how they avoided his eyes.

John Henry took a slow sip and became aware of a pleasing tinkle coming from the piano.

"Beethoven played by a Negro. What next?" The judge belched and patted his stomach.

He told John Henry that Gideon Wolf had a brother named Buck, from whom he'd been estranged for years. Buck had been an ambitious young man, the polar opposite of his brother, and had taken himself to California in search of a better life. Due to hard work and conniving, Buck had built a successful business making and selling oil rigging. He'd amassed a fortune, enough to attract and wed the daughter of oil baron Langston Adler. Buck's new wife had heard about Gideon Wolf's arrest—she'd followed the case of the missing boy, fancied herself an amateur sleuth—and, knowing her husband had a brother in the South, she asked if this might be the Gideon, *his* Gideon? Buck Wolf read the article she showed him and decided the man did indeed sound like his brother.

"So Buck met with his father-in-law to discuss the possible damage to their respective reputations should Buck's brother be found guilty. And Mr. Adler decided they needed to shut this whole thing down." The judge caught the eye of a drinks waiter. "Neither of them wants the infamy of having a convicted childnapper in their family. Adler has sent the top lawyer from his company's own firm to defend Wolf. I suspect he'll have plenty of money at his disposal to do what needs to be done." The judge lowered his voice. "Are you confident your man can argue a strong case for you? You've gone with Gomer Ellis, yes?"

John Henry glanced around to check for eavesdroppers. "Yes. Do you have doubts?"

"No. He's good, he wins. But it needs to be convincing. I can't have—John, it mustn't appear as though I've been compromised. You get Ellis to run over his strategy with you, plug any holes."

"I'll meet with him tomorrow. But I fear simple honesty won't be strategy enough for us to win. We need to find a way to put this Grace Mill story to rest."

Judge Roy stood up. "I didn't catch those last words. My hearing's not what it was." He walked across the room to talk to his good friend Mr. Collins.

Mary had challenges of her own. The boy hadn't warmed to her as she'd hoped, leaning away from her attempts to embrace him, refusing to try to speak. He was openly sad, and only seemed at ease with George and Paul. Which would have been fine, Mary thought, if their bonding was confined to playing hopscotch or tag together, collecting butterflies or sticks. But more and more often she found the three boys huddled around paper or slate, whispering, becoming silent when they saw her. The brotherly connection she'd long fostered had taken the form of a strange collusion she didn't understand.

She made deliberate efforts at spending time with them to counteract the secrecy. Today, while the boys sat either side of her on the sofa, Mary balanced a storybook on her lap and read.

"*The tigers were very, very angry, but still they would not let go of each other's tails. And they were so angry that they ran round the tree, trying to eat each other up, and they ran faster and faster till they were whirling round so fast that you couldn't see their legs at all. And they still ran faster and faster and faster, till they melted away, and then there was nothing left but a great big pool of melted butter.*"

George and Paul were transfixed but the boy, same as last time, let his eyes drift around the room. It was dispiriting, frustrating. She so wanted him to love her. And she wanted him to match her memory of him. After she'd read the last page, Mary slammed the book closed and rang the bell for Nanny Pru.

Ned could tell the lady was annoyed. She went from happy to angry fast, and he wasn't always sure what'd turned her. His ma wasn't like that. She didn't get mad about things like books, and she hugged without hurting him. When they did chores together, she kissed his cheek, sang the letters song, made up games. She could do pretty much every animal noise except buffalo, because what noise did they make anyway? He missed her smell of hay and cut onions, her eyes when they scrunched into a smile, and her voice. But he tried not to think about his ma too much because then he cried. Sometimes he couldn't eat for how much he missed her. He didn't miss the Cavetts, though, not one bit.

His ma had wanted him to go away with Gideon, and for Gideon to bring him back. He'd heard her say that a lot of times. He figured once Gideon got out they'd go home to the farm. He liked George and Paul, and it was nice enough to be in a big house, with toys, lots of food and a warm bed. Sometimes it was irritating for people to call him by the wrong name and make him wear clothes that weren't his, but it was just for a while. He was ready to leave now. His ma would sort things out.

One Sunday, John Henry suggested an afternoon of kite-flying, a return to an activity they'd enjoyed as a family when the boys had been younger. He'd asked Mason to fetch the paper kite from the attic.

"It's been too long since we had an outing. It might bring Sonny out of his sullenness."

"Yes," Mary said. "What a wonderful idea."

"You sound like a young girl." Perhaps they could return to a life of simple joys after all.

Rugged up in wool hats and thick scarves, the Davenports made their way to Golden Field. George and Paul walked down the street in parallel, each holding one pointed side of the large kite, with the boy following, making certain the ribbon tail and string spindle were carried high. Every now and then, Mary offered encouraging words about how near they were to the field. They didn't need her to jolly them, though; George and Paul discussed their undertaking happily, arranging and rearranging their hold on the kite, instructing one another to slow down or speed up. Occasionally one of them would turn around and talk to the boy.

"How high will it go?" Paul asked.

"Very high," George said. "This is a good wind for kite-flying, the right amount."

John Henry squeezed Mary's hand.

When they reached the field, John Henry led the family to a spot away from the old oaks, figs and elms. George and Paul placed the kite on the grass while John Henry explained how they would best get it up into the sky. The boy seemed incredulous this could happen.

Mary pointed up to the sky, where two starlings swooped and looped. "See how the air holds them up?"

"Kites don't work like wings."

"George, speak politely to your mother. Kites do work differently, but like those birds, they use currents and gusts of wind to carry them where they want to go." Reveling in the opportunity to educate, John Henry explained to his boys how a quadrilateral of paper, sticks, glue and string could fly as high as a bird.

The kite could not be piloted by three boys at once, so John Henry told George he could have the first go, as the oldest. After some tussling with the spirited kite, George shouted for Paul's help and, side by side, they held on to the wooden spindle and ran off. The other boy stayed next to John Henry, his head tipped up, mouth open in amazement. John Henry bent down. "You and I will fly the kite next."

Mary beamed in delight. How perfect to see her sons running across the field, the kite high above them, dipping and soaring; to see her husband standing next to Sonny, his hand resting on the boy's shoulder. Her family, outdoors, on a crisp day, with no one else around. John Henry was right to think this was the cure they needed.

Mary and John Henry shared a love of nature, but she recognized their inclinations were not the same. As a young man, her husband had wanted to be in the most rugged, untamed outdoors, clambering over rocks, hiking mountains, fording rivers, surviving nature, rejoicing in its power: this was the life he hoped to share with the boys when they were older, he'd said. But Mary found delight in the lines of a tree, the folds of an azalea bloom, the way cold water shivered around a dipped-in finger. And where John Henry worked diligently to know and control nature through an ax, knife, compass or map, Mary preferred to simply admire a blue sky, the curve of a polished stone, a crystal-clear river. She felt the same happiness when she stroked fur or listened to birdsong. Her joy was not a hearty, arm-swinging stride into the woods but a silent contemplation. Part of it, but apart. Sometimes she thought her husband put his love of nature into words to tamp down the feeling it gave rise to, to corral and shrink the emotion until it became manageable. Maybe that was wise.

As the boys ran back, Mary heard the paper kite battling the wind, snapping, and George and Paul shouting instructions to one another. The long red ribbons trailed the kite, whipping around wildly. She watched the kite as it flew closer, closer. The boys panted to a stop a dozen feet from her. The kite hovered. George made minor tweaks to keep it in flight, none controversial enough to be commented upon by his brother. Paul removed one hand from the spindle, shook his wrist out. The kite fluttered, as though saying it was happy to rest where it was a while.

Though they complained mightily, George and Paul finally passed the spindle to John Henry. As they did so, the kite dipped, lost altitude, and the family oohed in suspense.

Now that it was their turn, John Henry held one end of the spindle and the boy the other.

"And me too?" Mary ignored the boy's frown.

The wind picked up and the kite bucked, the paper rustling, quivering. Mary laughed each time the kite tugged them this way or that. "You'll be extra strong for me, won't you, darling?" she said to the boy. But she let go when John Henry said he and Sonny were going to run. George and Paul ran after them, yelling and waving their arms about.

On the way home, the boys barreled ahead of the adults, leaving John Henry to carry the kite. "I don't think we could keep up with them even if we tried," John Henry confided to Mary. "That's more running than I've done in years."

She rested against him as they walked. "I'll talk to Cook this evening about Thanksgiving. We'll serve a dessert of pumpkin pie, baked apple with cinnamon and cloves, gingerbread and cut oranges for the boys."

John Henry thought about whether to break the pleasantness of their outing by asking Mary the question that plagued him. But he needed to ask, out here where no one could listen in.

"He is—" He paused. It wasn't too late to stop. "He is ours, isn't he? He is Sonny?"

Mary stopped walking and let her arms drop to her sides. "Why would you ask such a thing? Why ruin our day?"

"My memories seem..." He spoke in a rush. "Is he ours?"

"Of course he is." She scowled.

"Yes, yes. It's my failing, I know, and it eats at me. But I feel no recognition when I look at this child. I yearn for your certainty. Can I not see Sonny in this boy because he's changed so much over the years?"

"He's changed, yes—how could he not? But he's ours in essence, John. And that's enough. It's more than enough."

"In essence? What does 'in essence' mean?"

"Mrs. Capaldi told me—"

"Who?"

"The spiritualist that Gladys—never mind, John. Mrs. Capaldi said he's here to teach us something. Our son may not have returned to us in exact form, but this boy is ours *in essence*. He's our reward for years of searching and suffering. He's here to make us whole again."

John Henry felt his throat tighten, his stomach knot. "Mary, if this boy is not ours—If Gladys Heaton has pushed you toward some charlatan—" He paused. "My love, tell me plainly, is he ours? Not *in essence*, in reality?"

She didn't answer, and he could see from her glassy eyes and set lips that she'd shut him out. She'd taken *in essence* and, as though under siege, bustled to a safe room in her mind, closed the shutters and bolted the door.

CHAPTER
TWENTY-FOUR

John Henry unlocked the door to his factory and stepped inside. He switched on the lights one by one and surveyed the cavernous room—spotless by the standards of any other factory. He liked his men to leave their workbenches in an orderly fashion at the end of the day: sawdust and shavings wiped onto the floor then swept up, tools aligned, pots of beeswax lidded, furniture-in-progress arranged ready for the next morning. Cleanliness was a mark of respect, he told his men, for yourselves, your craft and this company. The workers had seemed more receptive to him lately, he'd noticed, less standoffish than they'd been in months past.

The Southern American Chair Manufacturing Company made, as the signage attested, "Many Desirable Chairs": upholstered dining chairs, rocking chairs, bank and office chairs, and lounge-room furniture in solid oak with sprung seats. The chairs were of high quality and the factory, while preserving the reputation established by John Henry's grandfather, was known for employing modern methods not used by less progressive chair manufacturing companies. John Henry gave Hank full credit for this. Where John Henry's strengths lay in business growth, securing contracts and dealing with all things financial, Hank was passionate about developments in design and finish. Hank had introduced John Henry to the work of the Scot Charles Rennie Mackintosh and Austrians Koloman Moser and Josef Hoffman. Their designs were aesthetically disconcerting to John Henry, but he agreed with Hank that the new shapes heralded change. The world had enough Campeche chairs. Intrigued by the finishes coming out of the Cushman Manufacturing Company in Vermont, Hank was experimenting with sprayed shellac and varnishes. He'd also issued the Southern American Chair Manufacturing Company's first catalog.

While Hank kept them at the forefront of modern design, John Henry considered their next expansion. There'd been another worker rebellion at the Conroy mills, where the men were riled up about poor pay, long hours and a high rate of injury. Although the Conroys had a reputation for being skinflint and unreasonable, John Henry felt certain they'd sell their troublesome business for the right price. In which case, he could extend his reach from manufacturing all the way back to harvesting. He could sell lumber to his competitors (keeping it in the South), retain the premium wood for himself, cut out the market fees. There was potential there, definite potential.

To think about the business's future, to greet his men as they came through the door holding lunch tins and thermoses, to peruse the upholsterer's latest samples and the catalog pages before they went to print—all of this was a re-

lief from his home life. Mary's admission that the boy was
not Sonny but a simulacrum had been shocking; the one
blessing was that she hadn't shared Mrs. Capaldi's deranged
theory with anyone else. They'd argued ferociously, and John
Henry had sworn to Mary he would not allow a stray into
his family, no matter what twisted reasoning a mystic had
dreamed up. His first impulse on arriving home from the
park had been to contact Judge Roy, to confess and seek
advice on how to shield his family from any legal ramifications. But that would be to choose allegiance to cold and
inconvenient fact over his wife's happiness. It was clear she'd
come to the same sorry conclusion John Henry had, even
if she'd never articulated it: if Sonny were alive, they would
have found him by now. And, if he was honest with himself, had he not known, in the Birds' home, what Mary had
done? Had he not allowed his wife to bring home the boy
because in his heart he believed his son was in Heaven? He
was, now, an equal partner in his wife's admittedly imper-
fect solution. He needed to find a way to make it work.

Even more than before, John Henry wanted his family
out of the spotlight. But the court was taking an inter-
minably long time to clear its backlog of cases; until their
date was declared, the Davenport family had to wait. No
one seemed to care about Gideon Wolf languishing in a
cell—aside from Gideon Wolf, of course—nor did the delay
make any practical difference to the Davenport boys' day-to-
day life. The three were kept to a routine of schoolwork, eating, outdoor time and bedtime, with no discussions about
court cases or other mothers. The boy had remained silent
and reserved, and John Henry suffered no delusion that

his mood would lift at a jury's pronouncement. Time, he thought, was the thing that would melt him into the Davenport fold. Time. The same thing that would permit John Henry to forgive what he and his wife had done.

While John Henry was unlocking his factory door, Esmeralda was buttoning Mary into a blue pinstriped day dress. There were some tasks Mary still wouldn't trust Sula to do, and corsets, baths and small buttons were on that list.

"John Henry won't let me bring one home, of course."

"Oh no, he would not like that."

The pearls or the locket for me today?

Esmeralda paused in her buttoning to consider the two necklaces laid out on the wood. She held one up against the dress and then the other. "Pearls," they said in unison.

"But the boys will have such fun playing with them."

"Yes, ma'am. Hard not to be happy around a puppy."

"Though Gladys will be ridiculous, of course. She was almost delirious when she told me about them." Mary admired her reflection. "They're from her maid's dog. Did I tell you that?"

Esmeralda smoothed down the shoulders of Mary's dress. "Yes, ma'am."

"Oh, they'll be so happy, my rascals. What fun."

The Heaton house was too far to walk to, so Mary had Mason fetch the driver. She bundled the three boys into the back of the car and told them she'd planned an adventure. "And," she said, twisting around, "you must guess where we're going. To make the journey fun."

She was going to have a success of her own. Reading books bored the boy and kite-flying had been John Henry's moment. Mary gave them the clue that the day would involve wriggling. George and Paul bounced up and down on the back seat, shouting guesses at their mother. The boy, between them, smiled, enjoying their excitement while not understanding it. His few car rides had never offered up anything worth bouncing about.

"Is the circus here?" George asked.

"Carousel," Paul said.

"What wriggles on a carousel?" Mary asked.

"Are we going to the river? Are we going fishing?"

George frowned at his brother. "You're bad at this."

Mary worried that a basket of puppies might not be enough given their escalating expectations. She gave another clue to get them to the truth quickly. "They wriggle and squirm, and Sonny loves them."

"Them?" George said. "I know what it is."

"Worms?" Paul asked.

George snorted.

"It might be worms," Paul said indignantly. "It could be."

George and Paul groaned when the car stopped at the Heaton house. Granted, they weren't totally sure where they were at first since they'd only been there on two occasions, but once their suspicions were confirmed the mood turned flat.

"You won't be sitting in a dull room listening to women's talk, I promise you," Mary said. "What's your guess, George?"

"I think it's animals. Kittens? Puppies!"

"Yes, puppies! Won't that be fun?"

George and Paul clambered out and ran toward the front

door, where Gladys stood on the porch. "Wait for your mother," Gladys said. "Mary, come quickly. You must see these adorable little bundles."

Mary looked back to the boy, who hadn't moved from his seat. "Come along. This is for you most of all. You love puppies."

He shook his head briskly.

"Don't be silly. Come."

She stepped out of the car, then reached inside along the back seat and took the boy's arm. He left the car, but stopped partway up the path and pulled back like a mule. Mary firmed her grip on his wrist. "Do behave, Sonny." As he yanked again, Mary's shoe slid on the gravel.

"Whatever is wrong with him?" Gladys asked when they reached the porch.

"Nothing. George, take your brother's hand."

Gladys guided them into her living room, where a shallow, cushioned basket of puppies sat center stage. Her housekeeper was kneeling down, cooing at the six wriggling pups.

"Dalmatians." George knelt on the rug next to Paul.

"Can we pick them up?" Paul asked.

"Of course you can," Gladys said. "And give one to me."

Gladys and Mary sat on the sofa with a puppy between them. Although it was amusing, with its teddy-bear eyes and comically big feet, Mary's mood was dampened by the sight of the boy standing back near the door. What kind of child was frightened of puppies?

"He's forgotten. That's what it is. *His recollection held no other life.*" Mary stroked the puppy's soft fur. "Have you read the Tarzan stories?" She'd had no reason to see Tom McCabe in months, but suddenly felt an urgent desire to do so.

Gladys sighed. Mary could be so dull. Perhaps she wouldn't ask her to join her pinochle game on Thursday.

"Why are you over there?" Paul asked the boy. "They're puppies. It doesn't hurt. See." He pushed his finger in a puppy's mouth.

"How odd. You said he liked dogs. Oh, not again." Gladys told her housekeeper to deal with the yellow trail the puppy had made on the couch before fetching refreshments.

"He does." Mary smiled to temper the brusqueness of her reply, watched the puppy as it waddled away from its mess, wagging its stubby tail.

Having the boy stand in the doorway, unwilling to join in, made the gathering awkward. George and Paul grew bored of trying to persuade him and played with the puppies by themselves, with waning enthusiasm. Gladys's housekeeper offered him cake and lemonade, but he refused to move from his spot.

As Mary listened to Gladys complain about her mother's latest bodily woe, and detail the tactics she used to feign listening when Ira insisted on discussing his business successes with her, she fought to keep her rising anger in check. Once again, the child felt out of her control.

George walked to the doorway and spoke quietly to the boy. After a moment, George pulled a piece of paper and a crayon out of his shorts pocket and gave it to him. Paul, noticing they were up to something, joined them, and soon the three were sprawled on the floor, with the boy drawing and the other two watching and chattering to themselves. The puppies, now ignored, milled around their basket.

"For goodness' sake." Mary crossed the room. "What is this?" She pointed at the boy's drawing—the outline of a building, a stick-figure woman and a circle with a twirl attached to it—then reached down and took it from him.

"Give it back," George said.

"I beg your pardon?" Mary felt tears prick at her eyes. How had she become the outsider with her own children?

"Is it a piglet?" Paul asked the boy, who nodded. "He likes piglets."

"Piglets?" This was too much. Mary decided now was the time to end the adventure.

As they were leaving the room, a terrible howl traveled down the hallway toward them.

"The mother," Gladys said. "We have to lock her away or she won't let us play with the puppies."

"Can we take one home?" Paul asked. "I'll help him get used to it."

Though she couldn't tell whether he meant he'd help the puppy or Sonny, Mary said no. She turned to Gladys. "You'll let her go to her puppies once we leave, won't you?"

The mother dog howled anew.

"Oh yes, I suppose they're hungry." Gladys shrugged. "She'll have to get used to it though. They're being given away."

As they walked toward the car, George leaned close to whisper to the boy, out of Mary's earshot, "Piglets live on farms. Are you from a farm?"

CHAPTER TWENTY-FIVE

Grace set foot on the outskirts of Opelousas on a misty December evening, raggedy, unwashed and exhausted. After a long journey, during which she'd eaten little, crept into barns at night to sleep on straw, pushed through ice-cold rain and cutting wind, finally Grace saw a sign that told her she'd reached the Opelousas city limits. She stopped at the first farm she came upon after that, intending to ask for water and a place to rinse her milk-soaked shirt and clean Lily's red-spotted bottom. Seeing women's undergarments strung on the clothesline suggested this might be a safe place.

The stout, gray-haired woman who opened the farm door eyed Grace up and down and, ignoring her words, led her past a row of lined-up boots into a bright kitchen where a man and young woman sat at a wooden table.

"I'm Mrs. Penny—that's Mr. Penny, but you'll call him Farmer Penny because everyone does, and that's Anna Beth, our oldest." The woman regarded Grace, hands on her hips.

"White as a sheet, though you've clearly been in the sun. You'll need broth."

Anna Beth pulled out a chair for Grace. "A girl? When was she born?"

"August twenty-second."

"Oh, on the cusp. Leo–Virgo. It's hard to be certain which way she'll lean—fierce and passionate, kind, loyal if she's strong in Leo, or sincere, hardworking and generous if Virgo dominates. Either way, she'll be strong. People won't want to cross her when she's older." She smiled. "And you?"

"I'm not sure."

"Do you know your birthdate?"

Grace shook her head in apology. "The nuns didn't celebrate birthdays."

"Enough, Anna Beth," Mrs. Penny said. "Make some coffee."

"Where have you come from, then?" Farmer Penny asked. Grace was surprised to hear a man speak so softly.

"Give her to me." Mrs. Penny lifted Lily out of Grace's arms. "Oh, she's a dear thing. Isn't she dear?" Mrs. Penny lifted the lid off her honey pot, dipped in her little finger and popped it in the baby's mouth.

Farmer Penny smiled at his wife. Without warning, that simple act of affection, in a warm room with people who were unburdened and comfortable, made Grace feel a wave of exhaustion. Her shoulders dropped and her body sank into the cushioned chair. None of which went unnoticed.

Talking over Grace's objections, Mrs. Penny told Anna Beth to give Adam's old room a quick once-over and put another quilt on the bed. Anna Beth handed Grace a mug of fresh coffee. "I'll lay one of my nightgowns out for you."

"And I'll pour you a warm bath," Farmer Penny said as he stood up. "Plenty of time for talking tomorrow."

It was more care than Grace had received since she was a child herself and though she insisted none of it was necessary, she could tell she'd lost control the moment she'd crossed the Penny threshold. Alone with Mrs. Penny, Grace explained where she'd come from and why.

"And though I appreciate your kindness, I'll—" She stopped. It was late now. If she didn't sleep here in this lovely house, in a bed, where would she go?

"You'll wash and sleep is what you'll do. Once you show your face in town you'll be set upon like fresh meat. You'll need your strength." Holding Lily against her with one arm, Mrs. Penny dug about in her pantry.

"Because Gideon was arrested? But once I explain I asked him to travel with Ned, he'll be freed and we can go on our way. I don't think I'll be of interest to anybody once I speak."

"I'm afraid it's not that simple, dear." She stopped her rummaging. "Some jambalaya tomorrow, I think."

Though Grace tried to pry more information from Mrs. Penny, the conversation stopped there.

Once Grace and Lily had been fed, bathed and dressed for bed, Mrs. Penny insisted they lie down. She tucked them between crisp sheets and thick wool blankets, then sat on the edge of the bed. "This was my son Adam's room. Patrick, too, for a while." A round-faced ginger cat padded into the room and leapt onto the bed. "Mr. Miggs will keep you company for the night. Don't worry about him around your babe. He's used to being grabbed and prodded by our grandchildren. Never shows a claw."

As Mrs. Penny spoke, the purring cat kneaded, circled and lay down near Grace's feet. Grace thought that if Ned were with her, she'd never want to leave this room. She stayed awake long enough to watch Mrs. Penny walk to the doorway, but fell asleep without hearing her parting words.

In the morning, Grace sat at the kitchen table once again with the three Pennys. By the time she'd fed Lily and wrapped Anna Beth's dressing-gown around her, Farmer Penny had already lit a fire in the potbelly stove, fed the cows, goats, pigs and hens, and helped Anna Beth with the milking. Mrs. Penny had made a breakfast of eggs with creamed spinach and bread, and now, having placed Lily in a cot made from a wooden fruit box and soft blankets, she watched Grace eat while she folded laundry. A bowl of clementines sat in the center of the table, and Mr. Miggs was curled up in front of the stove. Through the kitchen window, Grace saw a grove of willow trees fringing a pond, a scattering of black-and-white cows, a piebald horse, a sapphire sky.

But the pleasure Grace felt in the presence of this comforting domesticity and bucolic landscape disappeared once Farmer and Mrs. Penny explained the situation.

"Another woman claimed Ned? But why? Is she barren, mad?"

"Neither, I don't think," said Farmer Penny. "But she's rich. And she says the boy is hers. They lost one of their own, you see."

"Then I need to speak with her right away."

Mrs. Penny smoothed the pile of folded pillowcases on the table in front of her. "Dear girl, the Davenports aren't going to give over a boy they've said is theirs. They don't know you, don't know us. They're about to go to court and say Gideon Wolf stole him." She rested one hand on the folded clothes. "You are sure this child is yours, aren't you?"

Grace flushed red. "Of course I am. Ned only needs to see me and it will be obvious I'm his mother. If we could go now—"

"Sit, sit." Mrs. Penny turned to her husband. "We need to take her to the sheriff."

"No, I need to go to Ned. Please, take me to the woman's house."

"You wouldn't be let past the front gate," Farmer Penny said. "Or granted entry through the back door. I'm not sure we've been clear about the type of people you're up against."

There was no question, however, that Grace should tell her story. So Farmer and Mrs. Penny drove Grace and baby Lily past fallow fields, over a rattling bridge, beside a winding river, into the town center of Opelousas.

Sheriff Sherman placed his coffee mug near a neat stack of papers and assessed the group seated stiffly in front of his desk.

"Pleasure to meet you, Miss Mill. I've been looking for you high and low."

"You have?"

"Just got back from the Cavetts' farm. That's an awful long way for you to travel."

"I'd go any distance to fetch Ned. I set out as soon as I heard Mr. Wolf had been jailed."

The sheriff rubbed his thumb along his bottom lip. "And when was that? Could you tell me again." He took in the heart-shaped face, apple-red cheeks and sparkling green eyes that showed undisguised concern and bafflement. She'd been dressed by Mrs. Penny, he could tell, in clothes too big for her but pressed smooth as her pulled-back hair.

"May I see my boy now, sir? Please."

"He'll be missing her something fierce," Mrs. Penny said. "And she's very loving to her baby, a good mother."

Farmer Penny tapped his wife on the arm, worried they were defending Grace from criticisms the sheriff hadn't leveled.

The sheriff stared at Grace. "Miss Mill, why exactly did you give the boy over to a tramp? Seems a strange thing to do if he means as much as you say."

"I thought that with a baby and my duties I mightn't manage. And the Cavetts made it clear—"

"You don't need to explain the Cavetts to me. But I'm stumped about why you'd part with a boy the Davenports say is no trouble, gentle and docile. Wouldn't he have been of use to you?"

"Oh, I wouldn't describe Ned as docile. That's an unlikely . . . And the Cavetts fight, so terribly."

"Have they ever harmed you or the boy?"

Grace shook her head.

"Miss Mill, I'm sorry, but I'm not sure I understand any of this." He paused. "He was your boy, wasn't he? The boy at the Cavetts'."

Grace reeled at the question. "Yes. Why are you all asking me that? He's my flesh and blood."

"Well, you understand it's a problem to have so many people claiming that. I think it's best for you folks to go back home. I'll speak with Mr. Davenport and we'll arrange a time that suits them to show the boy. I suppose the judge will delay the trial. Testing folks' patience as it is, but—"

"Show him?"

"With respect, Miss Mill, I've heard several stories and they don't line up. There's a man locked away here who's—"

Grace leapt up. "Gideon's here? Right here? Then that's the answer. Take me to him and he'll—"

"Oh no. The judge would throw the case out and the Davenports would have my badge if I let you talk to the accused childnapper. We can't have you two comparing notes. I mean it, Miss Mill, you can't go back there—Mr. Penny, I'm going to have to ask you to take Miss Mill home. I'll call on you soon."

Farmer and Mrs. Penny restrained Grace, urging her not to make a scene that would reflect badly on her, but Grace shouted out to Gideon. She kept shouting his name until they'd hoisted her back up into the carriage, but there was no reply.

Grace was fretful on the way back to the farm, and couldn't relax once they got there. "But when will I see Ned, do you think? Tomorrow?"

Farmer Penny tended to the animals' needs and chopped wood. Anna Beth worked in the vegetable patch. And Mrs. Penny, having put Lily down to sleep, told Grace that if she was going to stomp about she might as well have a broom in her hands. "I'd rather you slept, but it seems you have too much energy to spend." While Mrs. Penny peeled yams,

Grace swept the floor with a gusto the farmer's wife found alarming.

John Henry paced back and forth in front of Judge Roy's impressive wall of books until the judge, seated at his desk, asked him to stop. "I understand you don't want a spectacle—that is it, isn't it? The potential for this viewing to become some sort of show?"

John Henry swiveled to face him. "It's insulting."

"Well, you might see it that way, but on paper it's reasonable of her to want to see the child. And a necessary step for the jury to rule out—"

"Surely the act of ruling it out means we're taking this woman's claim of maternity seriously. How can we be seen doing that?"

"John, we must let Grace Mill clap eyes on Sonny in front of witnesses so we can put that part of the case to rest. The question is how to do it with as little fuss as possible. In chambers, with—"

"In my home, I beg you."

"Fine."

"And who must be present at this *performance*?"

The judge considered. "We can legitimately claim this is part of the trial, so I decide who's in the room. You, me, Grace Mill, your lawyer, Wolf's lawyer. That's all I'd say are necessary. Then—"

"Then no more. Not Mary."

"This is a formality to close off a line of argument. There's no need for Mary to be in the room."

"The problem is—" John Henry paused. "She's grown too

attached to this boy." Was it possible for Judge Roy to understand the damage that losing a child twice over would do
to his wife? The judge was older than John Henry by a half-
dozen years, a widower who'd never had children, who seemed
content for his whole life to revolve around his work. Even his
home was a workplace: legal books lined the shelves, chairs
were chosen for their suitability for reading rather than aes-
thetics or comfort for visitors, and John Henry had heard the
servants ask the judge if he'd wanted his evening meal served
in his library. There was no question Judge Roy had experience and knowledge, but did he know the heart of a mother?
How much had King Solomon drawn his wisdom from seeing
the bond between his many wives and their progeny? Could a
man with no children rule so wisely?

"John, we're on shaky ground now. This needs to be our
last private conversation until the trial is done. So, as parting
words, I want to be clear that a pre-trial viewing is not optional. Grace Mill needs to see a child…"

John Henry waited for him to finish his sentence.

"Don't make me spell this out. A child, *a* child." The deceit was
unconscionable. And there was a chance Wolf's lawyers might
cotton on. But how much worse it would be if the child did recognize Grace Mill and the Davenports lost a son once more.

"A child. Yes, a child," John Henry said. "But where does
one get—?"

"John, please." The judge rang the bell for his butler. "Give
my regards to Mary."

John Henry decided to stage the viewing after Christmas. If
he had to do it—and it seemed he did—he'd not allow it to

ruin the Christmas celebrations his wife had put so much effort into. Mary had worked with unwavering determination, instructing the servants on every detail of food preparation and decoration placement, encouraging the boys to help with hanging baubles and tinsel on the tree and endlessly rearranging the furniture in the living room even though the tree stood in the same spot it had every other year.

"Everything must be perfect," Mary had told him. John Henry knew why. The family was both remade and broken: Mr. Gould had sent a terse letter saying he would be enjoying Christmas abroad this year, in Vienna. With whom he did not say. Mary had received this news like a slap, holding the letter out to John Henry as though it might wound her again were he not to take it. He'd held her, wiped the tears from her cheeks and assured her they didn't need her father's presence to enjoy Christmas. In fact, his absence would lighten the mood. Mary had adopted that thinking with enthusiasm, and both Davenports knew the boys wouldn't miss their grandfather.

However, Christmas Day had an edge of anxiety to it, as the boy had no clue about the usual traditions. For the past two years the Davenports had suffered the awfulness of Sonny's absence, and Mary had deliberated over whether to hang Sonny's stocking, "in case he is returned," and had even bought him gifts. But now that he was here, she had to explain away the disconcerting fact that the Sonny of past and present were out of sync. "Two years," Mary and John Henry intoned to George, Paul and their staff by way of rationalizing the boy's unusual questions and preferences. Where once he'd loved pecan pie, now he did not. Where once he'd begged to play blind man's bluff, now he was unsure what the activity involved. The grandeur of the tree seemed to dazzle him, the carolers intrigued. At Christmas Mass, he'd sat between George and Paul in wide-eyed astonishment.

It was a relief for the Davenports to celebrate New Year's Eve at the Starry Lake Resort without their boys. An extravagant gathering with the theme of Arabian Nights saw men wearing bejeweled turbans and women in feathers and veils. There were stuffed leopards lunging from behind palm trees and giraffes bookending the long marble bar, and a tiled fountain in the middle of the ballroom. They danced under chandeliers swathed in colored silk, raised their champagne glasses high and sang in the new year with gusto. For one night, the powerful and well-informed members of Opelousas society shelved their worries about the war in Europe. No one mentioned the Davenports' troubles. The year 1916 would surely herald the peace and prosperity for which they all longed.

CHAPTER TWENTY-SIX

"Go on, then." Mrs. Penny stood next to Farmer Penny at the front door of the Davenport house, Grace behind her. "What are you waiting for?" Her words were confident, but Mrs. Penny's voice trembled. She pulled the folds of her skirt into line, picked fluff off Farmer Penny's sleeve then urged him again. "Knock."

Farmer Penny recognized his wife's tone for what it was. He, too, was fighting to appear at ease; he was not accustomed to raising his fist to such an impressive door, one that would open to reveal a grand entrance, high-ceilinged rooms, foreign rugs, servants. He glanced down at his boots, polished on top but carrying dirt beneath, probably a clod in the hollow formed by the oft-nailed heel. At the farm, Mrs. Penny made him leave his boots at the door. He banged his feet to loosen as much dirt as he could.

"Stop jigging about and knock. Knock before they see us standing here like we've never used a door before."

Grace touched Farmer Penny's coat by way of encourage-

ment, and when he saw her worried face he gathered his
courage then hammered on the door.

Mason led the three into the library then left them to stand
alone with a minimum of explanation.

"I didn't know we'd be the first," Mrs. Penny said. "That
fireplace isn't doing much, is it? I'd have thought they'd have a
bigger one."

"Maybe that's why their fellow didn't take our coats,"
Farmer Penny added.

"I suppose they figure this won't take long."

Mrs. Penny could see from the dents in the carpet and the
oddness of the furniture arrangement that chairs and sofas
had been moved. No one would ordinarily put their seats in
two lines at right angles facing nothing interesting. She pictured the armchairs back where they belonged, added a few
side tables, mentally relocated the vases of flowers—too few—
to better positions.

"Should we sit?" Farmer Penny asked.

"No, we should not. If they wanted us to sit their butler
would've said so." Mrs. Penny looked at Grace. "I don't imagine they'll apologize—wealthy people don't eat humble pie.
They'll make it right, though."

"No doubt," Farmer Penny agreed. "They'd be very educated, I expect."

Grace studied the room. It was vast, serious and still, with
shelves of leather-bound books, windows as high as a barn,
and potted tree-sized palms. Grace felt small and empty-
handed, having parted from Lily for the first time since she'd
been born. Mrs. Penny had assured her Anna Beth was com-
petent, and the two did seem relaxed when Grace last saw

them, Anna Beth snuggling Lily on her lap, reading from the *Astrological Bulletin*. Still, Grace wasn't sure what to do with her body when it was so entirely her own.

After a while, though, the Pennys and Grace relaxed enough to walk to the window and admire the expansive garden.

"Odd to see so much grass without an animal on it," Farmer Penny mused.

Grace murmured agreement, but her thoughts were on Ned. Had he been in this room? How mystified he must be at the Davenports' delusion. The woman's decision to take Ned showed she was unstable, no matter how indulgently Farmer Penny described her.

"A rare chance to be inside such an impressive house." Mrs. Penny examined the drapes. "And this will be over soon, Grace. Never fear."

They turned away from the view at the sound of the door opening. Mason stood to one side and five men in dark suits filed past him into the room.

The first thing Grace noticed was the sheriff's absence. Although he hadn't been helpful, he'd had a kind and trustworthy manner. She would've felt more at ease with him there.

One man was clearly in charge, indicating where the other men should sit and issuing a directive to Mason, then acknowledging Grace and the Pennys with a nod. The judge had told John Henry the girl would most likely be brought in by the farmers.

Grace noticed Mrs. Penny stop herself from dropping into a curtsy. She understood the impulse. The man was so imposing, and the room so magisterial. It was hard not to feel like servants.

Addressing Grace, John Henry said, "My wife and I were sad to learn that you, too, lost your son. We hope your child is found soon."

"Sir, once I see the boy—"

"We'll get to that, Miss Mill." He motioned toward the second, unoccupied, line of chairs.

"Very us-and-them, aren't we now?" Mrs. Penny whispered to her husband.

A black crow sat on the windowsill outside, watching them. Mrs. Penny made a mental note to ask Anna Beth if that might signify something.

"Miss Mill." A man older than John Henry, more portly and with less hair, stood in front of her, bending at the waist as if to examine a flower. "I'm Judge Roy. Those gentlemen are Mr. Wolf's lawyers, Mr. Gabino and associate, and Mr. Davenport's, Mr. Ellis. You are not to speak to them unless they ask you direct questions. Which they are entitled to do. Do you understand why you're here?" He paused. "Good." He turned to direct his next words to everyone. "What happens in this room will be admissible evidence, so I recommend you conduct yourselves with civility. It's my understanding that neither the Davenports nor Miss Mill have had any contact with Mr. Wolf."

Everyone murmured assent.

"Good. Mr. Wolf is claiming the child in this house is Miss Mill's son, Ned. This"—he waved his hand in Grace's direction—"is Miss Mill. Mr. Davenport, of course, believes the child to be his son. I think I need to point out the boy has been living here peaceably and happily—May I say happily? Yes. For more than two months." He glanced around the room. "I think we'd agree it's not an unpleasant house to spend time in."

Although John Henry's lawyer laughed at this, Grace bristled. She'd watched Ned walk away with Gideon Wolf. They'd been found together. Mrs. Penny said Gideon had told all of Opelousas the child was not Sonny Davenport. It was ludicrously, frustratingly plain that Ned was in this house because of the false claim of a madwoman and her husband. She wished they'd stop talking and bring him in. This could be resolved in an instant.

But the judge continued to speak. "Furthermore, I'm assured the lawyers have not entered into any pre-trial arrangements, and have not extended to any parties inducement to mislead us. I trust I've been told the full truth."

This Grace could not ignore. "Are you suggesting, sir, someone has paid me to lie? I'd never! I only want to be with Ned again, and to be away from here." She flicked her eyes to John Henry. "That your wife would lay claim to my boy, she must be a sad—"

"Grace," Mrs. Penny said.

"Do not," John Henry spoke loudly enough that all other talk in the room stopped. "Do not speak of my wife, Miss Mill. Ever." His cheeks flamed with rage. "I'll fetch the boy."

Esmeralda was dusting in the entrance hall when Mr. Davenport threw open the library doors and marched toward the back of the house. He didn't seem to notice Esmeralda on his way to—where, the kitchen? It would be strange for him to go there. Maybe Mason hadn't heard his bell.

A moment later, Mr. Davenport returned with a young boy in tow, the child scampering to keep up. Esmeralda hid behind a large vase filled with elephantine leaves and watched Mr. Davenport drag the boy into the room. All of which was unusual enough that she wanted to know more. But right when she decided to put her ear to the keyhole, Mason appeared and sat in the chair right outside the library. It was as though he was keeping guard, she thought, but why would he do that? She went upstairs, quickly so Mason wouldn't have any chance to stop her, to talk to Pru.

The nursery door was shut, but Esmeralda opened it enough to see that the three boys were in there, strange in itself for a late morning without rain. Though Mrs. Davenport was away in the countryside with Mrs. Heaton, she would've told Pru to take the boys outdoors. But there they were, absorbed enough in their game of jacks that they didn't notice Esmeralda. Nanny Pru saw her, though, and made a quick windmill of her hands, wordlessly telling her to go away.

Out in the hallway, Esmeralda leaned against the wall, bewildered.

In the library, Grace was also bewildered. John Henry had entered the room with a child she didn't know. A toothpick boy with bony legs and bottle-cap knees, wheat-colored hair, large fearful eyes.

They'd barely stepped into the room when Grace spoke. "This isn't Ned."

"That's correct. This isn't Ned. This is Sonny," John Henry said. "Thank you for clarifying that so directly."

"Why are you showing me this boy?" Her breath quickened. "Bring me my son."

John Henry led the boy to the center of the room. "Have you met this woman before?"

The boy shook his head. Two days ago he'd been taken out of the orphanage and put on a train going south to who-the-heck-knew-where, and now this. But the man had promised he'd be put up with a kind family who lived by the river if he did as he was told.

"Shaky as a foal," Farmer Penny whispered.

"Say your name," John Henry instructed.

"Sonny Davenport."

Grace scowled. "No."

"No to what, Miss Mill?"

"Ned can't—Of course this isn't Ned. Where is Ned?" Grace asked the boy. "Did you travel here with Gideon Wolf?"

"You may answer her," John Henry said.

"Yes, ma'am."

"Then you met Ned, didn't you?"

"I don't know any Neds."

"But you must."

"Miss Mill, *please*," the judge said. "You're frightening the child." He addressed the three lawyers seated next to him. "Gentlemen, we've demonstrated this boy doesn't recognize Miss Mill, nor does she recognize him. I can't think what questions you might have that haven't been answered already, but you may ask them now if you wish."

"Who are you?" Grace asked the boy.

"Miss Mill, the boy has already told you his name," John Henry said.

"But this makes no sense. If you were with Gideon then you were with Ned. You must know him." Grace knelt in front of the boy. "Where is he?"

The boy shrank behind John Henry.

"Make her stand up," the judge said to Mrs. Penny. "I insist. This is—"

"Don't you see?" Grace's voice was fast and high. "This can't possibly be the boy you found with Gideon if he doesn't know Ned. Is Ned somewhere else in this house?" She jumped up.

"Oh no." John Henry grabbed her wrist.

At this, Gomer Ellis spoke. "John, I'd advise you let go of Miss Mill." But Grace had shaken John Henry off before he finished his sentence.

Gabino and his assistant, who'd huddled in conversation, stood too. "With your permission, Your Honor, we'd like to leave to consult with our client."

"I imagine you would," the judge said.

"Oh, yes, you! Can you get me to Gideon?" Grace stepped toward Gabino. "We could go now."

The judge spoke up. "I cannot allow that, Miss Mill. And I think we need to stop this before it deteriorates any further."

"Your Honor?" Gabino asked.

"Yes, yes, go." The judge waved him away, turned to Grace. "Miss Mill, you wanted to see the boy in Mr. Davenport's charge, and you have. No one wishes to see you further upset. I'm uncertain whether either counsel will bring you to the stand but should they do so, you are compelled to tell the truth of what happened here today."

* * *

Esmeralda crept down the stairs, stopping to check if Mason was still outside the library. He'd gone, and she tried to think of a reason to knock on the door. It wouldn't seem too untoward for her to—but her thought was cut short by a woman's shout, then a cry rising in volume like an oncoming train. Esmeralda dashed to the far side of the stairwell, out of sight. The library door opened and, though it was impossible to hear everything that was being said, she caught snatches of conversation between a foreign man and his companion: "devise a new strategy," "small-town sheriff with no record of who spoke through those bars," "what incentive for her, unless she learned about his brother," "telephone California immediately," "who's playing who." Then an older couple comforting a younger woman: "makes no sense," "how much the sheriff knows," "Gideon Wolf."

After a moment's silence, Esmeralda stuck her head out to see if the room had emptied. She watched a lanky man walk toward the front door and outside with John Henry: "as well as we could hope," "put to rest," "no doubt." John Henry closed the front behind him, and the house fell silent.

In isolation, none of these snippets made sense. But Esmeralda figured that if she could piece them together she'd know what had gone on in the library.

That night in the kitchen, after Cook had gone to bed, as Esmeralda finished her game of solitaire and Mason lifted another bottle of wine from a newly delivered crate and ticked it off his inventory list, she asked him what the gathering in the library had been about, as though it was a passing thought.

"Why aren't you preparing Mrs. Davenport's room for her return tomorrow?"

"It's done." She crossed her arms. "Do I get an answer to *my* question?"

"No, because men discussing business is none of your concern."

"It wasn't only men in there. Who was the child?"

Mason neatened his cuffs. "I don't recall a child."

Esmeralda made a "ha" of disbelief and abandoned her pretense of disinterest. "Yes, you do. And I'm guessing he means something to the lady who was crying."

"For your own sake, I'd suggest you forget whatever you heard or saw." Mason's tone became stern. "This is nothing for us to get involved with, not now, not ever."

CHAPTER
TWENTY-SEVEN

Later that evening, Esmeralda went to Nanny Pru's room, sat gingerly on the squeaky wire-slung bed and asked why she'd kept the boys behind closed doors that afternoon. Mason would have no say in what Esmeralda did or didn't learn.

"Why'd you wake me for that?" Pru rubbed her eyes. "I was told to keep the boys out of the way while Mr. Davenport had important visitors, not to let them bother anyone. And that's what I did, exactly what I did."

"Did any other boy join you?" she whispered.

"What other boy? Am I going to have to mind another boy? *Merde*. Three's already too many."

Once she'd returned to her room, Esmeralda stayed awake trying to make sense of what she'd seen. She'd recognized Judge Roy. So it was something legal, which meant the woman was, in all likelihood, the out-of-town mother who claimed her son was also lost. She'd be Grace Mill, the woman Mr. Wolf had talked about when Esmeralda and Cook had listened to his spiel through the cell window on their way home from the market. The others—lawyers?

Maybe Mr. Davenport had found this woman's son and brought them together. But had he made a mistake, and the woman had become upset at seeing the wrong child? Or was she angry because the child *was* her son, and her chances of getting money from the Davenports or Mr. Wolf had evaporated? Had she been part of a scheme to swindle the family, a scheme being kept from Mrs. Davenport? Or, Esmeralda thought, she'd witnessed two reunions, in Mobile and Opelousas, in which neither mother nor child—? She paused mid-thought. No; she was missing a piece of the puzzle.

Over the next few days, Esmeralda learned what she could about Grace Mill. She spoke with the deliverymen, her Uncle Joe, her sister Annalise, each of whom had opportunities to overhear things on a regular basis. She asked the members of her church choir. One man said the woman was most definitely staying at Penny Farm, and that he'd overheard Mrs. Penny talking to her daughter as he'd helped Farmer Penny unload crates of oranges at the market. "She was worrying because the woman won't eat, pining for her son that bad." She asked Aunt Celestine to call on the spirits for guidance, but Celestine said the spirits couldn't make their way through the fog. "There are more children than you think, Es. Whole hive of them." Esmeralda asked Cook if she'd spoken with the boy or seen who'd brought him to the house, but she hadn't. Sula volunteered that she knew where Penny Farm was, because one of her nephews had picked apples in their orchard the previous July.

When Esmeralda had a bad tooth pulled out at the veterinarian's surgery, she learned that witnesses were being brought in from Alabama for the court case, that people believed Grace Mill had turned on Gideon Wolf after his lawyers short-changed her, and that Gideon Wolf would hang. She heard everyone who had an opinion—which was everyone in the town—say the judge would find in the Davenports' favor because the boy in their home was Sonny. It had now been proven. But once she put together what she'd discovered, Esmeralda was confident she'd been present at the making of a lie.

Mary Davenport returned from her stay in the country so cheery, from the second she entered the house issuing rapid-fire instructions for Cook to replicate the magnificent meal she'd enjoyed the previous night and Esmeralda to prepare the parlor for the arrival of new drapes and Pru to bring the boys to her room right away, that it was clear she was ignorant of what had happened in her absence. Unless she was happy because it had gone well, Esmeralda thought.

Either way, Esmeralda resolved to speak with Grace Mill before the trial, to tell her the boy she'd been shown was not the boy who lived in the Davenport house. She didn't dislike the Davenports, and she needed her salary, but to keep a mother and child apart was wrong. As wrong as it would be for her to sit with a lie. According to Sula, though, Penny Farm was more than two hours away by foot, and she couldn't be gone from the house for so long without anybody noticing. Her next Sunday off was too far away to help Grace.

She'd go to the sheriff, then. He seemed a reasonable man,

had always been polite to her, asked after her children. But, no, he'd traveled the country with Mr. Davenport. She'd seen them talking to one another on the porch before they set off on those trips, thick as thieves. He must be in on this, too. He presented the greatest risk to Esmeralda if he was helping the Davenports. He could lock her up to keep her quiet. Or worse.

But—yes. She could go to Tom McCabe. If anybody would want the truth, it'd be the reporter who'd followed the story from day one. He'd listen. It'd be for his own sake, not hers or anyone else's, but he'd listen. And good Lord, she'd heard him prattle about his treasured sources and integrity enough to know she could trust him. He'd probably try to convince her again they were friends. But she'd tolerate that, because he could talk to the Davenports as one white person to others, help them unravel a wrongdoing without anyone losing face. He liked John Henry and was soft-eyed for Mary. He wouldn't want them to do something so immoral, so born of pain.

CHAPTER TWENTY-EIGHT

Tom and Clara met with Eddie and Nora for dancing at Willy's Original Café. Eddie had been excited about this night all week, telling Tom how terrific it was sure to be: Kid Ory's Woodland Band was visiting from New Orleans.

"Word on the street is Jelly Roll Morton's coming our way, too," Eddie said, once they were seated in the crowded room.

"You look like the cat that got the cream." Nora blew a plume of smoke over his shoulder.

"Here, give me that." Eddie reached for the cigarette.

Clara was eager to chat about the upcoming trial. Everybody was talking about it, except Tom. She'd asked him for updates, but that seemed to annoy him. Mostly, she thought, because he'd started to think of himself as one of the Davenports' friends, only to be cut off. Since they'd returned with their boy there'd been no more reading, no social calls. He hadn't even met the boy. Clara had mixed feelings about this: on the one hand, she'd hoped the Davenports might be their passport to Opelousas high society; on the other, she was happy Tom wasn't spending time alone with Mary Davenport. It wasn't as if he'd do anything shameful; his infatuation with her wasn't a threat as much as a potential embarrassment. Clara imagined she'd been the only one who'd cottoned on to Tom's affection for the woman, but perhaps Mr. Davenport had, too, and had put his foot down. Why, Clara thought, if ever she were to meet Mr. Davenport she'd give him a great big kiss on the cheek to thank him.

When the band took a break and the café gave over to noisy chatter and gramophone music, Clara launched into the topic. Surely Tom would be more open to talking about it here, given the trial was due to start the following week, and Eddie and Nora were certain to have opinions. It would seem queer if he were to brush them off the way he did her.

"Will you go to the courthouse to watch?" Clara asked Nora.

"I wouldn't miss it," Nora replied. "Mother and I have followed the whole story right from the beginning."

"Tom, do you remember those days when I'd visit you at the Davenports' gate? How you spent your days on their front steps sitting in the sunshine with Walter? It seems a lifetime ago."

"Your visits were the best part of our day, Clara." Eddie grinned at Nora. "I hadn't met you yet, my sweet."

Nora raised her eyebrows. "I, for one, hope they let the boy go back to his real mother. The more I think about it, the more I'm sure the Davenports made a mistake."

"Do you know, I'm thinking that, too," Clara said.

"Since *when*?"

"Since now, Tom. You know I wanted the best for the Davenports from the start. But something doesn't feel right to me. People say the boy cries day and night. Wouldn't you think he'd be glad to be home? Maybe Mary Davenport was so set on getting a boy she—"

"Ah, you're talking through your hat," Tom said. "The boy is with his 'real' mother, and I'm sure he's plenty happy about that. I don't know who these mystery people are who've seen him crying. You know nobody's been near him. Anyhow, none of this gossip counts for anything. I've told you a hundred times the trial is between the Davenports and the tramp. It's about a childnapping. Wolf dreamed up the idea of the other mother so he doesn't get hanged."

"Dreamed her up? Oh, she's real. People have met her," Clara said.

"Listen, there is a woman." Tom spoke slowly, as though to a child. "But she's not the boy's mother. She's some poor girl Wolf's rich brother is paying to give him an alibi."

"They say the boy has her eyes," Nora said.

"Does he?" Clara leaned forward.

"Mind you, I also heard she was in the same room as the boy and he didn't recognize her. Screamed in fear."

Eddie joined in. "I've heard that, too. But it's not in any of the papers. Why is that, Tom? Seems to me, it's awful similar to what we saw—"

"It's not the same, not at all." Tom turned to Clara. "I'm astonished you'd want to see the boy go to an unwed woman with no means and no home. What kind of life would that be for him?"

"Well, I'm astonished you think the Davenports should get whatever they want just because they want it." She spoke

again to Nora. "I've been reading the old clippings Tom keeps
in a box and—"

"Those are my work papers!" Tom said.

"Well, what am I supposed to do when you won't talk
to me about the most sensational thing that's ever happened
around here? Even though you're smack in the middle of it."
She softened her shoulders. "Oh, the band's back."

Eddie ordered more drinks for the foursome.

Clara fiddled with her teardrop earrings, refusing to meet
Tom's eye.

Tom was troubled by her flippancy. She'd made sharp re-
marks on a few occasions, but he hadn't known how whole-
heartedly she'd turned on the Davenports, on Mary.

"Grace Mill is bedbound with fever right now, anyhow."
Tom raised his voice, to be heard over the band. "On top
of her marital status, lack of money and having a newborn,
she can't leave her room. She's in no fit state to care for the
boy."

"Sick people can recover," Clara said.

"And the rest? I don't know why you're siding with her.
She's the type of woman you'd cross the street to avoid."

Eddie and Nora watched the band, moving in time to the
music.

"It's like you're inclined to side with the Davenports no
matter what. That doesn't seem like the behavior of a newsman, more of—" Clara pursed her lips.

"More of what?" Tom asked.

Clara looked toward the stage.

Tom drank his whiskey and watched the band, but with
none of Eddie and Nora's evident enjoyment.

In a break between songs, Eddie turned to face Clara. "I'm with you. Never did think the boy was theirs."

Tom thumped his glass onto the table. "Have you all gone crazy? What is it you're drinking?" He pointed at Eddie. "You know John Henry, how long and hard he searched for Sonny. And Mary almost died of heartbreak at losing her boy. I can't believe you'd want them handing him over to a tramp."

"You're right. I want them to hand him back to his *mother*," Eddie said. "I've heard you wax lyrical about the rights of poor people before. And Grace Mill is one of them. John Henry is sincere—yeah, of course he is. He sincerely wants his life to go back to normal. But you can't put their needs above hers because you like them better."

Tom glared at Eddie. "The boy belongs with Mary."

Clara put down her glass. "Why, Tom, I think it's Mary Davenport you're thinking of, not the truth, not the boy, and not Grace Mill."

"Oh boy." Eddie reached out for Nora. "C'mon, honey, let's dance."

CHAPTER TWENTY-NINE

Fate smiled on Esmeralda. On Monday morning, as the house was waking to the day—fires lit, beds made, Cook washing the remains of *pain perdu* and honey off breakfast dishes, Mason greeting Gladys Heaton at the front door; the boys using their early energy to up-end domestic order through pillow-fights, digging through drawers for preferred clothing and laying magazines on the carpet to play slip-and-slide hop-scotch, the ruins of each game gleefully ignored—Esmeralda was once again trying to figure out how she could get to Tom McCabe without her absence being noticed. As she was folding Mary's nightgown, Pru rushed into the bedroom.

"No need to run." Esmeralda placed the nightgown in a drawer. "Not many things that important."

"He wants you in his library, *tout de suite*."

"Couldn't use the bell? Never mind, I'm going."

She found Mr. Davenport at his desk, the window flung open though it was close to arctic outside. Esmeralda stood in front of him, thinking it wouldn't be too great a politeness for

Mr. Davenport to pause in his paper-arranging. She was keen to go back to the more civilized warm rooms of the house where he never ventured. She coughed.

"I need you to deliver a document to Judge Roy's house." He slid a large sealed envelope toward her. "You remember where he lives?" His tone was stern, underlining the gravity of his question.

"Yes, sir."

"Remember to wait this time to see if he has a reply."

Esmeralda left the house and walked along the laneway that led to the judge's Daffodil Road home. It was no more than ten minutes away, less if she moved fast enough to warm herself, and that extra pace would leave her time to make a detour via the *Clarion*.

The front door to the *Clarion* building had a large brass lion's-head knocker in the middle and a fluted column either side. The door marked the entrance to a place of authority, and Esmeralda was not confident it was hers to knock upon. Indeed, she stood at the front because there was no accessible back entrance. "With Him at my side, I will not be shaken," she murmured, then crossed herself and grabbed hold of the lion's thick tongue.

A thin mustachioed man opened the door, with undisguised displeasure at seeing a Negro on the front step. After Esmeralda explained to him she was there to see Mr. McCabe, he closed the door and went to fetch Tom. Which meant more of Esmeralda's time wasted, each minute of which she might have used to explain.

By the time the door opened again she was anxious, impatient and chilled to the bone. She was relieved Tom was so plainly happy to see her. "What brings you here, Mrs. Somerset? Do you have an invitation for me?"

Esmeralda looked past him at the black-and-white checked floor tiles, the potted aspidistra, the dark wood staircase. So this was a newspaper office. Not as intimidating as any of the fine houses Mrs. Davenport had dragged her to over the years.

Tom read the anxiety in her face. "Is something the matter?"

"Yes, sir, there is."

"What's happened?" Tom stood in the doorway but didn't suggest she come inside. "Is it Mary, John Henry?"

She knew what a risk she was taking, but regardless of the danger, Esmeralda was going to speak the truth. Tom would stop treating her like an amusing child once she told him what she'd seen. "I'm here because I've been witness to an injustice. I've seen many injustices in my life but—"

Tom held one hand up. "Ah, I'm glad you feel you can be candid with me, but the *Clarion* is loath to publish stories that rile up Negroes. Sheriff Sherman might make a better—"

"No, sir, not an injustice of that kind." She silently asked for God's help once more. "Mr. Davenport invited Grace Mill into his home and showed her a strange child to trick her. It wasn't the boy he calls Sonny, wasn't any child I've ever seen before, though Mr. Davenport told her it was. Judge Roy was in the room, too. I believe they're conspiring to convince Miss Mill the boy they have is not hers. But Mr. McCabe, he is."

Tom stopped fidgeting. Esmeralda could see he understood.

* * *

Tom assessed his options. What Esmeralda had said was un-expected, and he wanted to ask for more details, but he didn't want her to think he'd entertain publishing it, not for a minute. He walked a slow arc away from her to gather his thoughts.

Everyone had known Grace Mill would need to see the child at some point. But Esmeralda had accused John Henry of deliberate deception, and implied Judge Roy was complicit. Whether or not that was true, he needed to stamp her accusations out immediately.

Tom's thoughts raced, but there was no question where his allegiance lay.

He'd tell her what a fanciful imagination she had, suggest she'd been drinking the cook's sherry. No—this was no time for deflective humor. Maybe tell her he'd look into it. Or that it was part of a legal strategy she didn't understand. (Mill's failure to recognize the boy must have thrilled Ellis. Gabino would have to argue—Lord, what would he argue?) But she'd ask what and how, and would push him.

Esmeralda began talking at him again, describing how the strange boy cried and Grace Mill shook as she left the house. She quoted this lawyer and that. She said, several times, that Tom needed to speak with Mr. Davenport before the trial, that he needed to—

"Stop, stop!" Tom had become angrier with every word she'd uttered. She'd piled detail on detail, boxed him into a corner, leaving him no easy way to dismiss her. And now, to tell him what he *needed* to do. Tom stepped forward, and although Esmeralda stood her ground she leaned back as he unleashed the force of his fury. "I *need* to share your tall tale about one of Opelousas' finest men? I *need* to defame a judge? I *need* to inflict further suffering on a woman who has already endured so much? I *need* to do none of that. Stop talking and let me think."

Esmeralda held her breath.

"I don't know why you're telling me this, I don't. For you to turn on the Davenports—"

"I'm not—"

"It's outrageous. They've been good to you, Esmeralda, liberal. Is this how you thank them, by spreading a lie that could ruin any chance they have of happiness?"

"This isn't about thanks. It's about a deception."

Tom stepped closer. "Listen, you think you saw something. But you don't know what happened in that room. You don't understand." Mason, Tom thought. He would speak to Mason, possibly the one loyal servant John Henry had. "You saw a boy going into a room, then he made some noise on his way out. I'm sure Sonny's made a fuss countless times. That's not unusual."

"Except the boy wasn't Sonny."

Her insolence, her refusal to back down, infuriated Tom further.

"I don't think you comprehend what a serious accusation you're making. It's a downright fabrication, I'd say. Do you have some grievance against Mr. Davenport? Because that would explain it. And since this is a legal matter, that's tantamount to interfering with the course of the law for your own ends. Is that what you're doing? Because there are severe penalties for that."

Esmeralda's eyes widened.

"Should I talk to Judge Roy, Esmeralda? Should I tell him how you came to me with a malicious lie, corroborated by nobody, with the intention of—"

"Judge was in the room. I told you that."

"Yes, you're claiming those educated, powerful men were in the room, but you were the only one who 'noticed' it was a different boy? The only one who could see the *true* nature of the gathering." Tom felt more confident now. "I expected more of you." He paused to consider how to proceed. "You should thank your lucky stars I'm not inclined to tell Mr. Davenport about your treachery. Unless—"

"No, Mr. McCabe—"

He stopped her. "Well, I won't, but not for your sake. This outrageous lie doesn't deserve another airing. Your story stops here." Tom marched toward the stairs. "Shut the door behind you."

Esmeralda stormed back to the house. So this was how it was. Tom McCabe had made his choice. When it came down to it he was a coward and abettor, no more interested in justice than the Davenports. But the lives of innocents were at stake, and Esmeralda would not shrug that fact off.

The newspaper was no good to her, nor the law. Mrs. Davenport might be in on it. Mason didn't want to help. Cook wouldn't understand. There was no getting around it: she needed to talk to the boy's real mother. She needed to go to Penny Farm.

CHAPTER THIRTY

To get to Grace Mill was to face a different world of dangers. Esmeralda would need to sneak out of the house, walk the streets at night to her Uncle Joe, convince him to borrow a horse and cart—stealing, if they were caught—to take her to Penny Farm, and then be on a road, two Negroes traveling with whatever plausible reason she could dream up between now and then. It could end badly. And she was running out of time.

Esmeralda put on her shawl, coat and bonnet. Without a candle to guide her, she tiptoed along the narrow corridors of the servants' quarters; down the creaky stairs; past the boys' bedroom, holding back a sneeze; past the Davenports' bedroom, eyes out for any sign that Mary was on one of her night-time wanderings, Esmeralda's fingertips grazing the wall, her footfall as light as could be; and down one step then the next to the entrance.

From there, Esmeralda scampered to the kitchen and out the back door, walking as fast as she could.

* * *

Joe worked at a livery stable on Bell Street—Adams & Sons' Livery and Sale Stables—and most nights, as his cottage was so far away, he slept at the stable, too. Esmeralda prayed he'd had no reason to be in his own bed tonight.

Ducking off the darkened street, Esmeralda passed the front of the two-story wooden livery building, with its dirty windows and enormous sign that read *Will Furnish Hacks, Carriages, Buggies and Saddle Horses, Prices Right*, and made her way to the back. The stable was only a few minutes' walk from the street, though since it smelled of manure and hay Esmeralda felt as though she'd already journeyed to the countryside. She checked the stable's main corridor for Joe, heard the horses stamping and grinding their teeth.

"Joe," she called in a loud whisper. "Joe." It was unlikely anyone else would be there, but she couldn't be sure.

Joe wasn't in the stable, so Esmeralda headed outside, past a cluster of unhorsed buggies waiting for cleaning or hitching. Nothing fancy here, she thought; richer folks went to the brick livery with the arched entryway a mile further on: *Harcourt Livery: A First-Class Stable, Gentle Horses and Careful Drivers, All Kind of Turnouts*. He wasn't there either. But it was a cold February evening so she figured he'd have sought out the warmest place he could. She went into the toolshed, and there was Joe—snoring, on a ticking-covered mattress on the far side of the room. Esmeralda knelt down and shook him awake, apologetic but insistent.

"You can quit whispering. We're alone." Joe sat up.

"I need you to take me somewhere."

Joe frowned at his niece in concern. "Middle of the night. Where is it you want to be?"

Esmeralda explained why she needed to go to Penny Farm.

"Lord, the lengths that family goes to to get what they want. Your farm girl doesn't stand a chance against them."

"She'd have more of a chance if you'd get up and into one of those buggies." She stood, waited for Joe to do the same. "You going in your undershirt?"

"I'm not sure yet I'm going anywhere. I'm thinking." He stared out the shed's open door. "It'd be a whole lot less dangerous in the daytime. Can't we do this tomorrow?"

"For a thousand reasons, we can't. I need your help now."

"Okay, okay. Don't get tetchy." Joe pointed to his folded clothes on a stool near Esmeralda. "Pass me those and turn around."

They went into the stables, where Joe took his hat from its peg, pushed one side of it back into shape and put it on, then lifted his coat from the rack. "We'll hitch the chestnut mare to that buggy."

"Let's take the worst one, the one poor folk might own."

"We'll take the one I choose is what we'll do," he said.

The two worked swiftly and quietly. Joe patted the horse once she was in place. "So these people don't know you're coming? You want to sneak up on them in the dead of night? They're white folk?"

"Yes. And we'd better hurry up about it."

Farmer Penny squinted through a slit made by the part-opened back door. Mrs. Penny, behind him, pulled it open wider so she could see, too. They were both in their sleeping clothes, with Farmer Penny holding a kerosene lamp. Once Esmeralda explained who they were and why they'd come, Farmer Penny raised his lamp higher to check they were alone, then pulled them inside.

The four sat at the kitchen table, wind rattling the windows and steam from the kettle rising. Joe flicked his eyes from Farmer to Mrs. Penny and back again, watching their wariness give way to curiosity then revelation, anger and forceful agreement. It seemed that Esmeralda's version of what had happened in the Davenports' library struck a chord with them.

"She's been had." Farmer Penny whacked the table.

"Quiet, she needs her sleep." Mrs. Penny turned to Esmeralda. "She had a long journey here with a hungry newborn, and then the shock of this. She's been in bed on and off since that day at the Davenports'. I don't know how she'll take this news."

Esmeralda shook her head.

"Question is what we do," Farmer Penny said. "Your word against John Henry Davenport and the rest of them."

"Yes, sir, I know," Esmeralda murmured.

"They're all in on it. Have to be." Mrs. Penny wiped a spray of crumbs onto her palm.

Under the table, Joe prodded Esmeralda's foot. They needed to get home.

"Oh, Grace."

Esmeralda turned at the sound of Farmer Penny's voice and saw Grace Mill, wearing a long cotton nightdress with no shawl or coat to cover it, her hair in a long plait draped over one shoulder, pale-skinned and slight as a switch.

"Dear girl, what are you doing awake?" Mrs. Penny said, standing up. "Come back to bed."

"Who are you?" Grace asked Esmeralda. "I heard you say Davenport. Is this something about Ned?"

Farmer Penny addressed his wife. "She has a right."

Grace pulled out a chair and sat facing Esmeralda. "Please tell me."

"Let me get you back to bed," Mrs. Penny said. "We'll explain in the morning."

"Best sit down, Mrs. Penny. The cat's out of the bag," Farmer Penny said.

Once Mrs. Penny had assured Grace they would speak with the sheriff first thing in the morning then steered her back to bed, she walked Esmeralda and Joe to the door.

"We'll collect you from the back of the Davenports' house on the way to the sheriff's," Mrs. Penny said. "Be ready at nine."

"Oh no, ma'am. I'm done," Esmeralda said. "I wanted Miss Mill to know the truth and now she does. The law will take care of the rest. I don't expect that you and I will see one another again."

"That may be what you think, but it's not what's going to happen," Mrs. Penny replied. "Sheriff's not going to take us seriously if we tell him a second-hand story from a mystery woman. No. You'll come along, tell him in your own words what you told us."

"Mr. Davenport would skin me alive. There's a reason we're here in the dead of night."

"Well, y'all should've thought of that before. My loyalty is to Grace and her boy. I'm afraid I don't know about you one bit."

"I can't be involved any more than this. The only way— but she's too sick—" Esmeralda hesitated. "I could get you into the house, to the boy, tonight. It wouldn't be hard. And he could leave, with his mama, go far away, wherever they want."

"Oh, she's not doing that. She could barely make it into the kitchen. You saw. They'd catch her, no doubt, and she'd be locked up with Gideon Wolf in a day, us in the cell next to her."

"Time to go," Joe whispered to Esmeralda.

"Dig your heels in all you want," Mrs. Penny said. "Even if you don't go with us tomorrow, the sheriff will come for you after we've spoken to him, and you can't say no to that." She rubbed her eyes.

Esmeralda and Joe rode back into town silent and scared, the clip-clop of the horse and the shake of the wheels thunderous in the night.

Esmeralda had no trouble making her way through the dark kitchen on her return to the house or avoiding the squeaky stairs to the second floor. But partway along the hall she heard Mrs. Davenport muttering to herself. Esmeralda froze, back flat against the wall, listening. She heard the click of a door, the boys' bedroom door. Good Lord, she thought, she's still going to them at night. If that wasn't the sign of a troubled mind, she didn't know what was.

Esmeralda considered what she could say if Mary spotted her. She was fully dressed, there was no doubt she was coming or going from the house, and even if she could stash her coat behind a chair, how would she explain her presence on this floor at this time of night? She'd say her youngest daughter had come down with a terrible fever, and that her sister Annalise had asked for her to come and help. She hadn't wanted to wake the Davenports, so she'd taken the liberty of going to her sister's house. And thank Heaven, the fever had broken not long after, so Esmeralda wouldn't need to let any of this disturb her duties. The story was strong.

She considered running tiptoe past the boys' bedroom. Maybe she could get upstairs to her room before Mrs. Davenport even came out. Her convoluted tale would be unnecessary. But she couldn't see if the boys' door was fully closed. And before she'd made a move, Mary walked out, right toward Esmeralda.

"Sally? Oh, poor dear. She's fourteen now, isn't she?" Mary had known her daughter's name, her age; Esmeralda hadn't expected that. "Men circle around a girl of that age, as though she's a meal to be devoured. You'll pick wisely for her, won't you? Don't say yes to the first man who shows up."

"Thank you, ma'am. No, I won't. Can I get your bed ready for you, Mrs. Davenport?"

"Dear Esmeralda, you've done enough caring about others for one night. I'll get myself to bed. Do get some sleep yourself." She took a few steps then turned back. "That does seem to be the lot of women, doesn't it? Worrying about the welfare of others, keeping them safe, distracting them from hardships and horrors. Though without that role we'd be nothing, I suppose."

Esmeralda willed Mrs. Davenport to stop talking, but to no avail.

"Did you know that Mr. Davenport has a sister? He never mentions her. Lord Brandt might love her, I wouldn't know. Her portion of the Davenport inheritance likely played a role. But now," Mary whispered conspiratorially, "there's only the two of them in that enormous English mansion and no chance they'll ever have children. Village named after his family, hundreds of servants, thousands of acres. He might regret his choice. A woman who can't produce an heir—no matter how lively—well, he got half of what he wanted, didn't he?" Mary's eyes widened. "I have exactly the thing to cheer your Sally. Come."

In the guest bedroom, Mary riffled through drawers of dresses folded in paper until she found the one she was searching for. She lifted a pale blue evening gown, beaded, slippery, shimmering, opalescent, and held it up next to her, admired it as though it were a third person in the room. "It'll be a little long, but that's easily fixed. I expect she's as able as you are." She held the gown out. "Take it, please. It's lovely but I've worn it so many times. It's such a waste to have it sit here when your girl could be cheered by it."

There was nowhere, ever, that Sally Somerset could wear such a gown. People would think she'd stolen it. Esmeralda felt a flash of anger at being forced to muster gratitude for useless hand-me-downs from the lady of the house. All she wanted to do was go to sleep.

Oh, but how much her daughters would love to prance around the house dressed like royalty. Yes, she'd give this to them, this luxury she could never afford. Esmeralda put her hands out and let Mary, glowing from her ingenuity and generosity, give her the dress. Then after a fast goodnight, Esmeralda walked upstairs to her room, the gown draped dead and damned across one arm.

CHAPTER THIRTY-ONE

Farmer Penny decided—ignoring his wife's wishes this once—to speak to Sheriff Sherman alone. He had no desire to get Esmeralda in trouble, and didn't see how the presence of a gaggle of women would help explain anything. Contrary to Mrs. Penny's expectations, the sheriff bypassed Esmeralda and went straight to John Henry.

"My housekeeper thinks I have a stash of young boys in my home that I trot out on a whim?" John Henry raised his palms toward the ceiling. "Where? Where are these mystery children?"

The sheriff could see that John Henry was as wound-up as a hay bale. "It does seem far-fetched, but this can be answered in a minute. I only need to talk to your boy. Ask him about that day. I know he doesn't speak—nods and shakes will do fine."

"Absolutely not." John Henry stood up. "I'll not subject him to an interrogation. Especially one requested because my housekeeper snooped, snuck out of my house and spread lies—the contempt, the audacity of her!"

"Now, John, Esmeralda's feisty but she's not malicious. Have you crossed her in any way? Does she have a gripe?"

"A *gripe*? She's treated like royalty. I've bent over backward to be solicitous to her. There's no Negro anywhere, in any house, who's been more accommodated. And now I find she's spreading vile rumors about me. Oh, there's a lesson. Why did I ever think mutual respect was possible? Do you know I was even going to invite her lad to join—Never mind."

"If I could talk to Esmeralda myself—"

John Henry didn't skip a beat. "She's not here. Who knows where she is, or what fresh slander she's spreading."

The sheriff believed it would be remiss of him not to also tell Judge Roy about Esmeralda's claim of a surrogate boy, so he went from the Davenport house to the judge's chambers.

"If there's any doubt about the viewing, this trial can't go ahead. Esmeralda's story casts a new light on the situation."

"Not to my mind," the judge said. "I was there. I don't have any doubts about what happened."

The sheriff frowned. Judge Roy was as brusquely adamant as John Henry. None of this was sitting right.

"Still, it might lay the issue to rest if there was another viewing, Your Honor. This time in the presence of people who know the boy. If I could be permitted to attend—"

"I know the boy. I hope you're not suggesting I'm lying, Sheriff."

"Not at all. But I do think the housekeeper's accusation demands—"

"Then the result of the viewing stands, and I'll allow it as evidence. I won't have my trial derailed because of one troublemaking servant."

Once the sheriff left, John Henry tracked Esmeralda down. His bellowing started the minute he glimpsed her through the kitchen doorway. While Cook stood at the stove, wooden spoon raised, not daring to move, John Henry yelled. He hit the wall hard, turned beet red and yelled some more. He circled Esmeralda around the chopping table, demanding she stand still so he could give her what she deserved. But Esmeralda matched each of his lunges to the left or right, so they came to a stalemate, facing one another, panting—one in fury, one in fear—as Cook held her breath and backed out of their way.

John Henry glared with steel-cold eyes, and lowered his voice to a growl. "How dare you, Esmeralda? After everything I've done for you."

"The boy you showed Miss Mill was a stranger to this house. You lied to that poor woman."

"*I* lied?" John Henry thumped the chopping table. "It's you who dreamed up a pack of lies. And to go to the sheriff and McCabe behind my back—By God, Esmeralda, the damage you've done." He narrowed his eyes. "We'll go to the sheriff right this instant and you'll tell him you were wrong. That's what will happen. And then you'll leave this house."

"No, sir. The boy belongs with his real mama. You can make this right."

Cook made a fast suck of air.

"Oh, I'll make it right. Even if I have to drag you by your nappy hair, on your knees. You *will* tell the sheriff you lied."

Esmeralda shook her head.

"So help me, I'll beat you to within an inch of your life if you don't do this, Esmeralda."

While John Henry was speaking, Esmeralda inched her way around the table.

"None of this is your business. You have no right to any opinion," he snarled at her.

As Esmeralda made a move toward the door John Henry lunged at her again, but she remained out of reach. Esmeralda flicked her eyes down the corridor that led to the cellar. John Henry smirked. "Go on. I'll leave you there to die."

Esmeralda made for the back door, desperate to be outside, gone. But this time John Henry was so fast she couldn't avoid him. He pushed her hard, his lead-heavy hands on her chest, and she stumbled backward until she was against the kitchen wall. She looked entreatingly at Cook, who whimpered but did not, could not, do anything.

John Henry brought his face close to Esmeralda's, breathed hotly on her eyes. He poked his finger into her ribs, digging it in until she thought he would pierce her. "You'll do as I say or I'll make your life a misery. I'll come after you at night. I'll come for your children."

Esmeralda pushed back, with all the force she could muster. John Henry swore at her, told her she'd swing from a tree, and Esmeralda hit him. She hit John Henry's face as hard as she could, striking his cheekbone and shocking them both.

Mary came rushing into the room, the three boys behind her, to find out the cause of the noise.

"John, no!" Mary shouted. She put one arm out to stop her sons from getting any closer.

John Henry raised his arm and punched Esmeralda once, twice, knocking her to the floor. Mary ran forward and grabbed his wrist mid-flight, barely deflecting his aim, as he brought it down to strike Esmeralda again. John Henry roared, and shook his wife off so ferociously that she stumbled back and fell against the oven, sending Cook's full pot crashing to the floor.

The boys ran over to help their mother.

"Get out of this house and never come back," John Henry shouted. "If I lay eyes on you again you'll be to blame for what happens."

Esmeralda, breathing hard, struggled to stand.

John Henry clenched his fist again. "Now."

"John, what is this about?" Mary's voice was shaky and small.

"Go upstairs, Mary."

"But I don't understand."

"I feel sorry for you both," Esmeralda said, her voice shaky and hushed. "Whole world in your hands and look what you do with it."

She walked out of the kitchen. And after a blink, Cook scurried out behind her, the smell of burning pie in their wake.

PART FOUR

JUDGMENT

CHAPTER THIRTY-TWO

On Monday, February 10, 1916, the first morning of the trial, Barbers Smith Senior and Junior sat at their kitchen table eating bowls of puffed wheat with milk and drinking strong black coffee, while Mrs. Smith juiced oranges. Outside, the air was colder than it should have been, a low fog still hovering over the garden bench. Mrs. Smith let herself enjoy the pleasing thought of the coming hours, when she and her tabby would have the house to themselves. Were that to last forever she wouldn't be entirely sad.

Once the two men had finished their breakfast, they would walk to the courthouse to sit on the jury for the Davenport-versus-Wolf case. It was exciting and annoying, an unrequested break from routine, a chance to be part of the biggest show in town, a day's lost earnings.

"Still," Barber Smith Senior said, "civic duty is not optional." He smoothed the newspaper with a wooden block. The *St. Landry Clarion* had published a front-page article by Tom McCabe describing how Grace Mill had been shown the boy pre-trial and neither had recognized the other. Tom's article argued that this alone should be sufficient evidence to put Wolf's ludicrous story to rest. Furthermore, he wrote, people had a right to know Grace Mill was holed up in the Penny farmhouse on the outskirts of town refusing to talk to reporters. She spent her days lounging about while the farmer's wife cared for the baby Grace Mill had had by an unnamed man.

Barber Smith Senior tapped at the story as he spoke to his son. "You should read this before we go."

"I've already heard enough to last me years. I'm fed up of these people's names, this pointless arguing over a child. It's not like either woman can't have another one, is it?"

Mrs. Smith thumped the two glasses of juice onto the table. "The things you say. Have another one—maybe that's what I should've done. Traded you in for another son, one with a heartbeat?"

"Now now, Mrs. Smith," her husband said. "Rest assured we'll be fair and reasonable." He drank his juice and patted dry his mustache. "A man's life hangs in the balance."

She looked down at him. "A man, two mothers, a father and a child. There's more than one life that's about to change."

Paul Davenport saw the front page of the *Clarion* that morning, too. The newspaper wasn't something he had any interest in, but after breakfast, when his parents had left the house, he'd snuck into his father's library to reclaim the ball that had been taken away from him when he'd been caught kicking it indoors. He didn't find his ball, but while he was exploring the off-limits room, he caught sight of his name on the newspaper that lay on his father's desk—his last name, in any case. That was enough to pique his interest. He was excited to see the article was written by Tom, and after he'd read enough of it, he had an idea. Paul folded the newspaper, hid it under his vest on the chance he bumped into Mason, and bolted upstairs to George.

Mary Davenport sat at the front of the crowded courtroom next to her husband and had to twist in her seat to look around. She saw Gladys and Ira, Tom, Eddie, two young women she assumed were their companions, Sheriff Sherman and seemingly all of her sons' tutors. Everyone was there, but Mary had no idea how their presence helped anything other than to feed public curiosity. John Henry had said the only people in the courtroom who mattered were the judge and jury. And surely they wouldn't be swayed by the number of spectators the Davenports or Wolf had drawn to the room.

The jury seats were empty and Judge Roy had not yet arrived. Mary placed a gloved hand on John Henry's. He twitched, then patted her briskly in response. She'd been told countless times by countless people that the case was a rude formality, that she was not to worry, so she was troubled by his palpable tension. Like her, he was unaccustomed to being in a courtroom, but Judge Roy wouldn't let anything bad happen to them. Hank would keep the factory running smoothly. Was there a real chance they could lose the case, lose Sonny?

Mary felt a wave of nausea roll through her. Even after sunrise there'd been a layer of frost on her lawn, but the courtroom was oppressively warm. *Surely* there was no reason to have let so many people in. The room was already stale with hot breath, the smell of damp coats and hats, oft-worn cotton.

And—Mary thought, as she pulled her hand back onto her lap, dropping it on the other with a quiet slap—as if the waiting, the clammy air, the hard seat and her roiling stomach were not enough, she had to find a new housekeeper, and cook. Her house was bedlam and she had no time to attend to it. Sula was sloppy and forgetful, and to have Mrs. Billingham's cook on loan was a temporary assistance but not without emotional cost. While it was a kind gesture, knowing Mrs. Billingham was staying with Gladys and Ira added enormous pressure for Mary to find someone quickly. More than anything, she missed Esmeralda to the point of tears.

John Henry still hadn't credibly explained why he'd struck Esmeralda. He said he'd caught her stealing, that Cook was part of it, too, but no matter how Mary pressed, he wouldn't say what had been stolen. Mary looked in the obvious places and couldn't see that anything was missing. Esmeralda was important to Mary—it would be wrong to say she was a friend, but she was more than a servant—and John Henry didn't seem to realize the impact on Mary of his impulsive behavior.

She worried, also, that the boys would never forgive John Henry for what they'd seen. Mary had offered them ambiguous answers in an attempt to explain the unexplainable: "would never be angry without a good reason," "sorry for frightening you," "she's welcome back if she's willing to apologize." Mary had taken to eating breakfast with the boys rather than with John Henry, and had made time to go outside with them in the afternoons and sit on the porch while they played. At first, they'd treated her presence as an oddity, but after a while they included her, Paul showing the bird's nest or strangely shaped rocks he'd found, and George and Sonny letting her help with their pictures. They'd been delighted at how good she was at drawing. Against John Henry's wishes, she'd granted the boys a month away from studies, to play as they wished. He was aware she was working to repair the damage he'd caused, so aside from grumbling his objections he did nothing.

Mary had asked Sonny that morning if he'd like a kitten, since they were most definitely the best pets to have, "soft and gentle." She'd promised to take him to the postmaster's house after Mother and Father's business—not trial, but business—was finished, as Mason said the man had a litter of kittens to be homed—not drowned or made mousers, but homed. All three boys had greeted her suggestion with such joy that she'd finally felt she had their approval. Which, of course, had been the point of her tireless attention. Sonny had beamed when she told him the kitten would mostly be his, so he could pick it from the litter. That had sustained her on the way to court. She'd expected John Henry to be more pleased with her victory, but he'd merely said, "Better than a dog."

Composed. She needed to remain composed. She glanced toward the back of the room again. John Henry had told her to be prepared to see Grace Mill and to ignore her, but Mary had never laid eyes on the dreadful woman so wasn't sure who to look for. As she perused the faces, she ended up at Tom. He smiled, and she wished he could sit beside her. She'd missed his company.

* * *

The day before the trial, while John Henry was at his factory, Mary had sent for Mrs. Capaldi. It seemed wise to gird herself for the coming days. Usually, Mrs. Capaldi made Mary feel calmer, stronger, but the moment the spiritualist had sat opposite her at the table, Mary willed her to leave. Everything about the woman was irksome, from her patchily powdered cleavage to her hideous jewelry. Mary looked for something to ease her eyes. A vase of white camellias sufficed until she saw a crack in the porcelain where none had been before. And the fold mark on her freshly laid tablecloth would not stay smooth.

"Mrs. Davenport."

The tablecloth was fine as long as Mary's hands were pulling it flat, as long as she was observant, but when she relaxed—She lifted her hands. The crease bounced back. Was this a new thing, for a crease to be ironed in? Who was she to talk to about it?

Mrs. Capaldi watched. "Perhaps you would prefer to sit on the sofa."

Mary shook her head. She was cross at her tablecloth, at Esmeralda for vanishing, at Mrs. Capaldi for not being more attuned to her mood and for smelling so strongly of vetiver. She was cross that Tom never came to visit, cross at her father for his cold silence, at John Henry for letting things get to this point, at the woman who would take her son away. That Mary had to even appear in a courtroom was ridiculous.

She used her water glass to press on the crease. "I think you ought to lay out the cards now. Right here."

Mrs. Capaldi was taken aback. Mary never directed the course of their time. "*Prego.*" She placed her tarot cards on the table, thinking she had precious little chance of accessing truths while Mary's emotions bubbled like boiling water in a pot. The cards needed stillness to unpack the present and anticipate the future.

"Composure is the idea you must hold center of mind, Mrs. Davenport. Be serene and at ease. *Donna dignitosa*. You have been wronged, but you are composed."

"Yes." That seemed a wise approach. "Composed." She looked away from the crease. What was it to her anyway?

Mrs. Capaldi placed her arm on the table, palm up. "Please, give me your hand."

The medium's hand was plump and warm. Even her rings gave off an almost living heat.

"Your heart line is strong. You have many loves."

"Many?"

"Your husband, sons, the things that enliven you—your music, your beautiful dresses. Your life will sing often if you let it."

Mary stared at her palm.

Mrs. Capaldi held Mary's hand between her own as though she'd caught a tiny bird. "Love can be a tiny flutter or a great soaring roar. Accept whatever form it takes, Mrs. Davenport. Be sure and still."

"Composed."

Mary watched the jury file in and arrange themselves on two long wooden benches. One by one they were sworn in by the bailiff. She glanced at the lawyers' tables in front of her, one either side of an aisle as though they were at a wedding. Everyone stood as the judge entered the room and took his place with three flags behind him: one for the nation, one for the state and one for the Confederate.

She and John Henry had been spared the indignity of sitting with their lawyer, but Gideon Wolf sat, rather self-importantly Mary thought, with his legal team of two.

She turned around to see the upstairs gallery was full as well, the colored people having found their seats via the internal back stairway. Would Esmeralda risk an encounter with John Henry in order to watch the trial, to wish Mary well? It seemed not.

Judge Roy reproached Gideon Wolf for talking to the jury.

"Forgive me, Your Honor. I was asking Ben whether his arthritis was still troubling him. They say it'll ease if you give up the good things in life. But a good life's better, eh?"

Several members of the jury laughed at this. John Henry noticed the casual affection they were showing Wolf, and Mary noticed John Henry's clenched jaw. As she turned back toward the jury, she saw a young juror—the barber's son—glaring at her. The air was so hot, her collar too restricting. She'd never wanted to run from a room more.

It occurred to her in a panic that John Henry had somehow found Esmeralda with the blue dress. Mary hadn't told her husband she'd given it as a gift for young Sally, hadn't thought to do so. And now Esmeralda had been beaten, fired, thrown out of their home. *That* would explain him thinking she was a thief. But she had Mary's permission to have the dress—more than that, Mary had given it to her. If only Esmeralda had spoken up when Mary had come into the kitchen. She reached out for John Henry's arm then pulled back—he was radiating prickly fury, and although she was desperate to tell him about the dress, she saw this wasn't the moment to do so.

Mary hadn't looked carefully at the colored section. Esmeralda didn't sit front and center—she wasn't a fool—but she was there, wouldn't have been anywhere else.

She'd walked to the courthouse staying to the edges of the street, near closed shop fronts with drawn shades, and thought that once she got into the courthouse she would blend in with the upstairs crowd. Some part of her wanted Mr. Davenport to look her in the eye and feel ashamed at what he'd done, and see she was unbowed. But the consequences of being seen were terrifying. She didn't dwell on that, instead put one foot in front of the other.

The day was picture-perfect, with a clear blue sky and honey-yellow sun. Esmeralda noticed that the people around her—all walking in the direction of the courthouse—seemed upbeat, were babbling to their companions.

But if everybody thought this bright, sunny day bode well for them, some of them had to be wrong. The verdict would either allow them to congratulate themselves on their prediction or bemoan the unfairness of the system, to cheer the underdog or stand up for the respectable elements of society.

Esmeralda joined the swarm of people shuffling up the courthouse steps then squeezing together to funnel through the doorway. In the passageway, before colored people went one way and white people the other, the townsfolk mingled like river stones. Their clothes carried smells from factories, stables, grand mansions: oil, cabbage, cigar smoke and rose-water. Esmeralda imagined the talk floating over her like a cloud, the men's baritone staying close to hat height, the women's higher notes soaring above. Once the crowd split in two, the air felt lighter and less pungent, the building more spacious, and Esmeralda relaxed.

She moved close to the railing and looked down on the main room, where the white men and women were dropping into their seats. When there were no seats left to fill, they stood in rows at the back. And when there was no room there, an official closed the doors.

Esmeralda saw John Henry and Mary Davenport sitting near the front. Behind them, Mrs. Billingham clutched a white handkerchief to her nose. At the back of the room there was Tom McCabe, holding his notebook, and Eddie, without his camera. No sign of Grace Mill or the Pennys, though. She glanced at Mary in time to see her look toward the colored section. Esmeralda eased herself back from the railing.

"You like to live dangerously." Joe sat down beside her.

"Hush. It's only dangerous if some boob lets the Davenports know I'm here."

"No different from hiding in plain sight, I guess."

Esmeralda was staying with her sister. The three-room wooden house, which would have fit ten times over inside the Davenports', was already sleeping Annalise, her two children and Esmeralda's three. It could hardly hold one more person without bulging at the seams, but it did. Esmeralda hadn't once worried that staying there would endanger anybody, including herself. Her sister lived a fifty-minute walk from the Davenports, so it wasn't as though she'd taken extreme measures to hide. Her safeguard was simply that nobody had ever asked where her sister lived—those who cared she had a sister—so that once she left, they were confounded.

Judge Roy banged his gavel again and Gomer Ellis stood, ready to make his opening statement.

CHAPTER THIRTY-THREE

Grace woke to the smell of eggs frying in butter, rolled onto her side and dangled her head off the bed to vomit into a bucket. She heard the pang of liquid on the tin base; someone had emptied her night's expulsions already. As she blinked into the bright light coming through the curtains, she listened to the clatter of plates being unstacked on the kitchen table, mugs filled.

She took a sip of water from the glass Anna Beth had left for her. As she stretched her legs, her toes touched the cotton-wrapped warming pan Mrs. Penny must have recently slipped into the bed. The blankets were firm and smooth over her legs, tucked in after another sleepless night.

When she wasn't filling the tin bucket, Grace felt she'd crack a rib from coughing. She wheezed when she breathed, struggled to keep her eyes open for more than a few minutes. She'd already tried to get out of bed once that morning—had it been this morning?—but her body had failed her. She'd managed to sit on the edge of the bed, but when she attempted to stand, her legs shook and buckled. She'd lain back perspiring, then cold. Then asleep again.

If it was after ten o'clock, the trial had begun. She knew that much. She wanted to be in the courthouse, but two days ago Gideon Wolf's lawyer and assistant had come to the farm to speak to her about the trial. Mrs. Penny had done her best to make Grace presentable, but Grace was sure she'd appeared like a bedraggled lunatic to them. She'd registered their expressions when, supported by Farmer Penny, she'd lowered herself into an armchair in the Penny living room.

"You'll be required in court on day two," the lawyer had said.

"Not day one?" Grace asked.

"Day two," the assistant reiterated. He'd glanced at Mrs. Penny. "Does she understand?"

"Of course she understands," Mrs. Penny tsked. The foreign man was a mite intimidating, but his underling was barely out of shorts. "She's sick, not stupid."

The lawyer had listened intently while Grace explained what Esmeralda had told her.

"We'd suspected some version of foul play, but not quite this." He'd seemed impressed by the ingenuity of the set-up, had spoken over the top of Grace's feelings about it, ignored the Pennys. The lawyer repeated—more to his assistant than anyone else—that he had a great deal of experience in the courtroom, that they should stay with their strategy and keep knowledge of the truth up their sleeve, to be played only if it could work to their advantage. He said the part of Grace's story that relied on information supplied by a Negro housekeeper wouldn't take them where they wanted to go, was unprovable and inherently suspect. Grace's task was to reaffirm that she'd willingly given her child over to Gideon Wolf.

"Is that enough, though?" she'd asked. "Shouldn't the jury hear the Davenports are conspiring to—"

"No. You are to be polite and demure, speak when spoken to and refrain from extended answers. You're part of a larger argument, Miss Mill. Please trust we know our business."

While the lawyer talked Grace through the various ways in which Gomer Ellis would attempt to derail and undermine her, Mrs. Penny asked her husband to join her in the kitchen.

"I don't think they're interested in helping her get Ned back. They only want to get that tramp set free," she whispered. "I fear she'll be lost in all this."

"But if the tramp's story is proven right she gets her boy back, doesn't she? Stands to reason."

"I suppose so, but I don't like the way they're talking to her It seems wrong."

Farmer Penny agreed. "Does she need her own lawyer, do you think? How many are let in the room?"

"As many as are needed, I imagine," Mrs. Penny said, shrugging. "But the sheriff would've told us if she was supposed to have one."

"Well, we can help her if it comes to that."

Farmer Penny's father had been one of the few men in Opelousas to buy into the Louisiana Lottery twenty-five years before. When the two boys from the Asylum for the Blind had picked his ticket from the barrel, Penny Senior had something to pass down to his son. Those winnings had spared the Pennys the horrors that befell other farmers when the weather turned on them, and had enabled Farmer Penny and his sons to add extra rooms: a second bedroom, then a third, a lean-to, a chicken coop. Even with last year's remade barn, and gifts to both the Macdonald and Lamott families, whose crops had been decimated by boll weevils, there was money to help Grace.

Grace was distraught by the time the Pennys re-entered the living room.

"It's merely a question of letting the Davenports save face," the lawyer said.

"I don't care about that," Grace replied.

"But *they* do, so *you* must. You cannot think that accusing the most powerful man in Opelousas of childnapping and deceit will get you what you want, Miss Mill. That is not how the world works."

"But I'm yet to hear you explain how you'll convince the jury they have my Ned."

"That seems a reasonable question," Mrs. Penny said in the gaps between Grace's fresh coughing fit.

"More a statement than a—" The lawyer's assistant stopped when he saw Mrs. Penny's stern expression. How, he thought, did every woman of advanced age know that same look of admonition employed by his mother?

The lawyer reclaimed control of the conversation. His assistant lacked the deft touch required with anxious women. "I've won many cases in my time, Miss Mill. That's why I'm here. Your job is to get yourself into the courthouse on time and do as I've said. Let me manage the rest."

After the lawyers had left, Anna Beth helped Mrs. Penny take Grace back to bed. Anna Beth returned with Mr. Miggs and placed him on the bedspread near Grace's feet.

"You've no intention of keeping to his script, have you?" Anna Beth asked.

"None at all."

Grace was sure the judge would want to learn he'd been hoodwinked along with her. Once she explained what Esmeralda had said, the judge would surely dismiss the case and Ned would be returned to her. The truth would win out.

She lay in bed with the sheet held to her face to soften the smell of vomit. She felt it too much of a liberty to ask one of the Pennys to empty the bucket again. They'd attend to her when they could, as they had for weeks. Grace promised herself she'd find a way to repay them.

But first, she needed to reclaim Ned. He'd be awake now, as his fate was decided by the trial-in-progress. Had he been outside somewhere or in the house, upstairs, when she'd been shown—who *had* she been shown? She replayed that day over in her mind, wishing she'd run from the room, shouting Ned's name.

With a stab, the thought occurred to her that the Davenport woman would've tried to win Ned over. What if she'd succeeded, and he didn't want to come back to Grace? She yanked back the tight blankets and turned to hold her head above the bucket once more.

CHAPTER THIRTY-FOUR

Gomer Ellis didn't surprise anyone with his opening statement. The Davenport story had been written about endlessly, so though he summarized it with gusto, people in the courtroom used the time to continue preening and looking around for familiar faces. Tom, who did listen since he needed quotes, recognized some of his own sentences in Ellis's speech. "Stalwarts of our community, a respected family that's contributed enormously to our town." That was his. Not even his best work.

But Opelousans sat up straight for Wolf's lawyer. They'd seen Gabino on the streets, agreed among themselves that he was polite and dapper. He began his statement confident, poised, restrained. He felt sad for the Davenports. "Only savages would be unmoved by a fine family having gone through such an ordeal. We are not savages." His lolloping, accented English made his sentences sound like a haughty song. People couldn't tell from his appearance alone—his broad jaw, equine nose—if he was usual or exceptional for someone from his country. He came from an influential family, was a man of good breeding, though he lived in San Francisco, which was troubling. ("Mexicans, heathens, unionists and bears. How a lawyer of merit could come from somewhere so lawless is beyond me," Mrs. Billingham had said. Gladys had shrugged away her mother's criticisms. Merit was such a subjective notion.)

Gabino was dismissive of the idea that Ellis would be able to argue anything worth the jury's time of day. "You see, the Davenports' loss, however poignant, has nothing to do with my client. Nothing." But the men of the jury seemed no more moved by his eloquence than by Ellis's pragmatic delivery.

Barber Smith noted the elegant cut of Gabino's suit. Ben Fleury hoped he'd fully turned off his leaky bathtub faucet that morning. And Martin LeMaire recalled an Italian customer he'd once had in his bakery; the man had acted suspiciously, had been more than a little arrogant.

Gabino could tell he didn't have the jurors' full engagement, so he injected a touch of outrage into his speech: "Desperate for someone to blame, someone to be responsible for their years of pain, Mrs. Davenport's descent into madness and—"

"Objection," Ellis said.

The judge agreed. "I see no grounds for you to discuss Mrs. Davenport's state of mind."

Mary scowled at this half-defense: no grounds to discuss and, they had not added, no evidence of any such state.

Sitting a row away from the jury box, Sheriff Sherman wondered where Gabino was getting his information from. The Davenports might have a genuine fight on their hands.

He glanced toward the back of the room. Where was Grace Mill?

Gabino walked toward the jury. "Let me be frank with you, gentlemen. I think that's what we all want. In order for the Davenports to win, which is to send this man, Gideon Wolf, to a lifetime of penury or death, *that* man and woman"— here he pointed to where the Davenports sat—"need you to believe they've captured the villain who stole their son. Now, that would provide the closure you've wanted after following the story for years. I understand. But their case is built on thin air. And you need more than that to convict an innocent man. So," he said, tapping the polished balustrade separating him from the jury, "I hope you will allow me to explain, methodically and comprehensively, that my client has committed no crime, certainly no crime that involves this family. In fact, if the Davenports were inclined to civility, and we'll get them there"—here he winked—"they'd admit they owe my client a debt of gratitude. For Mr. Wolf did indeed meet their son, fed him, returned him—"

Upstairs, Esmeralda whispered to Joe. "Why is he saying the boy with Gideon Wolf was Sonny? Pennys didn't talk to him?"

Joe shrugged. "Maybe saving them for a big finish."

"He can't argue the boy is Sonny *and* Ned."

Gladys was about to say to her mother that she was finding Gabino's reasoning quite compelling when Ellis stood up.

"Objection, Your Honor. Gideon Wolf did not *return* the boy. He was apprehended by Sheriff Bird in the company of the boy, at a time when Sonny Davenport's kidnapping was public knowledge. Had—"

The judge waved at Ellis to sit. "Counsel will stick to the facts. Jury members, please note Mr. Wolf did not *return* Sonny Davenport. Were that true, none of us would be here today."

Gabino smirked. "Semantics aside, the fact is that Gideon Wolf, a luckless tramp without a mean bone in his body, came upon a lost child and helped him, because he is a man of good conscience. What's more, when you hear the remarkable specifics of his generosity, you'll be convinced beyond doubt that Mr. Wolf should be set free." He slapped the balustrade. "Applauded."

Esmeralda narrowed her eyes. How did this story include Grace Mill and Ned?

The jury stared at Gabino eagerly but, confident he now had them in his pocket, the lawyer walked back to the table and set about arranging his papers.

Majestic, Gladys thought. She wasn't often taken with foreigners, but this one gave her goosebumps.

Gomer Ellis stood once more. "Gentlemen of the jury, I know every one of you. And you're far too smart to be taken in by amateur dramatics. There are no 'remarkable specifics,' no cloak-and-dagger reveal. The only unexpected part of this trial is what you may have learned from the newspapers—that the tramp has a rich brother who's willing to send his fancy lawyer to our town to keep a guilty man out of jail. But where is the justice in that? We know the truth." He paused for a breath, anticipating Gabino's objection, but it didn't come. Interesting. "John Henry and Mary Davenport's boy was kidnapped by Gideon Wolf. Sonny was playing with his brothers when he was *snatched* onto the train by this vagrant, and sped away to another state. The Davenports did what any loving parents would do—more, in fact. They searched for their child for years, across hundreds of miles, never giving up, suffering hardships most of us won't experience in our lifetime. And their efforts paid off when Sheriff Bird found Sonny in the clutches of *that* man." He pointed at Wolf. "That man who sits with his brother's out-of-town lawyer, telling you he did nothing wrong. Nothing wrong? How can it be right to roam the streets with a young boy stolen from his parents?" Ellis appeared incredulous. "It isn't. It simply isn't."

Gabino stood up. "Is the defense calling a witness, or have I misunderstood court procedure?"

The jury members laughed.

Eddie turned to Nora. "Cocky as all get-out, this guy."

"I was, indeed, building to that." Gomer Ellis cleared his throat. "We call John Henry Davenport."

Gomer Ellis guided John Henry through a serviceable statement. But Gabino, having identified his strengths with this jury, played up both his exoticism and the lure of his "remarkable specifics" to keep them interested. "So no one saw the train at Half Moon Lake, in fact. Or saw Gideon Wolf on this imagined train," he said to John Henry. "Curious that something so large and loud could pass through unnoticed. And your older boys gave no explanation for why the youngest ran off alone? One does question why he ran." He raised his eyebrows at Ben Fleury, shared a moment's surprise with Barber Smith Senior.

John Henry didn't find the lawyer either novel or intimidating, and Gabino saw this. He knew they recognized themselves enough in one another—their fine cloth, their assured carriage, their easy politeness; the courtroom and Gabino's personal lineage affording the lawyer enough status to become John Henry's equivalent—that the interaction could have been almost fraternal. Although they were on opposing sides, it was clear they started from a place of mutual understanding. But they both hungered to win, and were equally versed in the lunge and parry of argument.

None of Gabino's questions—no matter how blunt or provocative—ruffled John Henry. He matched the lawyer in volume, vocabulary and tone, and seemed prepared for every line of inquiry and veiled insult even though Gabino's repetitions were designed to catch him out. He even knew to speak from his heart, in an almost womanly way, to appeal to the jury's sentimentality. "To bring an end to my wife's pain, to embrace my son after years without him—I know that every man here would feel the same relief I felt when I found our boy," he said.

Gabino gave John Henry a nod of respect. But he hadn't traveled to this two-horse town to lose.

"Is it conceivable that your desire to relieve your wife of her misery might have caused you to accuse my client of a crime without comprehending his true nature or the full complexity of his actions?"

"No. I am, I believe, a good judge of character. Also, I understand the solid nature of fact. My son was found with Mr. Wolf, and Mr. Wolf is his captor."

"Unless," Gabino said, "he is his savior."

Ellis, at his table, swore under his breath.

* * *

Upstairs, Esmeralda and Joe whispered to one another, confused as to why Gabino hadn't asked John Henry about the viewing in his home.

"Cat-and-mouse game is keeping people interested," Esmeralda said. "But what's stopping him from mentioning Grace? They're acting as though she doesn't exist."

"Only thing I can think of is that he's trying to lay some hay so Mr. Davenport can have an easy landing. He's more likely to admit a wrongdoing if he can walk away with his head held up," Joe said. "Rich people give each other outs."

"I don't know. I think something else is brewing."

Ellis called Mary's doctor to the stand to confirm he had caused the mark on the boy's arm while using forceps during delivery. Ellis had decided to plow on with his strategy, no matter what Gabino was doing. He could only assume that Gabino was going to introduce Grace Mill to his storyline soon to pull the rug out from under John Henry and Mary. Grace must be his "remarkable specifics." Ellis needed to eradicate in advance any thoughts that the boy was not Sonny Davenport.

"I was compelled," the doctor explained, "to use some amount of force to pull the baby from the birth canal before his life became compromised. It was quite…physical." He stopped to see if Ellis wanted him to explain more fully, but the lawyer's expression of distaste made it clear he'd heard enough. "Of course, I'd sedated Mrs. Davenport so she was unaffected by the procedure. The forceps, while necessary, did make a curved mark on the baby's left arm, a permanent mark."

The doctor also confirmed he'd examined the child living in the Davenport home, and he was the same child he'd delivered. The boy's muteness was a mystery, "though most likely due to shock."

Ellis addressed the jury. "Sirs, you may hear argument from the defense that the boy found with Gideon Wolf was not the Davenports' son. I know you will have heard many versions of this nonsense in your day-to-day life. I trust the doctor has now put that to rest. The defense has spread this theory to provide a reason Gideon Wolf should be released. Do not be fooled."

Mary Davenport was escorted to the stand, and guided by Ellis through her statement with gentleness and deference. No one was interested in the facts she agreed to. Mary's job, as Gomer Ellis and John Henry had explained to her, was to help the jury see how much her sons meant to her, how loving a mother she was, how devoted a wife, how courageous, dignified and reasonable she was. As unnecessary as it should be, she was demonstrating her superior nature. This would hold her in good stead when she would be, unavoidably, insultingly, compared with the unwed farm girl later on.

Ellis explained to Mary that the Italian would speak to her in ways she wasn't accustomed to, and that she needed to fortify herself.

"Remain composed," she'd said. "I understand."

Gabino had looked forward to speaking with Mary Davenport the same way he looked forward to fox hunts. She was the quarry, the kill. Here, he'd learned (delighted by the ease

with which a middling detective could entice locals to di-
vulge everything they'd heard about the Davenports), was
a woman who hadn't recognized a child she moments later
swore was her flesh and blood, who'd turned to psychics and
occultists for life advice, who'd had verifiable bouts of insanity, and was unnaturally attached to her Negro housekeeper
and a newspaper reporter. There were so many tracks down
which he could pursue her, it was thrilling. He'd been anticipating this for weeks.

He took in her smart white blouse and tailored navy skirt, a
modest and dignified outfit Ellis must have advised her would
be suitable to win over the jurors. House of Worth, if he'd had
to guess.

Gabino weighed his first move. He didn't need to reveal her
as the unreliable individual he knew her to be now that he
had a hidden card to play, the one that would stop the jury in
their tracks. He needed simply to establish she'd been affected
by the press and some members of the public to believe stories
about Wolf that were not true. Upholding Wolf's character
was his priority, but the thought of cutting her down was ir-
resistible. He'd not deny himself. He'd met so many women
like Mary Davenport: rich, sheltered, patronizing, with a confidence as smooth and brittle as an eggshell. She'd end up with
the child, had to, but he'd let himself blood her a little first.

As Gabino walked toward the witness stand, Mary unex-
pectedly transformed before his eyes. Already elevated above
him, she grew perceptibly straighter and taller. Gabino paused
mid-step. He had an easy first sentence he anticipated would
make her fumble, but as she locked eyes with him he saw
she was—today—as self-assured as a monarch on her throne.

Gabino had met many lesser royals, though, so he wasn't shaken by her demeanor. In fact, it gave him a shiver of pleasure. He would rise with her.

"Madam, may I," he began, "take you back to that . . . some might say confusing, others might say difficult . . . night at Sheriff and Mrs. Bird's home?"

"You may. It could be the word you want is 'remarkable' or 'wondrous.' 'Blessed,' even. English can be so challenging."

"It is, indeed—no more challenging than my other three languages, but I thank you for your politeness." Gabino smiled. "It must have been unpleasant for you to even be in such an inferior environment. I imagine a sheriff's home in Alabama is less than refined."

In the gallery, Mrs. Bird, Sheriff Bird and Sheriff Sherman bristled as one.

"The Birds' home is lovely. And Mrs. Bird had taken very good care of—"

"Witnesses say you had to kneel on the floor to look at the boy. Is that true?"

"He was on the sofa. It was the best way—"

"And your Negro housekeeper, for reasons unknown, was seen wandering around the Birds' front yard talking to strangers."

Mary frowned. "I have no idea what you're—"

"It certainly sounds like an unusual night, one that I imagine you'd rather forget, with the squatting on the floor and—"

"I never—"

"—ramshackle houses and wayward servants—all that, of course, before you declared the boy wasn't yours, and then was. I know I'd rather put that right out of mind, were it me."

Ellis stood. "Where is counsel going with all this speculation? I've heard no question for my client amidst his entirely
false imagining."

"Do you have a question, counsel?"

Gabino nodded to the judge, touched his forefinger to his
lips, changed tack. "Mrs. Davenport, it's true, I think, that
you've never met Mr. Wolf before today."

"That *is* true."

"So you never heard him explain how the child came to be
his ward?"

"Ward?" Mary looked to Judge Roy for help.

"Yet another curious choice of word," the judge said. "And
unfactual, in any language. The jury will disregard it."

"Is it also true that your entire understanding of the circumstances surrounding Mr. Wolf's capture and undeserved
imprisonment have come to you via your husband and your
reporter friend, Mr.—" He waited.

"McCabe."

"Tim?"

"Tom." Mary felt her cheeks flame.

"Yes. Tom McCabe. He spent a lot of time lifting your
mood while your husband searched for Sonny, didn't he?"

"Relevance?" Ellis asked, but the damage was done. The
jury could see Mary Davenport was flustered.

Tom, startled and offended by the insinuation, pushed
himself off the back wall he'd been slouching on. What was
Gabino doing? He glanced at Clara and muttered, "Who does
this guy think he is?" But she didn't respond, and kept her
narrowed eyes on Gabino.

"You see, I worry, Mrs. Davenport. I worry you don't

have the facts at your disposal, and that you may have been led astray, condescended to, told half-truths. That's not your fault, but I do need to point it out. Men sometimes think women don't need facts. But I'm not inclined to believe that. I think you deserve the full story of how the boy became Mr. Wolf's traveling companion—"

Mary flicked her eyes to John Henry. No one had warned her about this path, and she wasn't sure how to walk it.

"Objection," Ellis said.

"—and you will get it in due course," Gabino finished.

Sheriff Bird replied to Ellis that John Henry had agreed when Mary Davenport declared the boy was theirs. And told Gabino that Mr. Wolf had put up no resistance to being arrested, and the boy showed no fear of him, no matter Mrs. Potter's observations.

A discordant note came from Mrs. Bird. "The boy was a treasure. Kicked up a little fuss when I bathed him, but that's nothing. Mostly he was no trouble. And six-year-old boys aren't always easy."

Ellis nudged her back on course. "Everyone in town was thrilled at his rescue. And they all showed up on my front lawn to say so," she said. The courtroom laughed in understanding. Mrs. Bird described how anxious Mary had been to see the boy, and how—

"How touching it was to see them together?" Ellis prodded.

Mrs. Bird froze.

"Witnesses say you were visibly moved when Mrs. Davenport arrived at your home, that you ushered her inside with great compassion. As one mother to another, you must have felt glad for her?"

Mrs. Bird considered. "She was unsure."

"I don't think anyone would say that's so strange?" Ellis smiled at the jury. "Women are unsure about a great many things." The men snickered. "But in seriousness, once she was certain, did she seem quite certain?"

"Oh yes, most firm." Then Mrs. Bird added, "But I can't say the same for the boy." She looked for Sheriff Sherman, but before she could say anything more, Ellis indicated for her to return to her seat.

Gabino waved away his chance to cross-examine Mrs. Bird, which left her words hanging in the air as she made her way back to her husband, casting a quick glare at the man who'd disparaged her housekeeping. Ellis considered his opponent's decision: the man was savvy, but where was he going with his odd defense?

Sheriff Sherman, when questioned by Ellis, answered that John Henry was a model father and loving husband who had applied himself with patient persistence to the search for his son. And that Mary, while at first overwhelmed at the Birds' house, had been resolutely certain by the end. Ellis nodded. "Mrs. Davenport showed the thoughtful caution such an important moment deserved."

Gabino pursued an entirely different line, asking the sheriff how thoroughly he'd interviewed Gideon Wolf. "While I'm told you're experienced in law enforcement, it does strike me that you restrained rather than engaged with Mr. Wolf."

"*Engaged* with him?" Sheriff Sherman said. "He was caught

with a boy who wasn't his own. That's a crime and now he's on trial for it. What more would you have had me engage with him about?"

"Did he not plead his innocence?"

"Every criminal does."

"In this instance there may be good reason for that. Were this case about you, Sheriff, I'd suggest a degree of negligence in not giving a man's honest statement due consideration." He didn't elaborate on that. Gabino knew to be careful; that in his critique of the sheriff there should be no whiff of him thinking the man had done a shoddy job because he was a yokel, a person who would not have been elected to the office in another town. The jury might see this as casting aspersions on Opelousas more generally. His attention had to stay on Wolf's innocence. He told the judge he had no more questions for the sheriff.

Like Esmeralda, the sheriff was baffled that neither lawyer had mentioned the viewing of the boy in the Davenport house. When Gabino freed him to step down from the stand, he hesitated. "Your Honor, may I speak?"

The judge nodded.

"It's important to note that two women are laying claim to this boy. I'm not sure at what point that gets brought up. But I'd like to offer some information about the event that involved Grace—"

The judge interrupted him. "Were you present at the event you'd like to discuss? No. In which case, it would be hearsay. I won't allow that."

"But it seems a crucial part of the—"

"This is a trial between the Davenports and Gideon Wolf.

You've answered the questions put to you, Sheriff. Return to your seat."

Gabino pursed his lips. He could press the judge to let the sheriff bring up the topic of Grace Mill, but he'd prefer to introduce her later, as he'd planned. He stood aside for the sheriff to walk to his seat.

At this point, Esmeralda bent low and edged toward the upstairs exit. Though she was curious about what was coming next, she needed to get to work. Without her income, her family was struggling to get by. Esmeralda helped her daughters with the laundry and piecemeal mending farmed out to them by well-to-do families, hoping that work wouldn't dry up once word of her departure from the Davenport house spread. When they weren't working, Esmeralda, Annalise and Joe made plans for the group to travel north as soon as they'd raised enough money for train fares.

Joe followed Esmeralda, whispering, "I'm coming, too. Had enough of this. They're going to cut that poor girl out of her own story."

Back at the Davenport house, the boys had come up with a plan. Pru was always more relaxed when their parents were gone, so while she ate a leisurely breakfast in the kitchen, the boys took the newspaper into their bedroom and wedged a chair under the doorknob. George read Tom's article out loud, and stopped when he got to the details about Grace Mill being at Penny Farm.

"Grace Mill is your real ma, isn't she?" George asked. To the boy's nod, he said, "Okay, then."

Paul grinned at his brother. "We're thinking the same thing. I bet we are."

George would miss the boy. They made a good gang, now that they were used to one another and the boy had learned their games. But Esmeralda had said it was the right thing to be kind to him. And taking him to his ma, no matter what Tom wrote about her, had to be the kindest thing to do.

"Then let's get you to Penny Farm."

Paul leaned over George and read aloud, "Johnson Street. That's the one that goes to the kite park. If we can get on that without anyone noticing it's a long straight line, pretty much."

"We'd go out through the backyard, down the milk cart lane, circle around to Johnson, past the vacant lot where the black boys play chickamy."

"How's that game go?" Paul asked. They paused in their planning to talk about the rules and requirements of chickamy.

Afterward, while the boy was drawing a map, Paul said, "Madame Caron lives near that lot."

"We'll have to be real careful."

"I'll bring my knife and compass. Rucksacks."

"Camp blanket, in case. And we'll hide away some of our lunch and dinner. We'll need food." George saw the disappointment on the boy's face. "We'll get ready today and go tomorrow."

"Remember how I told you about Scouts being prepared?" Paul asked. "Says here they think the trial could take a week, so tomorrow's as good. We want to plan this right."

"I reckon it's going to take most of the day to get there. And it'll be cold. But so long as we stick together, we can do it."

Without Pru, the new cook, Sula or Mason paying any

heed to what they were up to, the boys gathered supplies in preparation for their journey, spreading the load between two sacks that they hid under their beds. And after lunch, when Nanny Pru said they could play outside a while, they explored the backyard with escape in mind.

CHAPTER THIRTY-FIVE

Gabino walked the length of the jury box as if he had all the time in the world. He passed close enough to Barber Smith Junior, sitting at the end of the front row, that the barber was able to place his cologne: Cantonese lime, a refined choice. Meanwhile, in the gallery, Mrs. Billingham fanned herself. Gladys admired the glint of afternoon light on her pearl buttons. Tom whispered to Eddie that if Gabino said his name again he'd sock him once the case was done. Clara and Nora, standing next to one another, slightly away from Tom and Eddie, whispered loudly. Tom didn't even try to listen in: he'd get an earful when they left the courtroom.

"I know you're waiting to hear from Mr. Wolf," Gabino said. "And you shall. But first, let me tell you my client has never been anywhere near Half Moon Lake. I doubt he could find it on a map. But that's no crime. Gideon Wolf is guilty of one thing: compassion. Two, if one counts kindness as a separate attribute."

He examined his buffed fingernails. "You see, Sonny Davenport was not *kidnapped* by Mr. Wolf. No. He was *found* by him in Mobile, Alabama, the poor boy drifting about without a custodian, while our client was going about his lawful business of tuning pianos and church organs. And the reason the child approached Mr. Wolf was because he could tell he was a trustworthy man. How? Because on the day young Sonny met Mr. Wolf"—Gabino took the time to make meaningful eye contact with jurors in both rows—"and here I will keep my promise to you, gentlemen, and explain the *remarkable specifics*—my client was already in the company of a child with whom he had permission to travel. That's right—another child. There were *two boys*."

The people in the jury box and courtroom gasped as one.

Gabino spoke louder. "Gideon Wolf traveled through Alabama with *two boys*. Two!"

"Objection, Your Honor," Ellis said, leaping up. "This is the first we've heard of—"

Judge Roy banged his gavel.

"Two boys, *neither* of whom he stole. Masters Sonny Davenport and Ned Mill."

Reporters from the *Bugle*, *Daily* and *Louisiana Times* ran out of the room to get the news back to their editors. This was enough to write their front-page stories. The details could come later.

Mary sat wide-eyed and unmoving. John Henry had told her to display no emotion, no matter what she heard in court, but it was clear everyone was shocked to hear this. She tried to catch her husband's attention but he was looking straight at Judge Roy. As she reached out for him, John Henry stood up, and made his way to Ellis. She watched the two huddle and confer at the table, their faces furiously animated, while she concentrated her energy on how to comport herself.

"Yes," Gabino raised his voice louder above the ruckus, "two boys. Ned Mill, son of Grace Mill, was traveling with Mr. Wolf not only with the mother's permission but also at her *request*. That is how trustworthy a man our client is— a woman asked him to be her son's guardian. And while he was undertaking this duty, he came upon Sonny Davenport—"

"Your Honor, may I approach the bench? This is absurd," Gomer Ellis spluttered.

"Quiet!" Judge Roy shouted. "And yes, both of you, come here."

The judge spoke first to Gabino. "I'm not averse to some element of drama in my court. You've woken up the jury. But you best have some evidence to back up your claim. As far as I'm aware, this is the first time anyone has suggested Mr. Wolf traveled with two boys."

"I believe Mr. Wolf's testimony today and Grace Mill's tomorrow morning will—"

"You're not serious," Ellis said. "Your Honor, Gideon Wolf hasn't stopped talking in months, and he's never mentioned anything about being with two boys. No one has. And when he was arrested he was with *one* boy. It's clear this is a complete fabrication, a last-minute gambit."

The judge considered. "Mr. Gabino, I don't want to hear another word of soliloquy. Get your witness up here right now. I'll let you follow this line of questioning with him but I'm warning you, don't waste my time."

* * *

Once Gideon Wolf had sworn on the Bible, Gabino walked to the witness stand and got right to the point. "Mr. Wolf, did Miss Grace Mill give you permission to travel with her son, Ned?"

"She did."

"And so you did?"

Gideon nodded.

"And did you also travel with Sonny Davenport?"

"I did."

"Two boys? You're sure?"

Gideon Wolf shared his amusement at the question with the jury. "I don't know many things, but I know the difference between one boy and two."

"Of course you do. So tell us, how is it you came to be in the company of two young boys?"

"The thing is, it started out simple. I took to the road with Ned, with Grace's blessing, and she was about to birth her second. We'd agreed I'd circle back to her in a month or so. And when I got as far as—now, it's hard to say, some places are so small they don't have a name, not an official one, any-how. I once passed through a town—they called themselves that, 'town'—of three families, that named itself Xanadu. Ha, I guess there's no amount of—"

"And then you met Sonny Davenport?"

"Yes, let me think. I'll get this right. We'd gone as far as—"

Ellis stood. "Your Honor, Mr. Wolf is speaking to a script. This is insulting to—"

The judge stopped him. "I'm more intrigued than insulted. I'd like to hear where it's going. But consider yourself on no-tice, counsel."

"This stressful situation is testing Mr. Wolf's memory, Your Honor. I promise there's no cunning at play."

Gideon clicked his fingers.

"Mr. Wolf, please," the judge said.

"Sorry, Your Honor. Things come back all of a sudden. I was in Appleton with Ned, making for the river. We were ambling along, happy enough in the sunshine, when I saw the boy sitting on a rock, nobody near him. And without me doing anything about anything he decided to follow us. Didn't say a word. Could've been Ned's twin—peas in a pod."

"Your Honor, this is a ridiculous story, entirely unsubstantiated," Ellis said.

"Possibly so, counsel, but let's hear the whole of it. Mr. Wolf, you were traveling to a river for an unexplained reason when you found yourself in the company of two uncannily similar children. Go on."

"Now, I understand how peculiar that sounds, sir, but there are scads of young ones on the streets, orphaned or unwanted. They look for other children to travel with, safety in numbers."

"And what made you suspect this boy was Sonny Davenport?"

Wolf jerked his head back. "I didn't. Wouldn't. I'd never heard of the Davenports. Just met this lone boy. The two lads seemed companionable enough at the river, and I had no reason to chase him off. But he never answered my questions, didn't even say his own name. Shock, most likely, the way the doctor said. I've seen—"

Ellis stood again.

"Yes," the judge said, nodding. "Mr. Wolf, as you lack medical training I'd ask you to resist diagnosing the boy."

Ellis spoke anyway. "Your Honor, this is the first any of us has heard this story since Mr. Wolf arrived in Opelousas. And he's had ample opportunity to speak. There's no proof Mr. Wolf ever came upon another child—no witnesses, no evidence. We haven't heard from Miss Mill that any of this is true. There is only proof that Gideon Wolf was caught with Sonny Davenport."

The judge grunted. "Mr. Wolf, I trust your lawyers will guide you to explain why you've waited so long to share this part of your story with us. In the meantime, I urge you to remember your oath."

"Ran off," Gideon said. "He ran off."

"Who ran off?" the judge asked.

Before Gideon could reply, Gabino spoke. "Your Honor, Mr. Wolf didn't have all the information at his disposal until recently. He's explained he didn't know the name of the other boy since the boy didn't offer it. He had no idea the Davenport family had been searching for their son."

The courtroom erupted into laughter.

"Back then!" Gabino shouted.

"Is there room under that rock for me, too?" Eddie called out.

Mrs. Billingham turned to Gladys and said, "Oh, for Heaven's sake."

"Your Honor," Ellis said loudly and gestured with a sweep of his arm, "the response from the courtroom is telling, is it not? Even if neither of the sheriffs used Sonny Davenport's exact name in front of Mr. Wolf, which I'm certain they would have, every person who visited Mr. Wolf did. And he swore black and blue the boy was not Sonny Davenport but Ned Mill. His story has more holes than a colander."

"The other one," Gideon said. "I meant the other one ran off."

"Your Honor, I ask you—" Ellis stopped and shook his head in disbelief.

"Back then, at the time," Gabino said. "How could he know *back then*?"

The judge banged his gavel. "Mr. Ellis, would you approach, please?" As Gabino moved to join them, the judge waved him back. "I have a comment on procedure that's relevant to the prosecution." He addressed the jury, "Allow us an administrative moment, gentlemen, then we'll continue."

The judge spoke quietly to Ellis. "I want to check that you recognize this tale, though unexpected, can work for your client if you guide Mr. Wolf in the right direction. I can't tell you what to say, other than to note you'd be remiss if you fail to think through how this can be incorporated into your strategy."

"But the idea there were two boys traveling with him is patently a fiction."

"Might it be a fiction that would let your clients live their truth?"

"It might be." The judge's suggestion alarmed Ellis, both for its betrayal of legal principles and the bias of his advice. Ellis wanted to win his case, of course, but not by throwing his professional ethics into the fire. The advice, however, could not be dismissed.

Ellis walked back to his table, shaken.

"Mr. Wolf," Judge Roy said, "a question has come to my mind. I'd ask you to think carefully before you answer it. Which boy was with you when you first encountered

Sheriff Bird? Your interjections suggest you want us to understand one of them had run away by the time you reached Mobile."

Wolf shuffled his feet in the witness stand. "You're asking me to recall a long ways back."

"I am."

Mary tried to make sense of what Wolf was saying, and whether she wanted it to be true. If she believed the line of reasoning Mrs. Capaldi had persuaded her of—that the boy was not exactly Sonny but Sonny in essence—and if Gideon's story was true, then was the boy who'd run off her real Sonny? If so, then they did, indeed, have Ned Mill and this whole case was an abhorrence. John Henry should be traveling to this unnamed river, this rock in Appleton, to continue searching. But if any of this had occurred to John Henry he showed no sign of it, staring straight ahead, expressionless. Had he heard the same words she had?

Tom also puzzled at the ramifications of Wolf's story. It was a lie, that much was clear. But it'd be a tricky one to prove or disprove, and so served mostly to confound the jury and muddy the waters. Unless...Ah, if they discounted Esmeralda's third child story, and it didn't seem as though that was going to be brought into the defense, then the boy in the library viewing could be said to be Sonny, while Ned had run off in some nowhere town. And though this scenario was devastating for Grace, she was worth nothing to either side. It might work. Though, dear God, it was a brutal thing to do to a woman.

Judge Roy grew impatient. "Mr. Wolf, can you tell me if you believe the child with you at the time of your arrest in

Mobile—the child who did not run off—was Sonny Davenport?"

Even the more naive jurors recognized this as a leading
question, a shocking intervention from the one neutral party
in the room to whom they could look for guidance. The judge
continued, undeterred by the room's reverberations.

"What I am asking you, Mr. Wolf, is this: was the boy who
ran away from you Ned Mill?"

Both Gabino and Ellis sat forward in their seats. Though it
would've seemed unlikely a few hours before, both the prosecution and defense now wanted Gideon Wolf to say yes. Were
he to utter this one word, Gabino could close his case by arguing Wolf had rescued the Davenport child who, struck mute
by circumstance, did not tell the tramp who he was. That
child had been co-operatively returned, and no crime had
taken place. Since Wolf's story vindicated the Davenports and
there was no further incentive for them to proceed, Gabino
felt Ellis could convince them to withdraw their case. And
certainly, the judge seemed inclined to that outcome.

Gideon Wolf's years on the road had honed his talent for acting. Many times when he'd pleaded for a warm meal, a bed,
loose change or work, he'd embellished the truth so persua-
sively he'd almost believed that every word he said was God's
truth. He needed to use those talents now. Gabino had re-
hearsed the story with him over and over. But he was glad
Grace was not in the room. She was a loving mother, and he
was about to betray her.

He looked at Mary Davenport, finely dressed, anxiously
stiff. Gideon had heard the rumors about her wild mind, but

Ned would be given a wholesome life, a grand home, all the goods money could buy. Grace would suffer, but not so much as he would hanging from a rope if he didn't say what the Davenports wanted to hear right now.

He took a deep breath. "I don't know who it was stole that child away from his loving home but cursed be that man, for I've never met a more agreeable child than Sonny Davenport. The child has seen some hardships, but not at my hand. From the time he came to me, I made sure he was fed, and put him on my back when he was too worn out to walk. I committed no crime. It was lucky I met Sheriff Bird when I did and he was able to find the boy's family. And yes, it was Ned Mill who ran from me. I'll never know why. Truth be told, I was ashamed of that. I wanted everyone to believe it was Ned still with me. I couldn't let Grace down—that kind, suffering woman—couldn't go back without her boy. And I didn't know anything about the other boy, if he even had a family anywhere. I do know I took care of him. But I admit I lied about the boy, and that was wrong." Gideon looked out at John Henry. "I'm glad to see Sonny Davenport back home where he belongs."

The courtroom erupted into noisy talk. Tom bolted out of the room to get his story to Mr. Collins. John Henry patted Ellis on the shoulder, then returned to his wife to embrace her. Mary hid her face in her husband's shoulder. The judge banged his gavel and declared an end to the day's proceedings. People flooded out of the courtroom, a riot of eager talk. They would return tomorrow; no one would miss it. Because though the day had been action-packed, Grace Mill had yet to take the stand.

Sheriff Sherman walked outside slowly, disturbed by what he'd witnessed. He'd met plenty of criminals who considered adherence to truth and laws as optional, but it was troubling to watch people in power do so. If laws weren't followed by the very people who wrote and enforced them, then what use were they?

CHAPTER THIRTY-SIX

At nine-thirty on the second morning of the trial, a day as pitilessly bright and clear-skied as the one before it, once the public, judge and jury sat down, the bailiff opened the double doors to admit Grace Mill and the Pennys to the courtroom. Everyone watched in silence as the Pennys helped Grace walk the aisle to a bench behind Gideon Wolf.

Judge Roy had hoped she'd be too ill to attend, but now she was here he needed to choose his next move. After Gideon Wolf's testimony, the judge felt certain the jury would find Gideon Wolf innocent, and the Davenports would go home with Sonny. He needed to make the road to that end as smooth as possible. He could instruct the lawyers there was no need for the woman to testify, and send the jury in to deliberate now. But it would appear heartless to deny Grace Mill the chance to speak, and may cause additional, unnecessary controversy. She couldn't possibly say anything to change the narrative; Gabino's two-boy story would hold. At most, people would feel sorry for her, and outraged at Wolf's carelessness.

Judge Roy beckoned the two lawyers to come to him. "The woman is observably ill, so use a light hand. None of us wants to be seen as bullies. Do only what's necessary to get both your clients what they want."

Grace sensed the stillness in the room, saw that everyone had turned their eyes to her, an attentive herd. She'd smiled at Gideon, but he'd turned away without returning the gesture. That was odd, but maybe he felt as nervous as she did in this room. She studied one face after another, trying to read their expressions. The curiosity and pity were understandable: she was unknown, unwell, and Anna Beth's clothes were ridiculously big on her. But she'd also prepared herself to face animosity—she was here to reclaim a son that one of Opelousas' gentry had stolen: a popular and beloved family, as she understood it—and she saw none of that. A pretty woman at the back of the room had placed one gloved hand on her chest and looked at Grace with undisguised sympathy. Another woman had muttered "courage" as Grace walked past. And there was the sheriff, nodding in a way she read as encouragement. Well, she thought, no matter what the prevailing mood in the room, she would say her piece. The Davenports and their friends wouldn't like it, but once Grace and Ned left, the town would find a way to forget. She needed only to summon the strength to get through this part of it.

Gabino turned away, briefly, from his conversation with the judge to greet her. Grace supposed he'd tell her what to do when the time was right, though she wished he'd given more advice before now. He'd told her what he wanted her to say, and how to answer the questions he anticipated from the Davenports' lawyer, but he hadn't described the odd geography of the courtroom, and how she was to appear at ease in it. Was she supposed to stand and speak from this place where she sat; did the jury ask questions as well as the lawyers, and if so, was she expected to walk over to them when she replied? That would be tricky in her state, but the Pennys would be able to help.

Upstairs, Esmeralda fumed. When she'd taken her seat, minutes before Grace arrived, the woman next to her told her about yesterday's revelation. As Esmeralda digested the story, and took in fragments of added information as they came at her from every person in the gallery, she watched Grace and the Pennys enter the courtroom. She hit a fist against her thigh in frustration. She could see Grace was almost eager. Was anyone down there going to tell her what had happened? Everything was now so unfairly stacked against her.

As if reading her mind, Joe mumbled to Esmeralda, "Don't even think about it. You got three of your own depending on you."

From the moment Grace Mill had entered the room, Mary's eyes hadn't left her. Grace didn't look as Mary had expected. She was delicate, frail and appealing, with such a sweet face, though wan. That she'd come into the room ill, and would now learn that Gideon Wolf had lost her son—Mary felt some sympathy for her. Mostly, though, she wanted all of this over.

"Miss Mill," Judge Roy spoke directly to Grace, "welcome to my courtroom. We appreciate the effort it must have taken to travel here."

"Answer him," Mrs. Penny whispered.

"Do I tell my story now?" Grace asked. "I'm ready."

The judge put one hand to his ear. Grace repeated her question. He sighed. "Yes, I suppose you should."

Gabino stood and asked Grace to come to the witness stand. Seeing her confusion, he pointed at it. The judge gave Farmer and Mrs. Penny permission to help Grace into the stand. Once Grace was seated, and the Pennys had apologized their way back to their own spot, the room fell quiet again. Grace coughed, a rattly, wheezy wave of coughs.

Judge Roy looked down at his papers. The entire room was waiting for Grace to gather herself so she could hear something that might be the death of her. What a case this was.

Gabino approached Grace with his arm extended, offering her his embroidered handkerchief, along with words of praise for her fortitude in leaving the bed she so clearly required. He told her she'd only be here for a short time, then he paused. Very soon Grace Mill would regard Gideon Wolf as a villain, and that was neither here nor there. Gabino's job was to keep the tramp alive and out of jail, and he would do that. But the woman was so feeble, and so attached to the boy . . . This would be one of the more distasteful tasks of his legal career. "Miss Mill, do you know the man seated at this table?"

"Yes, that's Gideon Wolf. Hello, Gideon." Still, he wouldn't meet her eye.

"And is it true that you permitted your son, Ned Mill, to

travel with Mr. Wolf while you gave birth to your second child?"

"Yes. But they didn't come back. And when I heard from Matthew Cavett that Gideon was locked up in Opelousas, I was worried for Ned. Gideon, too, but my little boy. If I could see him, then we can—"

"To be clear: your son, Ned, traveled with Mr. Wolf with your permission?"

"I've already said that to the sheriff. He can tell you himself. He's—"

"I have no further questions, Your Honor."

Ellis narrowed his eyes at Gabino, aware he'd been set up to finish the job.

"Your Honor, there's been a terrible—" Grace coughed mid-sentence.

"Miss Mill." The judge stopped her. "I'm aware you may not be familiar with court protocol, but I'd ask you to answer the questions that are put to you and not speak to me directly."

"Oh, but sir—"

"Miss Mill." Gabino stood up and shook his finger at Grace.

Ellis walked slowly to the stand. "It seems I have been charged with telling you what took place here in your absence, Miss Mill. Yesterday afternoon, Mr. Wolf's legal team—oh, and that man Gabino, he's not your friend by the way, any more than Wolf is, oh no. Yesterday, Miss Mill, Mr. Wolf told us that he had lost your son."

"Lost him?" Grace stood up. "You *lost* Ned?"

"Ran off," Gideon mumbled. "Not my fault."

"What are you saying, Gideon?" She looked at Judge Roy. "What is he saying?"

"Please sit down, Miss Mill, before you faint. Mr. Ellis, I warned you both."

"Your Honor, I thought it best to simply state the truth. Miss Mill, you believe the Davenports have your son, but they do not. In front of this room, Mr. Wolf said your son, Ned…ran away from him. He lost your son, Miss Mill. And was found with the Davenports' son, as he'd traveled with both boys from—"

"He wouldn't do that."

"I'm sorry?"

"Ned would never run away. He wouldn't. Gideon, you know that."

Gideon stared at his lap.

"Ned is with them." Grace pointed at John Henry then looked up at the judge. "Have you not figured that out?"

Judge Roy glared at Gabino. "For the last time, tell your witness to direct her comments to you. And do not make Mr. Ellis shoulder this entire burden."

Gabino approached the stand. "Miss Mill, this is terribly sad. But with my hand on my heart, I confirm what Mr. Ellis has said is true. Mr. Wolf admitted under oath that he did, indeed, travel with your son. And then your son ran away from him."

But Grace ignored the lawyer, her focus on Gideon. "You were supposed to bring him home. No more than five weeks." She turned to the jury. "I know my boy. In a new place without me, there's no way he'd run off anywhere. He would have stuck to you like glue, Gideon. Unless you were treating him badly. Did you? Did you mistreat Ned?"

"Counsel," the judge snapped. "How many times do I need to ask you to do your job?"

"Miss Mill," Gabino said, "Given what we've heard, I think there's no further reason for you to remain on the stand. You are distressed and the comfort of a bed"—he gestured for the Pennys to come help Grace—"would be—"

"I don't believe any of this. Gideon, you're wily," Grace said. "It was your silver tongue got you called back again and again to the Cavetts'. You never made that piano sound any better than a pile of old teeth. You've invented a tale to escape punishment. But I've been told the real truth by another." She looked at Gabino. "I told you when you came to Penny Farm that the Davenports' housekeeper, Esmeralda, knows the child I was shown by Mr. Davenport was neither Ned nor Sonny. She's worked for them for years, knew their son since his birth. And why would the Davenports deceive me with a different child if they didn't have *my* son? Ned is in their home. I'm certain of it. Their boy is lost and gone, and they took my Ned to replace him. *That* is the truth and you know it. You must all surely know it."

Again, the room exploded into loud chatter.

"We've been deceived, Your Honor. That viewing was a scam."

"Miss Mill!" the judge bellowed. "May I remind you I was in the library that day but the housekeeper was not. So her opinion is based on subterfuge and guesswork. And as such it is worth nothing."

"She wasn't in the room, sir, but she heard and she saw. And she knows the boy they're calling Sonny. He has no voice, like my Ned. There aren't many boys without the ability to speak. When Esmeralda came to the Pennys' farmhouse, she told us—"

Judge Roy gave up on Grace resisting the urge to talk to him directly. "You're telling me the Davenport Negro traveled, without permission, to a farmhouse where no one knew her, to spin you a web of lies about her employer? And that we are to take her falsehoods—motivated by an animosity I have no wish to fathom—into consideration? Madam, I understand your thinking may be clouded by sickness and shock, but this is preposterous."

Upstairs, Esmeralda sank low into her seat. It was enraging to hear insults about herself, beyond frustrating not to be able to shout out in agreement with Grace, but the judge's feelings had escalated enough that she was in fresh danger. She could not be seen. Everyone around her understood the precariousness of her situation and arranged their bodies to help Esmeralda fade into the crowd.

Downstairs, Mary was stung at the news Esmeralda had gone to the Pennys' farmhouse with the sole intention of betraying her. Was that where she was coming from when Mary had presented her with the beautiful blue dress? She reached out for John Henry.

"Miss Mill," Gabino said as he stepped forward, alarmed at the judge's anger, "you need to accept it is you who has been deceived. The housekeeper you met is wicked and aggrieved, and has concocted a story that in your desperate state you've believed. But please cast it from your mind. She lied, then fled. And her incredible story has served only to hurt you and the Davenports."

"She's gone?" Grace asked.

"Yes." Gabino waited for this news to return Grace to the beaten and pliable witness he could control.

"Gone where?"

"Whoever knows?" He turned to the jury. "But I believe I can say we are sorry to see how much distress an irresponsible servant has caused."

The jurors murmured their agreement.

At this point, Gabino expected that Grace might begin to sob, or shake. The farm folk would comfort her. And then, after a quick deliberation by the jury, this nasty business could be ended.

Grace, however, raised her chin and met his gaze. "You're lying. All of you, lying." Unassisted, she stepped down from the witness stand and left the room, the Pennys behind her.

Sheriff Sherman watched Grace leave, moved by her dignity, ashamed he hadn't taken her side from the moment he met her. She was right, he thought. But it was too late, and there were too many forces against her.

Esmeralda tapped Joe on the arm.

"Let's wait a minute," he said. "Too much coming and going for it to be safe yet."

"Now."

Joe mumbled his misgivings then followed Esmeralda through a tunnel of shielding bodies to the stairs.

Esmeralda had a fresh idea. Grace's boy was inside the Davenports' house, and Esmeralda knew that home and the habits of its occupants better than anyone. She could get the boy out and back with his mother before the court case was over. But she needed Grace and the Pennys to come with her to the Davenports'. If they distracted Mason at the front door, she could count on Sula to help her scuttle the boy out the back where they could collect him. Pru: well, she'd lose her job, but she'd find another. Esmeralda and Joe couldn't ferry Ned to the farm—she was sure of that from the story of Clarence Tine and a hundred others. Two Negroes with a white boy... But the Pennys with him wouldn't raise an eyebrow.

"Your Honor," Ellis said, "we contend that Miss Mill is not in her right mind due to her unfortunate illness and personal loss. We are satisfied with Mr. Wolf's admission that the child now with the Davenports is, indeed, their son. And my clients are prepared to drop their—"

He stopped at the sound of a chair scraping loudly on the floor and turned to see John Henry standing, and Mary briskly making her way for the door. Reading John Henry's confusion, he asked if his client could have a brief recess.

Seeing there would be no way of stopping Mary without causing a fuss, the judge agreed.

"I need air," Mary had whispered in John Henry's ear. "I can't breathe."

Under any other circumstance, John Henry's main thought as he followed Mary to the door would have been the humiliation of such an untimely public exit, but what he worried about instead was if there'd been enough time for Grace Mill to have left the building. Even an invalid would have been outside by now, though.

Yet there she was, sitting on a wooden bench near the doors, between the Pennys: marshaling her strength to get to their buggy, he supposed. He tried to direct Mary away from them but wasn't quick enough to stop the two women from seeing one another.

"Don't do this," Grace called out.

Mary let go of John Henry's arm and walked toward Grace. "I won't ask what *this* is because you've been very clear about what you think, Miss Mill. But you're wrong. I'm keeping my family together. What you're doing, I don't know. Causing chaos."

The courtroom door shut with a bang as a scattering of people also in search of fresh air stepped into the hallway. Most of them, observing the tinderbox combination of individuals, and knowing the die had already been cast, chose to walk away. Two women from the Ladies Aid, though, stood against the nearest wall, watching, ignoring John Henry's glares.

"I saw your face in the courtroom," Grace said. "You weren't aware of your husband's deception, were you? But now you are, so everything is different."

"Mary, you don't need to speak to her," John Henry said in a low voice. "Come with me."

"Different how?" Mary said. "You're right I had no idea of the falsehoods in your head. Nor did I know my housekeeper had betrayed me. But neither of those things changes the facts."

"Your husband showed me a boy in your house and said it was Ned but it wasn't, nor was it your Sonny. The child said he'd traveled with Gideon but had never heard of Ned. That makes no sense with Gideon's tale. He must have been a foundling, or one of your other sons told to lie."

"You're mistaken, Miss Mill. There's no reason my husband would manufacture something so odd."

"But that's my point. He crafted that bizarre situation to throw me off. I believe Esmeralda—Ned is in your house, under false pretenses. If the lawyers cared about the truth they would've found your housekeeper and let her speak."

"Your son ran off, Miss Mill. We heard Gideon Wolf say so."

"He'd say anything to escape the noose. Him with his fancy lawyer and you owning this town—I wasn't worth enough to be heard."

"Money has nothing to do with it," John Henry said.

"It has everything to do with it." Mrs. Penny stood up next to Grace. "Let's go home now. We'll work something out."

Mary struggled to find her breath, yanked at the band of her skirt, but there was no loosening it. "I'm sorry your boy is gone, Miss Mill, believe me. But the person who's wronged us both is Gideon Wolf. You should direct your bitterness toward him, not me."

Grace stared at her. "How can you go on this way? You know he's not yours. You *must*."

John Henry grabbed Mary's arm. She shrugged him off.

"Miss Mill, I'd no sooner take another woman's child than I'd harm a puppy. I don't know anything about your boy. Why," she said, shaking her head, "I'm flabbergasted at your suggestion there's some nefarious plot against you. I tell you—no, John, let me—we've done nothing other than recover our son."

"You madwoman. You mad, deceitful pair. Do you want me to bow and scrape to get him back, to beg? I'll do that."

Grace dropped to her knees on the cold stone floor.

The Ladies Aid women gasped. One whispered, "We really must get someone." This time, the second woman agreed. The pair scampered back into the courtroom.

"Miss Mill." John Henry moved toward Grace, but Farmer Penny shot him a look of such fury he stopped.

"Stay away from her." Farmer Penny bent down to help Grace up. "This is no good for you."

"Oh, this is infuriating!" Mary stamped her foot. "Why are you doing this to us?"

Grace spoke slowly, refusing to move from her knees. "Whatever that group of strangers decides, Ned is my son. To you, he's property, a replacement for something you lost. But that boy is my flesh and blood. You will never rest if you do this."

"Miss Mill, get off the floor. Why must you keep shaming yourself? Mary, come, now."

"And you, Mr. Davenport? Do you lie awake at night and think about your true son? He's alone because of you, with no one searching for him anymore. You've condemned your own child."

Mary strode forward, quick as lightning, and slapped Grace hard across the cheek. Grace fell sideways onto the floor, her hands splayed to support her.

"You're nothing, no one," Mary hissed. "And you'll never see that child again."

And the two Davenports walked back into the courtroom, bound.

Esmeralda and Joe were far enough away, on the stairs, that no one noticed them. But they were close enough to hear the slap of Mary's hand.

Such a violent outburst disappointed but did not surprise

either of them. Mary Davenport, despite any kindnesses she'd shown Esmeralda, was the same as every rich white person: enraged and hurt when confronted with the idea that the world and everything in it was not hers for the having. She'd been benevolent when things were going her way then outraged when they were not, like the worst kind of indulged child. And what spoiled, impulsive child can raise a good one? If she didn't get the boy back to his mother the line of poison would drip down for generations.

An official stepped into the hall to call out to any other members of the public that the doors were closing. He waited a minute, and held the door open as a man ran toward him. By the time Esmeralda and Joe were able to dash unobserved to the front of the building, Grace and the Pennys had rounded the bend on Main Street and were headed home.

"We'll go to the livery," Esmeralda said to Joe. "Take a buggy out to the farm."

"Uh-uh, no. We're not doing that. The Pennys aren't going to let her steal the boy back. They already made that clear, and they're right. Grace would've been locked up for it before this, and she'd be worse off now. Time to worry about your own."

CHAPTER THIRTY-SEVEN

In the courtroom, everyone waited for the jury to return. No one thought the deliberations would take long, and they were right. As the jurors filed back in, Tom shushed the two women seated in front of him. "It's over now anyway," one said. She pointed at John Henry and Mary as they entered the room and walked toward their seats.

The judge read the verdict to himself then frowned at the jurymen. He signaled for Ben Fleury, the head juror, to come closer, whispered in his ear, then the jury filed back out to the room in which they'd deliberated. The judge joined them.

Once the judge closed the door everyone in the courtroom spoke at once, upstairs and downstairs. The lawyers and their clients were visibly confused. Even those who'd never been in a courtroom before knew this was when the verdict was supposed to be announced.

"Judge didn't like what he read," Tom whispered to Eddie.

"And so what if he didn't? That's their part of the job, isn't it?" Eddie replied.

Another reporter nearby joined in. "Could be it's a tie. And now he's giving them a talking-to, making them vote again."

The woman sitting in front of Tom turned to face them. "That's *interference*. He can't *interfere*."

"Seems to me he's interfered plenty," Nora said.

Eddie nodded and lit a fresh cigarette.

"Maybe he's telling them to disregard Gabino's lies," Tom said. "I've never seen anybody spout so much garbage in a courtroom."

"I'm sure it wasn't all garbage," Clara muttered.

Nearby, Gladys Heaton refolded her gloves in her lap. Mrs. Billingham closed her eyes for a second's respite. Ira picked fluff off his waistcoat while Tom watched John Henry and Mary fidget in their seats, as worked up as he'd ever seen them.

Clara eyed the Davenports, too, and realized right then that Mary Davenport was no threat to her. Tom had been called out in public, humiliated. There was nothing guaranteed to snuff out a secret infatuation as having everyone's eyes on it. Clara felt relieved, glad even, of how the day had gone, no matter how it ended for the Davenports. Though it certainly would be the icing to see the boy go to Grace Mill.

In the back room, Judge Roy spoke to the jury at length, explaining to the men why, as a matter of law, he could not accept their unexpected verdict. With no other legal expert present to contradict him, the judge improvised a convoluted explanation as to the formal reasons they needed to reconsider. How on Earth, he asked himself, had they been more

persuaded by Grace Mill than Gideon Wolf? He could not allow the Davenports to suffer the results of such foolishness.

After a half-hour, the jury re-emerged and Ben Fleury once
again handed the judge a piece of paper. This time, Judge
Roy read out that the jury had found Gideon Wolf innocent of child napping, agreeing that Ned Mill was lost and
Sonny Davenport was in his rightful home. The judge declared Gideon Wolf a free man.

The unfairness of it maddened George. They'd got an hour
away from the house—and that had taken considerable
doing—and on their way to Penny Farm when Mason saw
them. The boys couldn't have known he'd be in a buggy on his
way back from running their father's errands. The second he'd
spotted them walking on the fringes of the vacant lot where
the colored children played he'd yanked the horse to a stop,
shouted, then jumped out to chase after them.

George and Paul were quick, and Paul clever enough to
split off in a different direction, but Mason caught Ned easily.
Once he'd grabbed him by the shirt, he held him high, the
boy's feet pedaling madly, his arms lashing out for any part
of Mason he could reach. When George saw Ned had been
captured, he slumped. There was no point running anywhere
without him. Paul, however, preferred action to acquiescence,
running at Mason and kicking him in the legs as hard as he
could. Unfortunately, Mason was built more solidly than the
boys had ever noticed, so Paul's blows did no more than annoy him. George stood out of arm's reach, imploring Mason
to let the boy go, saying he didn't understand what they had
been doing. But Mason ignored both George and Paul, and

hauled Ned to the buggy. He understood enough, he said, to know they were in big trouble.

Paul raced to the buggy and added closed-fist blows to his kicks, telling Mason that he hated him, had always hated him. George screamed. But after a short while they gave in, knowing that as long as Mason kept his iron grip on Ned—which he did, no matter how George and Paul hit, poked and railed at him—the escape was finished.

Back at the house, Mason dragged the boys up to their bedroom. All the servants were angry, and seemed more worried about getting into trouble themselves than the fact the three boys were upset.

Once George gave up on shouting out for the adults to see reason, he dropped onto the floor next to Ned. "Don't worry. Not every plan works the first time."

Paul lifted his head from his knees. "We'll be lucky if they ever let us out of the house again."

CHAPTER THIRTY-EIGHT

Grace sat squashed between Farmer and Mrs. Penny on the black leather buggy seat. There was enough room for the three to have spread out more, but the Pennys stayed close to keep Grace from flopping over like a dying daisy.

Grace felt the warmth of them through their wool coats; felt the cold wind swishing around her back, darting about her waist where Mrs. Penny's shawl fell short; felt her nose twitch at the strong smell coming off the horse's rump. Her throat hurt from trapped pain, her jaw ached, her body was heavy yet drained. As she swayed in rhythm with the buggy, her pain grew darker, deeper, even as she willed herself to stay afloat for Ned.

Without warning, the knot in her throat rose up and unfurled out of her, an agony too enormous for words. She howled, alarming the Pennys, causing the horse to startle. Grace howled without pause all the way back to Penny Farm. Dogs howled back to console her, house lights flickered on and curtains were pulled aside so people could see the source of the noise, men smoking on porches in the gloaming bowed their heads by way of respect. They knew there were only a few things that could call forth such savage sounds.

When Anna Beth opened the front door of the farm, Grace's expression told her everything she needed to know. She put her arm around Grace's waist and guided her straight to where baby Lily slept safely in her cot. Farmer Penny added logs to the fire. Mrs. Penny took Anna Beth's cake from the oven. Outside, light rain fell, spotting the pond. Farmer Penny closed the curtains.

The Pennys formed a protective circle around Grace, made their house a warm cocoon. They would help her survive this, and whatever came next. And, as Anna Beth whispered to her mother in the kitchen soon after, what came next was rage.

Mason held the front door open and said he hoped it wasn't an impertinence to ask Mr. Davenport if the trial had gone well. The servants had been worrying.

John Henry answered it wasn't impertinent and yes, the jury had done the right thing. It was over, and now they could move forward with their lives.

Mason said how glad he was, that he would tell the others. Mary watched his face for signs of an undercurrent of doubt, since whatever Esmeralda knew Mason must also. Nanny Pru and Sula, as well.

"I'm sorry to be the bearer of bad news, then," Mason said, taking John Henry's hat, Mary's coat, "but there was something of an incident with the boys while you were—"

"Are they hurt?" Mary asked.

"No one is hurt." Mason considered how to tell the story

so that the boys' infraction and his role in correcting the situation were fully understood. Before he could begin, Mary
walked toward the stairs.

John Henry, however, wanted the whole story. "Spare me
nothing, Mason."

Mary had imagined she'd feel happy when the trial was over,
joyous, close with her husband after the inevitable shared victory. But it didn't feel like a victory. John Henry had barely
spoken on the way home, and Mary was left to wonder if he
was as shaken as she was by Grace Mill, or if he was angry
at having been called on a genuine deceit. She rubbed that
thought out of her head. If John Henry had done anything
others might label untoward, it'd been for the greater good.
She would not question him about that.

And now an "incident." Mary had barely moved past the
top of the stairs when Paul came running toward her, Pru not
far behind him, her mouth open, about to yell. Mary had
never seen such a ferocious look on Pru's face. Without her
usual docile expression she was suddenly frightening. When
Mary said her name it was as much in shock as reprimand,
but it stopped Pru in her tracks.

At the sound of her voice, George and the boy came hurrying toward her, too.

George and Paul yabbered at her at once. This was not
how Mary had envisioned her homecoming. She'd wanted to
tell them the judge had made the bad people go away. She'd
even thought she'd suggest they collect the new kitten the
next morning. But this chaos! Pru saying something in French
about running on streets and breaking doors, Paul proclaim-

ing unfairness, and George urging his mother not to believe Mason.

Everyone fell silent at John Henry's bellow as he stormed past his wife and commanded the boys to get back into their room. He followed them in and slammed the now damaged door.

After Pru explained to Mary in a rush what had happened in the Davenports' absence, Mary went to the boys. She found John Henry sitting with Paul facedown on his lap, walloping him.

"Enough!" Mary shouted. "No more beatings in this house."

John Henry roughly pushed Paul away from him. The boys ran together into the center of the room, magnetized into one shaking lump.

John Henry crouched down and, eyes on the boy, explained some of what had happened in court. "So you are officially part of our family. The smartest men of Opelousas have decided. And do you know why?" He took a deep breath and softened his voice. "Because she doesn't want you."

Mary hung her head. It had come to this.

The boy remained silent, so John Henry continued. "The woman who used to be your mother doesn't want you. But we do. Stop crying now. You have a fine home, brothers and the chance of a bright future." He stood. "From now on, there'll be no secret scheming, no running away. There's no place for you to run where you'd be welcomed. This is where you live. George, Paul, you disappoint me."

He turned to Mary. "Tomorrow we'll go to Starry Lake. Tell the nanny to pack their things, and the maid to arrange yours."

* * *

Mary rang the bell for Sula then sank onto the end of her bed, begging the thousand particles around her to cease their agitated, noisy swirling so she could think. She waved her hand in front of her eyes to clear a path. This wasn't dust in the bright sunbeam, not a horde of mischievous tiny fairies, but her own mind come into the air, her anguish manifest. She wanted nothing to do with it.

For her family to pass through this liminal moment to something better, Mary knew she had to be strong, to bury any hope of seeing Sonny again. She had to grieve in lonely secrecy, and rejoice in public. She would try. She'd tried every day since she'd claimed the boy, had endured complicated sadness and encouraged helpful delusions. It required constant vigilance.

She'd learned to force pleasing thoughts into the foreground of her mind, had sung aloud, walked out of one room into another to escape melancholy or panic, picturing the unwelcome sensations as a pile of rubble left behind a slammed door. Still, terrible thoughts came at her when she was on the edge of sleep, then filled her nightmares.

So what viciousness for Grace Mill to blurt out the one thing Mary and John Henry could never discuss: Sonny alive and abandoned. Even an instant with that thought was unbearable. And there, in the courthouse, with everyone else wanting the best for the Davenports and the boy, Grace Mill had said the unsayable.

Mary snatched at clothes and threw them at Sula, annoyed the girl was packing the wrong things. She shouted at her, told her to leave, then demanded she return.

Of course she'd doubted herself, her choice at the Birds' house. But she'd been sure at the time. Hadn't she? Sure enough to say yes, a word she'd spoken not only for herself but for her whole family.

She'd trapped them. John Henry couldn't continue to look for Sonny now they'd said he'd been found. The boys were forced to pretend the boy was their brother. But what if John Henry had failed to check in the one place Sonny was, had missed a clue or ignored a key letter? Here they were, living with a child who was not a reward or even a substitute, but a constant reminder of their terrible choice to take him.

Surely she'd freed them, though, too. Because how could they have kept searching forever? John Henry, the boys, she wouldn't have survived it.

The one thought that brought Mary peace—the blackest of ironies—was that Sonny was dead. That was her solace: thinking her dear, sweet child was dead. Every alternative was horrifying.

Mary forced her thoughts to Starry Lake and the ease she'd feel in those amiable and ordered rooms. The air would sound with tings of crystal and silver, piano music, harmonic murmurings. She'd be given champagne and Oysters Rockefeller, freshly cut lemon, on a polished tray. She'd stand on a candlelit porch, feel the breeze on her neck, pearls cool on her skin. And life—ineffable, overwhelming—would be made beautiful. Bearable.

But, wait. With a shiver, and too weakened to block the thought, Mary remembered her last visit to the resort. Late October, dropped leaves in heaps beneath naked trees, a crisp, still night. She'd walked outside for a break from the chatter of the Governor's Ball, stood on spongy, wet grass under a bloated moon. She'd breathed the alyssum-scented air, let her eyes rest on a line of arches draped in clematis, then gazed out at the lake. The lake, sprinkled with sparkling reflections of the stars, so like the real thing. The same stars would be reflected in Half Moon Lake, and would be shining above the forest, her house, her Opelousas house, her father's house, Arlington Grove, her sons.

As Mary had looked up at the vast night sky, clouds had rushed in to shield the stars.

The night turned on her. Whenever she'd had this feeling before, of the world revealing its consciousness, its ferocious aliveness, she'd been indoors and able to escape with a quick close of the drapes or change of room. But this time she was alone under the gray sky, surrounded by skeletal trees, and though she thought she'd only walked a dozen or so steps, the resort building seemed far away. A breeze had arrived, the sound of music replaced by agitated rustling—dried-up leaves and sticks. She'd watched a long-armed oak tree whack an upstairs window so insistently she was sure it was going to break the glass. With her eyes on the ground, she'd run back toward the building.

At the door she'd glanced down at a patch of mud beside an azalea bush and had known, without question, she'd once felt mud between her toes. A clear memory of staring at her feet as they pistoned up and down, barefoot, relishing the squelch of wet mud pushing between the gap of her toes. But that was impossible.

While Mary lay on her bed in Opelousas—now ignoring Sula as the girl packed her mistress's morning gowns, afternoon dresses, walking dresses, evening dresses, skirts, blouses, corsets, petticoats, drawers, stockings, nightgowns, coats, as Sula placed shoes and hats in individual boxes, slid covers over Mary's three silk-and-whalebone parasols, lined up jewelry for selection, brushes, ribbons and hair combs, toiletries—Grace screamed. So as not to wake Lily, Grace went into her Penny Farm bedroom, held the goose-feather-filled pillow to her face and screamed. Anna Beth closed the door with a gentle click, and the family sat around the kitchen table, talking quietly, letting grief flame as it must.

Grace's fingernails clawed then tore at the pillow covering. Her mouth left a wet ring and teeth marks. When her scream was spent, Grace threw the pillow away from her, knocking a painting off-kilter. What kind of people—Oh, but she knew. She'd known them all her life. She couldn't remember a time when she hadn't had to bite her tongue, deny her needs, placate insecure people who held power over her, when she hadn't had to hide her strength and lower her eyes. Restraint. Passivity. She'd behaved as they'd told her to from the time she was a child: had been grateful, hadn't fussed or taken more than she deserved. She'd labored for a pittance, and known none of life's ease, while others were born on a mountain of gold. And now her son—*her son*—stolen. Who would design a world of such cruel unfairness? Who had deemed Mary more important than Grace?

PART FIVE

THE TRAIL

CHAPTER THIRTY-NINE

John Henry's first duty as Republican nominee for the mayoral race of Opelousas was to judge the 1916 Parish Spring Fair pie competition, held on the first of May. Wearing a cream-colored suit and matching hat, he sauntered on the cut grass past a line of gingham-covered trestle tables, admiring the pies and chatting to the bakers. He was happy to stretch the afternoon out to show his lighter side.

Mary walked behind him, congratulating each of the women, asking questions about their techniques and promising their secrets were safe with her. They knew that to be true, of course. Mary Davenport would never bake a pie. Her job today was to show she could conduct herself as a mayor's wife. She'd dressed the part, wearing a fashionable but not ostentatious pale blue day dress with white piping, her raven hair swept up under a wide-brimmed straw hat.

John Henry could see his wife had taken trouble with her appearance, though he wished she'd put more energy into her conversations. He was the judge of the contest, but food was a topic a woman should be able to discuss with enthusiasm. The fair provided an opportunity for Mary to shine, though it was obvious to John Henry that the local women didn't like her. He worried they misread her reserve as superiority, and he supposed she still had work to do to vanquish the rumors that had spread during Sonny's absence. It was work worth doing since these women bakers were envoys to voters. Even the single ones had brothers, fathers, uncles. He was aware of the men hovering about, too, watching them.

"Rhubarb. That's one of your favorites, isn't it, Mrs. Davenport?" John Henry leaned toward the women closest to him. "My wife grew up eating rhubarb pie. But I won't let that sway my judgment, I promise you." They laughed politely.

Mary smiled but felt no joy. She felt only numb, again. Lately she'd worried she'd lost her footing in the world. She so often seemed to slide about, flailing, feeling for solid ground. There had been a time when she'd found it easy to traverse social occasions like the fair. She'd been comfortable with the rules, had grown up around them. Her words and actions had been second nature. But since the trial she'd lost her confidence. Sensing people's uncertainty about her made her uncertain of herself: had she unknowingly said what she'd been thinking, had she *not* spoken when she thought she had, had she let her face betray her? Ordinary life had become problematic, perilous. And she had no idea how to explain this to John Henry. If she'd been able to speak truthfully with him, she'd have said she wanted to be at home, in their garden, to read her magazine stories and play with the kitten. Instead, she dressed and redressed for endless functions, worked to conduct herself properly, strived to refashion herself as the person she'd once so effortlessly been.

And to pretend she cared whether he became mayor or not. Because what did it matter? She lived a lie neither of them spoke of, not even to one another. When they were alone, they discussed domestic matters (Mason should order more wine; the boys ought to begin tennis lessons; the new cook would serve turtle soup, crawfish étouffée or lobsters on rice, bread pudding with whiskey sauce, pralines afterward at Saturday's dinner party) and informed one another of events to be added to the calendar. Sometimes John Henry asked Mary to listen as he read aloud a speech he was writing. Or would ask her whether he should wear this coat or that. Mary knew about more than her husband realized, but they didn't discuss the Republican woman in Montana running for a congressional seat. (So strange, and her chances of winning were laughable. If we can't vote, we certainly can't be voted in, Mary thought.) They didn't discuss the Easter Rising in Ireland, the Germans' relentless attacks on the British. She hid her copy of *The Crisis* magazine, kept because Mary was transfixed by the cover photograph of the comely white woman holding the black baby. She hid her growing collection of *All-Story*, *Detective Story* and *Saucy Stories* magazines. She wrapped Hop in paper and placed it in a sealed box under her bed.

Mary smiled at her husband and the women bakers. "My goodness, the smell of these pies takes me back to my youth. There's some kind of witchcraft at work here." She'd meant it as a joke but it fell flat, so she went for a more familiar sentiment. "I don't know how you'll ever choose a winner today.

These pies all look like winners to me." John Henry beamed, relieved.

After perusing the pie display, the Davenports wandered around the fair. John Henry shook hands and answered questions. Mary watched her three boys run toward the ice-cream stand. Most times, she found a way to push to a far corner of her mind the hurt that arose when she tried to laugh or play with them, as they clearly didn't want her company. The silly faces of disapproval they made at one another that they thought she didn't see. She was their mother, though, not a companion, she told herself, so of course they didn't want to include her in their games. Or their secrets. And surely other children whispered, made clumsy attempts to hide nonsense nothings when their mother came near.

Her husband's stern words had at least put an end to what Mason, once, referred to as the boys' "jailbreak." John Henry told them Grace Mill had left town.

When John Henry stopped to speak with yet another stranger, Mary scanned the fairground for Esmeralda, as she did in every crowd. It had been hard for Mary to lose so many people in such a short space of time: Esmeralda, run off to who-knew-where; her father, not gone but refusing any contact with her (which, in truth, would not have bothered Mary except that a rift could reflect badly on John Henry); and Tom. She'd felt sadder than she could explain, had she anyone to explain it to, when she found out that Tom McCabe had married without inviting her to the wedding. She'd thought they were friends.

But Mary knew her husband was right: life goes on. What other option did any of them have but to go on with it?

Later in the day, once the winning pie had been announced, and ribbons for second and third prize placed on
the tables, John Henry stood at the podium near the lucky-
dip stall. He told the crowd he wouldn't ruin this exceptional
day with a speech, but he couldn't let the moment pass without telling them how much their support would mean to him,
and how tirelessly he would work to represent them.

"I may be the most cost-effective mayor you've ever had—
I'll work for pie!" Everyone laughed and clapped.

Any outside observer would've said this was the year of the
Davenports. Life was going their way: their son was returned
and their legal troubles were behind them. The couple attended balls and banquets at the Starry Lake Resort, the
theater in New Orleans, and mixed with the best people.
They sat in the front row of the Catholic Church every
Sunday at ten. John Henry drove a Pope-Hartford and his
business was thriving. In March, he'd bought the Conroy
mills and purchased revolutionary machinery to make the
most of them, and had promoted Hank to manage a new factory for modern furniture that was already receiving glowing
praise. John Henry had been able to make a sizable dona-
tion to the Westwood Academy, where his sons now attended
school. And the week before the fair he'd announced that,
inspired by Carnegie's philanthropy, he'd open a grand mu-
nicipal library that would put Opelousas on the map. After
this, the *St. Landry Clarion* declared that John Henry's ri-
val should throw in the towel. The mayoral election was Mr.
Davenport's to lose.

Ladies who saw Mary Davenport with her boys saw a

picture of moneyed serenity, maternal bliss, composed and assured, her worries gone. Her clothing and hair were the envy of her friends. And the children were strapping and healthy: George, almost ten, tall, a miniature version of his father; Paul, cheeky and gregarious as ever; Sonny, returned to the fold. True, he was often sullen and refused to play with anyone other than his brothers, and he never spoke. But who could say what terrible things he'd survived during his time away from his family? Everyone agreed, though, that he would forget.

With the many advantages the Davenports enjoyed, they both knew, deep inside, that life would eventually right itself. Their moment of scandal would be forgotten, papered over by their good deeds, generous hosting and John Henry's professional achievements. They needed only to stay the course, to live the lives into which they'd been born. For it was too exhausting for Opelousas to forever refresh its distrust and disappointment when it was clear the world was built for people like the Davenports, built to give and forgive them everything.

CHAPTER FORTY

Mrs. Penny and Anna Beth fed baby Lily cow's milk they warmed on the stove, placed her pram under the leafiest trees, sewed smocks and knitted sweaters, rubbed her gums with morphine syrup and sang her lullabies. Mrs. Penny talked of entering Lily in the Better Babies Contest at next month's spring fair, then decided against it after hearing that John Henry Davenport would be attending to judge the pies. "Let's wait for the state fair," Farmer Penny suggested. He carved a rattle for Lily, attaching a silver bell he'd bought specially, and set about unboxing Anna Beth's old dolls.

The Penny women cared for Grace, too, encouraging her to eat soups and stews, broth—though by April the weather was warm—and guiding her to wash and dress, when she often had no interest in doing so. Sometimes, in the early afternoon, Mrs. Penny and Anna Beth walked with Grace around the farm, stopping to feed the chickens, check if hung sheets were dry or cut herbs to go in the pot for dinner. The walks were slow, and the practical elements a ruse: the farm chores were done to a schedule, and the chickens, befuddled, pecked at the extra meals with a speed that suggested they knew the madness wouldn't last.

Mrs. Penny had long used walking as medicine for her children and herself. And Grace was more talkative when they were outdoors, moving, her eyes landing on fresh flower buds and seedlings opening to the sun, but the beneficial effects never lasted long. Once they returned to the farmhouse kitchen, though it was scrubbed and polished and there was a vase of pinks on the table, Grace fell back into silence.

Farmer Penny sat with Grace in front of the fire at night. He occupied one armchair, put his socked feet on the stool, smoked his pipe and chatted about the animals, the garden, as he'd done with his children when they were little and Mrs. Penny had needed sleep. Grace curled up in the other armchair, draped in a lamb's-wool blanket, and watched the flames.

Sometimes after midnight, when everyone else was in bed, Anna Beth took her father's place and kept Grace company, teaching her the wisdom that could be gleaned from the spirits and the stars. She sat on the floor and laid out her tarot cards, Celtic Cross her preferred arrangement, on a purple cloth, always with an eye to describing a bright future for Grace. The Justice card every time, which made sense. The Wheel of Fortune: a turn for the better, luck. That was good. The Ace of Cups, though? There must be some way of interpreting that aside from her usual reading of marriage and fertility.

When Grace asked her to, Anna Beth consulted the cards about Ned. Lily, at eight months, was too young. Ned's future, she said, would be positive, without a shadow of doubt. "See? King of Coins again." She couldn't make sense of the persistent message that the events of Ned's life reverberated after his death, so this wasn't something she discussed with Grace. The Temperance card, liquid flowing from one vessel to another, the rebirth of the soul. The Sun. Perhaps, she thought, the boy was more special than anyone realized.

When the rest of the Penny clan came to visit—Farmer and Mrs. Penny's grown sons, their wives and children—Grace and Lily were treated with gentleness and respect. They understood that Grace's loss was like a death, and no death was worse than that of a child. The Pennys told Grace to stay at the farm as long as she pleased, forever if she wanted: she was family.

And Grace might have stayed at Penny Farm, had it not been for Sheriff Sherman.

On a mild Saturday afternoon drifting into a rainbow dusk, as Mrs. Penny chopped carrots, with Anna Beth nearby washing Lily in the kitchen tub, Farmer Penny at the table cleaning out his pipe, and Grace folding clothes—determined to fight her lethargy and be of use—Sheriff Sherman knocked on the front door. Farmer Penny invited him into the living room and must have looked perplexed enough that the sheriff quickly offered that this was a social visit—no one had been hurt or arrested. There was no trouble of any kind. Grace and Mrs. Penny, hearing the sheriff's voice, rushed out from the kitchen.

"Have you come about Ned?" Grace asked.

"Grace, he's only just walked in the door. You might want

to start with hello." Mrs. Penny turned to the sheriff. "Please excuse her. She's not herself right now." She paused. "But *is* that why you're here?"

Farmer Penny, Mrs. Penny and Grace stood in a line facing the sheriff, waiting for him to speak. He exhaled heavily. "I'm sorry but no, I'm not here about Ned."

The three issued a soft "ah," then Farmer Penny made small nods at nothing and Mrs. Penny muttered, "Coffee," and disappeared into the kitchen.

"I'm sorry if I woke fresh hope about your boy," the sheriff said to Grace. "Nothing's changed. I came to—"

"Take a seat," Farmer Penny said, sitting down facing the sheriff.

Mrs. Penny returned with a tray holding full mugs, Anna Beth walking behind her with Lily washed, dressed and held against her shoulder.

The sheriff spoke to Grace. "I'm not here in an official capacity. I wanted to know how you were getting on, how you were managing after…I wanted to tell you I've been thinking about your situation a lot these past few months, and I feel badly about what happened to you. It wasn't right. I know that now."

Anna Beth swayed back and forth, then at Grace's request passed Lily down to her. "Ace of Cups," she said, smiling, though no one knew what that meant.

"Have you seen Ned?" Grace asked.

"I've seen him from afar, playing with his—the other boys. They get on well, those three. He has good company in them."

Grace had asked the Pennys countless times to drive the buggy past the Davenport house, but they'd resisted, saying were the boy to see her it would confuse and distress him, and in no way alleviate her pain. "What if we were to swoop him up and leave? Who could stop us?" she'd said. "That would be kidnapping, Grace," Farmer Penny had said. "I know it makes no sense, but your boy isn't yours anymore."

So though it pained her to think of Ned with another family, she was glad to hear he was happy enough to play, and had friends in the Davenport boys.

After a few moments of awkward silence, Mrs. Penny asked if anyone would like more coffee, but no one did. Anna Beth left the room without explanation. Farmer Penny smiled at the sheriff, nodded at nothing in particular.

"I never got to thank Esmeralda properly," Grace said, patting Lily gently on the back.

The sheriff hadn't expected to hear Esmeralda's name but was keen to show an interest in anything Grace said. "I'm sure she—It's kind that you'd want to—"

"She took such a risk in coming out here to help me. I can imagine the Davenports' rage. Do you know where she went?"

"No, I'm afraid I don't." The sheriff tried to think of anything more he could say about Esmeralda, but he hadn't seen her since before the trial, so was at a loss.

Mrs. Penny frowned. "It's never in your interest to side with a Negro, Grace."

"She sided with me. I can't see how that was in her interest."

"Well, it was her choice."

"A brave one, you have to admit," Farmer Penny said.

"Oh yes, she's brave," Mrs. Penny said. "No doubt about that."

Anna Beth walked back into the room carrying Mr. Miggs, placed the cat on the rug, then walked to her mother and whispered in her ear. She'd understood the situation more quickly than anyone.

"Oh," Mrs. Penny said, then asked Farmer Penny to join them in the kitchen. "That troublesome pantry door," she said, clucking.

As they left Grace and the sheriff together to talk, Mr. Miggs leapt up onto Grace's lap. Mrs. Penny reasoned that since they were a few feet away, Grace and the sheriff were not alone in any compromising way. Also, he was the sheriff. She wasn't one to jump the gun, but if there was any chance that Grace might have a suitor, how wonderful that would be. Anna Beth had good instincts for these things.

CHAPTER FORTY-ONE

By March, Esmeralda and her three children, Annalise and her two children, and Uncle Joe and Aunt Celestine had enough money to leave Opelousas. They were almost ready, and were excited and anxious in equal measure. The trip to New York by slow train would take several days, with three legs after New Orleans—north to Cincinnati, east to Philadelphia, then up to New York City—and many stops along the way. They'd heard from others that not every station had a coloreds water tap or food, and that they'd need to spend a sleepless night in Cincinnati station. The journey would be uncomfortable, dirty, crowded. Then, from Pennsylvania Station they'd need to get to a boarding house in Harlem, where a friend of Joe's had arranged temporary accommodation for them. After that, they were on their own, together.

They had to leave. Without a reference from the Davenports there was no work for Esmeralda in Opelousas, and neither New Orleans nor Baton Rouge was a safe place for women or girls. Esmeralda felt sure they'd find opportunities in New York. She'd say the old lady she'd worked for had died, get Celestine to write a letter from her. She knew how. "Mrs. Mary Contrary," Celestine had laughed. "Oh how she loved you, Es. Final moments on Earth and all she could think of was finding you a new home." Joe had a reference from the livery so he'd get work; his friend in New York had assured him of that. The railroads were in dire need of laborers. And the children would do what they could: domestic or factory work.

Once they arrived, they'd sell the fancy dress Mary Davenport had given Esmeralda—with thanks to Sula for having been brave enough to deliver it with the rest of Esmeralda's things—and the small mountain of jewelry Celestine had accrued over many years from the rich ladies of Opelousas in return for keeping them free from curses. "Should've given me more," Celestine said. "The things they'd done."

So, on a Monday afternoon, Esmeralda went into town with Joe to find out when trains went to New York. It was a warm day, bright, with cotton-ball clouds. Birds tumbled and played in the horses' water trough outside the barbershop. Women wearing white drifted along the brick sidewalk.

As Esmeralda and Joe walked up Main Street to the station, another batch of orphan children, freshly arrived, tagged, were being ferried out to motor cars and buggies. Some of the children walked in the company of a man or couple who'd pre-ordered them. The others, about two dozen of them, would be herded into the town square to be inspected for purchase.

"It's not right," Esmeralda said to Joe. "I don't care what

Mason says. Look at their faces. Terrified." She clicked her tongue and pointed at a knock-kneed girl in a worn cotton dress. "You know Mr. Conroy won't do anything other than work that poor little thing to the bone."

"Might do something worse than that," Joe said.

Esmeralda stopped and elbowed Joe when she saw Tom McCabe striding toward them. Joe made it clear they should keep going but Tom stopped as well, nodded hello, though he appeared far from pleased at seeing them.

"Mr. McCabe." Esmeralda bent down to pat Walter, who was as bouncy as a puppy at the sight of her.

"I heard you'd left town." Tom ignored Joe.

"We're about to." She kept her eyes on Walter. "Tomorrow maybe, depending. Oh rabbit-dog, I've missed you." Walter nuzzled into her apron and though there were no treats there, not even the crumbs of one, he stayed while she stroked his back.

Tom relaxed at Esmeralda's news. "That's for the best, I'm sure. Mr. Davenport will be mayor soon, and I can't think who'd hire the housekeeper that turned on him."

Esmeralda gave Walter a last pat then stood upright. Tom hadn't developed any subtlety. But she'd lost her income, her bed, her reputation, and she was leaving town, so Esmeralda wasn't sure she needed to be subtle either.

"Turned on him—that's how you're telling it?"

Tom shrugged. "That's how I see it."

"You know, for a while there, when you came to read to Mrs. Davenport, I thought you were a good man. Trying to get one up on the other reporters, I could see that. But doing it in a kind way—that meant something."

Tom gave a small nod by way of acknowledging the compliment. But Esmeralda wasn't done.

"Then as soon as you found your footing in that house you puffed up like a rooster, so proud of your own self, of your patience and the hours you were putting in. Started to think you were doing the Davenports a favor by showing up, started to think you were their friend." She stepped closer. "But the Davenports don't have friends like you. You were working for them, same as me, but without getting paid. So more fool you."

Tom's expression grew dark. Had there not been a sidewalk full of people he would've yelled at Esmeralda, maybe even struck her. "I'm no fool, I assure you. I'm a reporter. And I did my job."

"Did you? I thought it was your job to tell the truth. But I dropped the truth right in your lap and you brushed it off."

Joe coughed to get Esmeralda's attention. This was risky behavior. They needed to walk away, and quickly.

Tom had already been raked over the coals that morning by Mr. Collins, again. His editor prided himself on sticking by his reporters, but said he'd had to stick by Tom one too many times. And it was hard for him to defend his star reporter's lapses in judgment with the Davenport story. "Reporters aren't supposed to get sweet on the people they write about, McCabe," he'd barked at Tom. Since the trial, Tom had been relegated to less controversial stories, writing about Mr. and Mrs. Smith's *narrow* escape after their buggy fell into a crevasse, the *relieving* drop in the level of the Atchafalaya River before the May rises, the Daughters of Isabella *extravagantly* entertaining at the Knights of Columbus Hall. He didn't care about any of it and, according to Mr. Collins, it showed. He'd scrunched Tom's latest story into a ball and told him to take a walk and come back when he was ready to be a reporter again.

Now this. The whole world seemed to want to tell Tom he was failing as a writer and a man.

"There's no such thing as the truth, Esmeralda. There's your truth, my truth, Mary's, John Henry's, Gideon Wolf's. There's a gussied-up truth and one that's plain as Jane. You don't have any license on some single inviolable truth."

"That child was stolen from his mama. There's no getting around it. The Davenports may not pay on Earth for what they've done, but sooner or later they'll pay. God will punish them for stealing one of His own."

"Oh, yes, I see, God." She'd never heard him use a tone so simultaneously furious and mocking. "Wouldn't you say God made His thoughts clear when He let Judge Roy send the boy home with the Davenports? That must tell you something about God's will?"

"Tells me God has a plan we don't understand," Esmeralda said. "I pray for that mother and child every night."

"Thank you, Jesus," Joe murmured.

"Sonny Davenport lives in a mansion, with parents who can give him anything he wants. Seems you'd be better off praying for yourself."

"Money's no substitute for love," Esmeralda said.

"They love him."

"Not like his mother would."

Tom snorted. "His mother. It's a shame we've ended up here, Esmeralda. You really do think some great wrong has been committed, don't you? Well, I don't see it. I know that family inside and out, and I don't see it."

"You're seeing what you want to see, what's best for you."

"I see someone who doesn't know when she should leave well enough alone. Now, if you'll excuse me, I have things to do."

Tom clicked his fingers and whistled to get Walter away from Esmeralda, but the dog ignored him. It wasn't the departure Tom would've chosen.

"They've messed with God and Nature," Esmeralda said, as Walter leaned against her leg. "The Davenport line from now till eternity will be stained by the crime those two committed."

Tom whistled more insistently for Walter, then started to walk away in the hope he'd follow.

"The Devil will take them," Esmeralda called out. "He'll take John Henry and Mary Davenport. And the Devil will take you, too, Tom McCabe."

Tom stopped and turned. "What did you say?"

Joe tugged hard at Esmeralda's sleeve. "That is *enough*."

"The Devil sees every choice you make, Tom McCabe. It's not too late, though, never too late to stand up for the truth."

Tom looked around for the nearest building she couldn't enter. He marched toward the Opelousas Hotel saloon and pushed open the doors.

"Goodbye, rabbit-dog," Esmeralda said quietly.

So he was going to Hell. Might as well go drunk. Tom downed his whiskey in one gulp, shoved his free hand in his pocket and felt the silky lining on his knuckles, wool on the heel of his palm. But his lucky pennies weren't there. Which made some weird sense. His luck had dried up.

"Another," he said to the barman. The whiskey was fire in his throat, and Walter was whining to get back outside. The bartender seemed decidedly disapproving, Tom thought. Maybe he'd heard Esmeralda. But who cared what a bartender thought? Tom was tired of other people's opinions.

Even last night, in his own home, he'd been mocked by a man he'd never met. A poet, of all people. Tom had sat down happily enough to his book, Frost's *Mountain Interval*, fresh off the presses. He'd heard the poems were uplifting, inspiring, and he was in need of that. But the first poem he read was nothing of the kind. It read like a personal attack. Had the writer watched him from afar? It was possible. Tom's name had been on every story about the Davenports from the get-go. He'd even penned the celebratory piece that had appeared the day after they were awarded custody of the boy: "Pure Joy in All Our Hearts." Good grief.

Frost wrote of a wanderer who, coming to a fork in the road, chose a path that set the course for his life. Tom heard no positive note in the poet's surety that there was no going back, no chance to revisit the fork and choose differently. It was defeatist. He'd slammed the book shut.

Tom would never tell her as much, but Esmeralda was right. He'd walked the wrong road, left his integrity by the wayside, attracted by beauty and power and the possibility of small fame. He couldn't rewrite his past, but he could back up and return to the place where his life had forked. He could. He knew which road he'd walk from here on in, and it sure didn't end in leaping flames.

Tom slammed his glass on the bar and threw some money down. "C'mon, boy," he said to Walter. "Let's go."

A half-dozen blocks away, Mrs. Billingham and Gladys were strolling back to their motor car through the city square. The square was more crowded than it would usually have been, since the last few children from the most recent orphan train were being auctioned off.

"Don't gawp, Gladys. Do come along."

But Gladys kept her eyes fixed on the auction block. She edged closer.

"Gladys, I am not staying for this spectacle. It's charitable, I'm sure, but it's not ours to watch."

When her daughter didn't reply, Mrs. Billingham followed Gladys's gaze to the stage where a thin, bedraggled, fair-haired boy stood waiting to be bought. Crying, clipped on the head each time he tried to speak, though he seemed desperately to want to. "Impossible," she murmured.

"You see it, too? Why, that boy is the very image of Mary. Mother, what if he's—"

Mrs. Billingham grabbed her daughter's arm in a hard pinch, making Gladys wince. "Ow!"

"Be quiet." Mrs. Billingham glanced around to see if any of the men and women near them had registered Gladys's words but they were craning forward, concentrating on the bidding.

"But if that's their boy, then—"

"Then nothing. Absolutely nothing, Gladys. We go home and never speak of it."

"Mother, if that's Sonny, we can't possibly let him be bought by a stranger. He's a Davenport."

"There are three Davenport boys and they're safe at home. That child is an orphan. By tonight he'll have a family and a new name. In any case, it's been years. I doubt you paid enough attention even back then to recognize him for sure."

Gladys stared at the boy. "Oh, but I *am* sure. Very sure. We must do something—tell the auctioneer, tell Mary."

"We'll do *neither* of those things. Can you imagine the trouble you'd cause John Henry and Mary, and everyone who stood by them? The public disgrace, the mayoral election. No, Gladys. We'll not utter a word about this to anyone. We walk away."

ACKNOWLEDGMENTS

Thank you Dave, Liam and Milo for your love, support and patience. Writing a book takes years. This one felt like it took decades. And while it was thrilling for me to sit down day and night with my invented people, I know that made me unavailable to you for large chunks of time. I appreciate you tiptoeing around me, most likely wondering when I would ever finish, and why I was so intent on doing something that had delivered me no success. It must be strange to live with a writer... Thank you for accommodating the strangeness with such good humor.

Thank you, also, to the many friends and family members who continued to ask me how the book was going, long after politeness required. You've been unfailingly encouraging, even as I squirmed at the thought I would never live up to your kind words. To those friends who didn't know I was writing a book, my apologies. I wasn't sure it would see the light of day so it felt unwise to spread the word too confidently. And I wasn't lying when I said I was a dog walker: I do that, too.

I'm hoping I don't offend anyone by singling out two friends. Thank you Cathy Ford for being so smart, generous and empathetic, and showing me how a real writer conducts herself. I've benefitted from knowing you in ways I can barely articulate (while knowing it's not your job to benefit me in any way). I'm terrified at the thought of you reading this book. I mean it when I say I can't write as well as you, though it's good to have a goal.

Martine Thompson, thank you for years of friendship. I treasure every moment of it. Thank you for sending me gum leaves when I was in Banff. And thank you for letting me finish this book in your home: it was a perfect sanctuary (except for the part where I scared your cats).

Writing is a solo activity but publishing is not. I'm grateful to the people who stepped up to do the things I cannot. My thanks to my agent, Jacinta di Mase. You didn't throw me off your books even when my first manuscript was rejected by twenty-six publishers, though you could have. You calmly persisted and found a home for it and this one, simultaneously. I appreciate your hard work, dedication and talent.

Thank you to Penguin Random House publisher Beverley Cousins and editor Tom Langshaw. Beverley, I can only imagine how many manuscripts cross your desk. Thank you so much for choosing mine. Tom, I aspire to your impressive combining of wide vision and attention to detail. Both of you offered feedback and expertise that improved the manuscript immeasurably. (And offered it so diplomatically!) It's been a pleasure to work with you.

Elizabeth Sheinkman wrote a report on an early version of this manuscript in which she suggested that my attempt to braid together an historical and modern telling of this story wasn't working and that I had, in fact, two books on my hands. Her advice that I focus on the historical story first was right. And I thank her very much. The second book is in the offing. (A sidenote of gratitude for kind people who share their friends: thank you Joanna Hershon for introducing me to Elizabeth—and for your beautiful novels—and to Emma-Kate Croghan for introducing me to Joanna.)

Phil Dwyer gave detailed legal advice in language I could understand, and in a warm and thoughtful manner, for which I am forever thankful.

And a sweeping but heartfelt thank-you to writers everywhere. Reading is life-changing. It has brought me joy, information, enlightenment and solace. At every difficult or confusing juncture, I've turned to the written word. Reading has taken me across the world, across time, to other planets, into people's lives and minds. So, thank you to writers of fiction and nonfiction. You make humanity better. And to anyone aspiring to be published: please know the number of rejections I cited above is true, and only for that one manuscript. I've lost count of various other pitches that went nowhere. Rejection is awful, but readers like me are hoping you succeed. Please keep going.

YOUR BOOK CLUB RESOURCE

READING
GROUP GUIDE

DISCUSSION QUESTIONS

1. How do you think Mary Davenport's disquieting upbringing—her mother's miscarriages and sadness, her father's coldness and Mary's isolation on the plantation—has affected her role as a mother and wife?

2. The Boy Scout movement that John Henry Davenport so admires was founded in England in 1908. Baden-Powell wrote *Scouting for Boys* for use by existing youth groups, but his book was an immediate success and people set up Boy Scout troops across the world. What, do you think, was it about the Scouts that so appealed to people like John Henry during this era?

3. At Sheriff and Mrs. Bird's house in Mobile, John Henry agrees when Mary declares the boy is theirs. Was he right to put his wife's happiness and health above the truth? Was that, in fact, what he was doing?

4. George Davenport was seven years old and Paul was six when their brother went missing in the forest. How would this episode in their lives change the type of people they become? How do you think they understand the choice their parents have made?

5. What was it about John Henry's deception in the library that spurred Esmeralda to take the enormous risk of traveling to the Pennys' farm at night: her sense of justice, concern for the boy, identification with the mother or some combination of those things? Would you have done the same in her position?

6. In real life, the Orphan Trains movement transported an estimated 200–250,000 orphaned and homeless children from crowded and dangerous East Coast cities of the United States to rural parts of the Midwest and South, from 1854 to 1929. While *Anne of Green Gables* (1908) and *Pollyanna* (1913) offered up happy endings for rehoused orphans, the true stories weren't all as cheery. Do you think this was a good approach to housing hundreds of thousands of homeless children? Was Mason right to suggest the Davenports take in a train orphan?

7. Mary and Grace Mill meet for the first time in the hallway outside the Opelousas courtroom. Do you imagine that moment might have gone differently had there been no other people there?

8. Ned Mill won't be a child forever. Do you think that as a young man he might seek out his mother, despite what John Henry said about her not wanting him?

9. Do you think Grace and Sheriff Sherman might end up together? Would she be able to forgive him for not believing her earlier on?

10. At the end of the novel Tom decides he can do better—be better—and leaves the bar with a head full of steam. Where do you think he goes, and why?

11. On April 6, 1917, America joined the Great War. How do you think that might affect the characters in *Lost Boy Found*? Would Tom, Eddie or the sheriff have signed up? How would it have changed the lives of the women, if at all?

12. In the true story of Bobby Dunbar, the lost boy's descendants conducted a DNA test in 2004. It revealed that the boy had been given to the wrong family. How would you react if you discovered your ancestors had effectively kidnapped another woman's son?

AUTHOR ESSAY ON INSPIRATION AND RESEARCH

LOST BOY FOUND is a novel, but it was inspired by a true story I encountered on a podcast. "The Ghost of Bobby Dunbar" originally aired as an episode of NPR's *This American Life* in 2008. I didn't hear it when it first aired, but the episode was popular enough that they rebroadcast it in 2012. That was my introduction to the story of the four-year-old lost-then-found Louisiana boy who was claimed by two mothers in the mid-1910s.

The story is fascinating, but it raised questions for me: How could a woman not recognize her own son? Why didn't the boy tell them who he was? The podcast also delved into how the family's descendants were dealing with the discovery that, thanks to a DNA test in 2004, their ancestors had essentially kidnapped another woman's child, which raised both ethical and personal identity issues.

The NPR podcast creators Tal McThenia and Margaret Dunbar Cutright wrote a nonfiction book on the Bobby

Dunbar story called *A Case for Solomon*. While I enjoyed it, it left me wondering. My head wanted to work with the gaps in the story to imagine what might happen if I put some extra characters in the mix, moved the story a little closer to the start of the First World War, and talked about some of the other issues that were important at that time. What I really wanted to do was combine fictional versions of the past and present stories—the vanishing, the rediscovery, a town divided over which mother was telling the truth, and the modern-day discovery of what had been willfully lost over the years…

I tried, and I failed. Annoyingly, everyone agreed that I'd failed. My agent didn't think it was working, a freelance editor didn't think it was working, and then a savvy American friend-of-a-friend told me I had two books on my hands and that I should begin by telling the historic tale on its own. So, I took my braided 80,000-word manuscript and pulled it apart into two separate documents, strand by strand. I put the modern story (about 40,000 words long and smattered with song lyrics, photos, obscure pithy quotes) to one side and set about telling the historical story from the beginning, reading and researching along the way, reimagining the characters and the place, until it felt like its own novel. I hadn't set out to write a purely historical book, but the American reader's advice was right: This was its own story.

I made a conscious decision not to travel to Louisiana. *Lost Boy Found* begins in 1913, and I worried that seeing the modern-day Opelousas, New Orleans, and its surrounds would obscure the historical image I held so clearly in my head.

Instead, I researched intensively. The years from 1890 to the early 1920s are labeled the Progressive Era because so much changed. It was an incredibly significant time, with massive social and cultural shifts, the First World War (1914–1918, with the US entering it in 1917), the beginning of many technologies we now take for granted...

These things were invented during the Progressive Era: airplanes, crossword puzzles, stainless steel, zippers, bras, mousetraps, assembly lines, windshield wipers, electric blankets, parachutes, Formica, the Model T Ford, and traffic lights.

Music of the time included ragtime, Tin Pan Alley songs, the earliest versions of Jazz. There was a fledgling and overdue recognition of African-American musicians and gospel music in the South (though much of it was never recorded). It was an incredibly inventive time for traditional music including classical (the audience in Paris rioted when Stravinsky's "Rite of Spring" was first performed there in May 1913) and opera.

I read widely about topics from the Civil War to the bird life of Louisiana, from Jim Crow laws to women's suffrage, from the early years of the First World War to Southern music and cuisine.

I read fiction from the time: Edith Wharton, D.H. Lawrence, Jack London, Beatrix Potter and Mark Twain. I also read plenty of nonfiction: *Scouting for Boys*, John Muir's nature tracts, and books about the era such as Florian Illies's *1913: The Year Before the Storm*. I read old newspapers and magazines that I found online, too. (I cannot recommend this enough, just for fun.)

Films of the time featured Charlie Chaplin, Mary Pickford, and Buster Keaton, with directors including Cecile B. de Mille and D.W. Griffith. I watched more silent films than I needed to and revisited *Gone with the Wind* with freshly critical eyes.

And though I know the internet can be terrible, I can't imagine how much more difficult it would have been to research what people wore and drove in 1913 America, how much they earned, and what the laws of the day were without it. I spent hours learning about things that amounted to no more than a single line in the book, and I don't regret a minute of it.

I didn't give up on the modern story, by the way. There's something too interesting in the idea of discovering an entirely different version of one's family history and having to consider what it means for the here-and-now. Are we responsible for the actions of our forebears? Do their choices change who we are?

To my mind, the human experience makes no sense without exploring the stories from our past, imagining those from our future, and being clear-eyed and honest about our present.